About the Author

Following an abusive relationship Fiona found herself juggling home and work life commitments for many years before deciding to return to education. In 2011 she graduated from The University of Bradford with a BSc (Hons) in Psychology and is a member of the British Psychological Society. It was at the recommendation of one of her tutors that Fiona's debut novel came into fruition.

Dedication

To Dr Norah McWilliams for putting forward the notion that I should write as a career and to Claire Priestly for reading the first five pages and insisting I continue with the project, I owe you both a huge debt of gratitude. I would also like to thank Simon Waters for encouraging me to finish the book and his sister Louise Urch for conducting an initial proof read and providing constructive criticism. To my family and friends I will merely say I appreciate everything, and without words you know what you mean to me. Finally, a special mention to Dan, Courtney and Ethan for proving to be my driving force in life.

Fiona Winter

A LEAD TO LOVE

AUSTIN MACAULEY
PUBLISHERS LTD.

A CIP catalogue record for this title is available from the British Library.

ISBN 9781785542367 (Paperback)
ISBN 9781785542374 (Hardback)
ISBN 9781785542381 (E-Book)

www.austinmacauley.com

First Published (2015)
Austin Macauley Publishers Ltd.
25 Canada Square
Canary Wharf
London
E14 5LQ

I would like to thank the team at Austin Macauley for all their hard work and support and for making this book into a reality.

Chapter One

Jessica Wainwright could hear it; she was just trying her best to ignore it. The persistent repetition of her alarm going off had entered her subconscious and was now doing its utmost to drag her from her perfect sleep, the sleep in which she was sure she had married Gerard Butler. However, with each beep of the alarm, Jess's perfect world was slipping away. And so she did what every self-respecting person would, and decided to choose snooze. Another twenty minutes in her perfect world would be worth the ensuing rush. It would of course entail skipping breakfast in order to make up the time and ultimately being starving by eleven o' clock, but in her state of being half asleep, half awake, Jess considered it worthwhile to be warm and cosy with the fragmented memory of Gerard for just a little longer.

However, fumbling in the dark for her phone, Jess's brain slowly began to kick start into action and whilst still half asleep the self-talk began. *Is it a week day? No it's not a week day, then why is the alarm going off? That's because it's the phone you fool. But who would be ringing me at this time – it's still dark. I'll bet it's someone selling something. No it can't be, they're not allowed to ring before a certain time. If it's Brandon ringing to tell me again how great his relationship with Justin is working out I will kill him. But wait! No, it can't be him; he rang Thursday to tell me they were off to Venice for the weekend. Which can mean only one thing- Oh god, it must be an emergency!*

Reaching in the dark for the light switch, Jess was momentarily dazed. She felt terrible, dizzy from sitting up too fast, and the retinas in her eyes felt like they were on fire. This, she was sure, must be due to the stark contrast from dark to light and not the Shiraz she had shared last night with her best friend Kate. Jess clumsily pulled the tangled mass of long dark curls over her eyes, hoping this would form a protective shield from the harsh light. Gingerly, she began coaxing her eyelids to open and for a brief second they did, just long enough for Jess to acknowledge that her bedroom could do with a makeover. A couple of throws and fluffy pillows could not hide the drab magnolia paint of her walls even with her vision momentarily skewed. For one moment Jess was tempted to pull the duvet up, turn off the light and pretend that it was possibly a wrong number. But she couldn't because for some reason she just knew, she didn't know how she knew, she just did. And what she knew or at least surmised was that something was wrong, and so with steely determination Jess picked up the phone and pressed answer.

"Jess, is that you dear?"

For a moment Jess tried to place the almost whisper of a voice. Upon recognising the faint mumbling to be that of her usually confident speaking Gran, Jess immediately sat up straight and her eye lids no longer refused to cooperate.

"Gran, what time is it, and why on earth are you ringing me at whatever time of the morning or night it is? Is everything ok?"

Pain was clearly evident in her Gran's speech as she mumbled "Its seven am dear, you do remember it's January? It's always dark. Now listen I don't want you to panic but I could do with you coming over. You see I've had a bit of a fall, I'm going to phone for an ambulance but I won't be able to answer the door as I can't move and I wondered if you would come over with the spare key."

"You should have rung the ambulance first Gran, ring them now, I'm on my way."

Two minutes later, Ugg boots and sweater hopefully disguising the fact Jess was still in her PJ's, she was out of the door. Jess knew that her Gran would have played down the incident in the understated way in which she did everything; this ultimately meant that Jess's stress levels had been rising sharply since putting the phone down. It took only ten minutes to arrive at her Gran's house, primarily for two reasons. The first being that clearly Jess was not the only one who thought it too early to be out of bed. And the second reason for making such good time was that she had implemented a Formula One style of driving, except of course for having to stop at the numerous traffic lights across town. On an average day they were bad enough, however in a crisis they were making even the normally law abiding Jess consider whether it would be justified in jumping a red light in order to save time. Fortunately for Jess, in the time it took her to justify breaking the law, the lights had changed to green.

It may have only taken Jess ten minutes to get to her Gran's house but the stress and adrenaline had been building. This combined with being a little out of breath from running up the garden path meant that Jess could hardly get the key in the door, and having achieved this, she practically fell through it.

Clearly bursting into a fit of giggles would not have been high on the list of initial reactions upon coming to the rescue of a dearly loved family member and Jess later justified it as being an unintentional reaction to the stress. That and the fact that her Gran who was normally a stylish women, who always went to great lengths with her appearance, and could have easily passed for being a good ten years younger than her seventy-eight years, seemed to have developed an over fondness for fur. The image of Gran wearing a fake fur hat, combined with fake fur boats and coat, with even one of those hand warmer things in fake fur, was for a moment, enough to make her forget the seriousness of the situation. This, combined with the adrenalin, Jess considered as the causation of the inappropriate reaction.

"Gran what's with all the fur, has the central heating broken or something?"

"Don't make me laugh dear, now is really not the time for your silly jokes."

Seeing her Gran clearly in pain and laid in an awkward position on the floor in the hallway just at the bottom of the stairs had the effect of making Jess regain her composure and return to the heroine Granddaughter role. Grabbing a coat from the coat stand beside the door, Jess rolled it into a ball and kneeled down in order to gently place it as a pillow under her Gran's head.

"Seriously though Gran what happened? It's lovely and warm in here so you weren't freezing to death. In which case I'm guessing the reason for the fur number is that you were going out."

"And you would be right super sleuth" came the quick witted reply, though spoken in a way that only someone in pain has the sound of. "Now who's being funny?"

"But Gran it's the middle of winter and I'm sure snow was forecast for today. You should have just called me if you needed anything, though what could be so urgent that you had to go out at this time on a Sunday morning is beyond me."

"I would have sweetie but I didn't need anything." Jess and her Gran had always enjoyed this kind of casual banter, and it seemed that they each had chosen the method of remaining as normal as possible in a crisis as the best method of coping and so the banter continued;

"So why are you suddenly looking guilty Gran, it's not a crime to be over fond of fur you know!"

In response Jess received a steely glare from her Gran, however undeterred she continued. "Seriously though, the ambulance will be here in a minute and they're going to want to know what happened. Am I supposed to say you passed out with the most likely cause being that you over heated due to a new fur fetish?"

Momentarily her Gran's eyes closed as she took a deep breath, and then with an element of obstinacy in her tone she blurted out. "Oh for god's sakes Jess, it was because of Elvis!"

Not for minute did Jess suspect that actually Elvis was not indeed dead as is popularly believed, and that instead he had been hiding in her Gran's spare bedroom. No, Jess knew what the answer was going to be before she even asked the question, because hadn't her Gran being harping on about the same thing for ages now, and hadn't all the family tried to talk her out of it? However, Jess still had to ask the obligatory, "Who on earth is Elvis?" question, though she had to bite her lip so as not to start laughing again when she asked it, primarily because she was fighting with the mental imagery of the King of Rock emerging on cold wintry mornings to escort old ladies to the corner shop in a jewel encrusted jump suit.

By this point, Jess was trying really hard not to start giggling again and was biting her lip so hard she was close to drawing blood. Instead she managed to hold it together whilst she waited for her Gran to explain.

"He's my puppy and I was just about to take him for his first walk. I thought I'd go early so it would be quiet in order not to frighten him with too much noise and, well I think he was excited. Anyway, I tripped over him and then I think he must have left a little puddle by the door because I slipped and that was it. I knew I was going to fall and tried to grab the coat stand. That didn't help and as you can see I fell, but I landed funny and I knew something had broken. It's agony if I try and move."

"Well don't try and move then, but Gran honestly I can't believe you've gone and got yourself a dog, I thought we'd managed to talk you out of the idea. I'm guessing mum and dad don't know because they rang me yesterday and never mentioned it."

"Right again Miss Super Sleuth; you know you're not quite as dippy as I thought dear. I mean I know I have to look after your passport seeing as you've lost the last three and it's because of things like that that I forget that you actually went to University. I've often wondered why you didn't pursue a proper career in mind reading or whatever it was, instead of having a million different jobs. Though I must admit you've surprised me making a go of that flower shop."

"Stop trying to change the subject, and I'm not sure now's the time to be discussing career choices do you?"

Jess wouldn't have wanted to discuss her chosen career at the moment even if her Gran wasn't in her present dilemma because in truth, she wasn't quite sure herself as to why she hadn't tried a bit harder to become the country's leading expert on criminal behaviour which had been her intention her entire time at Uni. Of course, Jess having a career whilst being married to the dazzling Brandon hadn't seemed important. Instead she had loyally followed him around the country eventually settling in London, the only real place for a financial genius to flourish, which indeed he had.

She had been flattered when he had asked her to marry him on their graduation day, insisting that she was and always would be the only girl for him. And although her parents were against the idea of her marrying so young, when she stood in the register office and looked up at the handsome young man stood beside her, she had no doubt that her future would be perfect.

And it had been, well at least she thought it had. Right up until the point that the gorgeous dynamic Brandon had come home one evening and informed Jess in a not too sensitive manner that he had fallen for his personal trainer. A tale heard a million times, only Brandon's personal trainer was the equally gorgeous and dynamic Justin, all six foot two of tanned, toned muscles with twinkling eyes and a smile to die for. Jess had felt totally humiliated and inadequate, and had hot footed it back to Yorkshire where she spent the first two weeks crying into the pillows of the bed in the spare room of her Grandma's house.

Jess's intention had been to stay up there in her solitude forever, or at least for a very long time. However, it wasn't long at all before she had been enticed downstairs by the bribe of a homemade Sunday lunch. And so the recovery process had begun. Of course it had helped that she was back, where her Gran defined as "home" and "where she belonged," and of course the biggest added bonus was that her best friend lived only a few minutes' walk away. Kate had spent many hours passing tissues to Jess whilst she cried her way through the part where Brandon had told her that he couldn't live in denial anymore, that he loved her but not as much as Justin, and right on cue for what seemed liked the millionth time the tissues would come out. Six months later though and a few good nights out, and in, with the girls, and Jess was back to being herself. One surprising outcome of her new life was that she was now the proud owner of Funky Flowers, the somewhat quirky flower shop located on the corner of the village high street.

Yesterday had been the grand reopening in order to demonstrate Jess as the new owner. The shop had been redecorated and designed to combine both classic and contemporary and Jess had to admit, it seemed to be a success. In-between sipping champagne and schmoozing with the customers, she had mused upon the notion of what a funny old life it can be.

Jess had reflected upon how passing time by idly meandering down the high street of the little village on the outskirts of her beloved Bradford, could lead to such a dramatic change in career. She had merely been admiring the beautiful array of flowers in the window display when she noticed the advertisement for a shop assistant and on a whim had decided to apply. Jess had immediately loved working in the flower shop. After attending an evening course at college, and because she had always had a bit of a creative streak, it hadn't taken long for her to enjoy the challenge of creating something new and personal for customers. So when old Mrs Jacobs had decided to sell the business and adjoining flat, Jess jumped at the chance. She and Brandon had been fortunate enough to have a considerable amount of collateral in their London property, aided by the fact they had moved so many times. As such, the only good thing to come out of her divorce was that she had been fortunate enough to buy both the shop and the flat from Mrs Jacob's out of her settlement. And now, with the combination of the personal touch mixed with the unique designs Jess had created, the shop now had a new image and an expanding customer base.

It was hard work though, a lot harder than she had anticipated. Jess had to be up early in the morning for deliveries of stock. And though she was thankful that this element of her working day was made easier by merely having to walk down the stairs of her flat to her place of work, it was still not her favourite thing to do. It was well known to everyone who knew her that Jess was not what you would define as a morning person.

The organisation of it all was proving a bit of a challenge too as her Gran was right, organisation was not really Jess either. So having accounts and bills and delivery schedules and orders was driving Jess just a little bit crazy, though she considered it was worth it to meet lots of nice people who whilst placing their desired order, seemed to want to share their life stories. Jess loved the idle banter that took place whilst she created one of her unique floral designs primarily because one thing Jess thrived upon, was meeting new people, "A people person," her Gran called her. So albeit that she was somewhat disorganised, the business seemed to be thriving. This Jess knew, was partly because she had been fortunate to have retained so much of the original customer base, due to the fact that they had grown to know Jess over the time she had worked for Mrs Jacobs.

And Jess did love the independence of having her own business; her only concern was that having now achieved so much in such a short time, she would she get bored. She normally did, having kept most jobs for about six months. This she knew was because she enjoyed the challenge of learning something new, and once she had completed it, she would generally move on. This time though it wouldn't be so easy and maybe it was the commitment that she was worrying about. Last night whilst she and Kate had celebrated long after everyone else had left, Jess had voiced her concerns to Kate. Since the day they started primary school together they had become inseparable and had even chosen to study at the same university. Kate knew Jess better then she knew herself and as such Jess valued her opinion. Kate had told her to stop being ridiculous and that having your own business was completely different and she wouldn't have time to get bored and to some extent this had pacified Jess. However, as she drifted off to sleep that night she was already wondering what she might like to be next.

Jess decided now was not the time to get into that particular conversation. Surely the ambulance would be here soon. Jess hoped so because it was clear Gran was in increasing pain. For this reason she decided to stop giving her a hard time over the dog – that conversation could wait and in truth, Jess wasn't really that surprised. Ever since Jess's Granddad Bill had died two years ago, her Gran had been talking about getting a dog. Her Granddad had been a wonderful husband to Jess's Grandma Jean but he always refused to let his much adored family have a dog. He always insisted that he had an allergy to them, although the story was that he had been attacked by one as a child and had been scared of them ever since. And so his loving family which comprised of Jess's Grandma Jean, her father John and his sister Barbara had conceded, because other than his refusal to let the family have a dog, he had been the perfect husband and father. However since Bill had suddenly died of an heart attack two years ago, Jess's Gran, who had relinquished owning a dog for so long, had brought up the subject at every opportunity. Though coming to think of it, Jess realised that she hadn't mentioned it for a few weeks now. And no wonder, because having discussed all the negative things about owning one, her Gran had gone and got a puppy anyway. *Interesting,* thought Jess, *that blows the concept that you live and learn right out of the water.*

Jess was getting worried. Her Gran was beginning to look very pale and it was clear she was in a great deal of pain now, and the fact that she hadn't bothered to come back with a quick-witted reply or justify herself was worrying Jess even more. Gran always had the last word normally.

"So where is the furry assassin then because the ambulance should be here any minute, in fact I can hear it now and I don't want to have to go looking for it if it escapes while I have the door open?."

"In the kitchen, or possibly the living room, I'm not sure; I believe I scared him when I fell Jess."

"Well I can't find it now, because that's definitely your ambulance and I can't see it here in the hallway so I'm going to lock the kitchen and living room doors and I'll find it later."

Jess stood by the open door waving to attract the attention of the ambulance even though it was already coming to a halt outside the neat semi-detached and, in no time at all a short, stocky built paramedic of about fifty years of age had made his way up the garden path and was following Jess into the house. After an observation that identified a definite break in Grandma Jean's ankle, with the possibility of other injuries, Jess was locking the door to her Gran's house whilst Grandma Jean was being loaded into the back of the ambulance.

Jess locked the door and turned round to make her way down the path to join the waiting ambulance which now had her Gran loaded on board. However one of the ambulance crew was making their way back up the path looking very... *what was that look, worry, anxiety*? Jess could have sworn he had an element of embarrassment but either way she was beginning to get that panicky feeling again. "Now I don't want you to panic but we've had to call for backup."

"What the hell do you mean back up?" Jess almost shouted as she pushed past him and hurried back down the path and towards the back of the ambulance dreading what she might find, though needing to know. Jess couldn't see the back of the ambulance as it was facing away from the house. And as she rushed to find out what could be so bad that it required backup, she came to a halt so suddenly that the paramedic behind her nearly knocked her off her feet, although his lightning quick reflexes meant that he was now holding onto Jess by the waist. Jess was for a moment speechless, and as she regained her composure and steadied herself the only thing she could think to say was "I don't believe it."

The reason for the somewhat cliché remark was due to the fact that standing right there in front of her was the second ambulance crew member looking rather embarrassed, with a slight smirk on his face as though he was trying really hard not to laugh as he stood holding the ambulance door. Not open and attached to the ambulance, but actually holding *the* door.

"Sorry, about this. We have already called for some back up and I can assure you that the short delay won't affect your Gran's health or recovery. I just can't understand it, it were fine when we started our shift wasn't it Jake."

Jake, who had now let go of Jess, had hopped into the back of the ambulance to check on his patient and shouted from inside. "Yep I checked myself before the start of the shift, but not to worry there'll be another one along in a minute and it means that I get to chat to this gorgeous young lady for a bit longer."

Jess's Gran was giggling like a love struck teenager now instead of the injured pensioner that she was, and although Jess was beginning to feel more and more like she had somehow morphed into a Carry On film, she had to admit that the paramedics' smooth talking charm was clearly working a treat at keeping her Gran calm and entertained. Jess who had initially been stunned into silence by the ridiculousness of the situation burst into laughter as she took a seat beside her Gran. This ultimately had the effect of easing the tension from the

11

situation and resulted in a chorus of laughter. And although Jess could no longer see the paramedic who was now hidden from view behind the offending door, he too could be heard laughing as the ambulance door was moved back and forth in unison.

In the short time it took for the replacement vehicle to arrive, Jess found herself giggling along with her Gran to the stories being shared by the paramedic as he monitored her health. He clearly had a way of putting his patients at ease and was a fabulous story teller, and though she was somewhat embarrassed to admit it, as he had loaded her Gran into the replacement ambulance, she could not help but notice his fabulous physique.

Jess felt cold and tired as she made her way back to collect her car and the Furry Assassin from Gran's house. It hadn't taken long for a replacement ambulance to arrive and ferry them to hospital where it had been confirmed that her Gran had a fractured ankle and wrist along with some serious bruising, and the doctor had insisted she stay in hospital for a few days as a precaution. The bus wasn't Jess's favourite method of travel, primarily because it always seemed to take twice as long to get anywhere. Although Jess had patience when it came to creating fabulous floral masterpieces, in every other element of her life, patience was not one of her virtues. Now in the cold dark January evening, the journey seemed to be taking an age. Even though it was Sunday which generally meant there was less traffic on the roads, it still seemed like an eternity before she reached her Gran's house. Jess could swear it was taking longer than it normally should: typical considering she was still in her pyjamas, wearing no makeup and with hair that looked like it hadn't seen a comb in days. Just watch, any minute now Mr Drop Dead Gorgeous would get on the bus just to round the day off.

'Thank God for small mercies', Jess thought as she got off at the stop at the bottom of her Gran's street. Mr Gorgeous had not got on the bus, and as such Jess considered that at least she had been spared the possibility of meeting the love of her life whilst looking like a pyjama-wearing cave woman.

Jess switched on the hallway light and closed the front door behind her. Then remembering that her Gran had thought that the four legged fiend had last been seen entering either the living room or kitchen, Jess began her search. Opening the living room door, Jess took in a quick scan of the room, proudly reflecting on the fact that the living room didn't really portray a pensioner, although she considered that her Grandma Jean didn't really represent your typical blue-rinsed pensioner. She was instead a vibrant woman who retaliated against the ageing process with the deployment of a few successful tactics. These included dying her hair a lovely chestnut colour that off set her fabulous hazel-coloured eyes a treat. She also participated in regular exercise and wore really rather trendy clothes. The end result being one in which it was easy to forget that grandma Jean was in fact a pensioner.

Jess considered that the decor was representative of her Gran. It looked like a room from one of those 'Fabulous Homes' magazines. The walls were plastered and then finished in white with the recesses painted an unusual shade of dark turquoise, and the massive corner sofa and footstool gave a very minimalist finish. For one moment Jess made another mental note to give her flat a makeover.

Having quickly scanned the room, Jess decided the minimalist look definitely wasn't hiding any puppies. Never-the- less she decided it might be good to light the living room with a lamp in order to deter burglars and with this in mind, she headed toward the other end of the room. Although Jess had spent many hours in her Gran's house, it presented as an alien environment in the dimmed light. As she headed towards the lamp, she caught the edge of the sofa with her Ugg boots and although she tried unsuccessfully to retain her balance Jess began to fall.

As she toppled towards the floor Jess made a grab for the foot stool in an attempt to break her fall. It was at this moment that he was unceremoniously introduced to the somewhat startled Elvis, who made a strange whimpering sound and shot onto the sofa leaving Jess to break her fall by landing on the fake fur rug. *More fake fur* Jess mused as she lay there for a moment regaining her composure, *I must really talk to Gran about this.* Pulling herself up from the floor, Jess went to sit on the far end of the sofa, on the other end of which sat Elvis, who even in the dim light Jess could make out to be one extremely cute though very big puppy. She considered it an easy mistake to make that a puppy that large and curled up fast asleep could be mistaken for a foot stool.

How in the name of God did you sleep through me coming into the house? You certainly don't bode well as a guard dog do you? Jess stated, though more to herself than to Elvis.

Jess could see that the puppy was shaking with fear and so decided the best course of action would be to calm it down with the use of food. The "if in doubt, resort to food" plan had always worked for Jess and as dippy as she could be, even she knew that scared dogs are prone to bite. Though it may have been a puppy, it was already the size of a foot stool and Jess didn't fancy getting nipped by it. So she slowly rose off the sofa and backed into the hallway. Two minutes later she was back with a dish of water and a bowl of food. She deduced that the little rascal would be thirsty having been locked in the living room all day. She was right. Elvis was hungry and thirsty and whilst Jess was not overly fond of dogs, she was pleased to see him tucking into supper.

"Right little one, you fill your boots whilst I do a few security checks."

Having checked the living room windows, Jess headed back into the kitchen. Everything seemed secure so Jess picked up her handbag and turned to head back into the hallway, where she nearly fell over the puppy again.

"Crikey you really are like a furry assassin; you've already taken down myself and one pensioner and now you very nearly floored me again I think the best thing for now is if I just carry you so you can't make a third attempt."

With the puppy thrown over one shoulder and her handbag over the other, Jess struggled to lock the door, and then somewhat deflated, she said out loud to the bemused puppy, "Well for now Elvis, you are leaving this building and coming home with me."

Twenty minutes later and Jess was back in her flat. Kicking the door shut behind her, she made straight for the battered old sofa that had come with the flat, a house warming gift from Mrs Jacobs. The chocolate brown sofa may not have been modern in its design but it was soft to the touch and the arm rests were at the perfect level to rest you're head on and have a nap. Which Jess had often done after a particularly busy day in the shop.

Jess cursed out loud as she threw her handbag to one side and the array of contents spilled out, displaying a variety of random objects. Some of which included last year's diary, an empty crisp packet and a half full bottle of coke (diet coke) she noticed, proud of the fact that she was at least making some changes to her diet, albeit small ones. Rather than putting the items in their rightful place, i.e. a bin, Jess merely brushed the items off the sofa and onto the floor. She then placed Elvis on the middle cushion whilst she sank into the cushion at the end of the sofa. And for two minutes she just sat there with her eyes shut taking in the events of the day. Yep it was definitely up there as one of her worst days.

Not because of the frantic phone call, the crazy rescue drive, or the very random emergency services experience did her day represent as one of her worst. And it was not because her Gran was ill, as she had been reassured by the medical team at hospital that her Gran would be fine. And it was not the embarrassing bus journey home in her PJ's , no, it was not because of any of those things that Jess was now massaging her forehead in the hope of dissipating the migraine that was trying to materialise. It was because she knew that for the foreseeable future, she would be babysitting one very large fur ball with the ridiculous name of Elvis, and the truth of the matter was that, like her Grandfather, Jess was not overly fond of dogs.

Chapter Two

Monday morning on another cold dark wintery day and this time when Jess heard her mobile going she knew it was the alarm and that it was time to get up. However in keeping with her usual routine, she reached over picked up her mobile and chose snooze without even opening her eyes. Although she was still half asleep, she could feel the cold of her bedroom due to dodgy central that along with the dodgy old sofa had come with the flat. What this meant in real terms was that the heating was temperamental. In the summer, the flat was boiling as every radiator came on when she ran a bath and in winter, it was freezing as the heating went, well she was not sure where the heating went but it certainly didn't get to the radiators very often.

Jess began to turn over although it wasn't easy as the duvet felt like a lead weight. She had been curled on her side of the bed, the left side, a habit she had unconsciously continued to do since becoming single, as the right side had belonged to Brandon. However, now as she turned and peered over in the dim light of the room, she found that the space which had belonged to Brandon had now been replaced by one very asleep Elvis. Jess peered at the puppy, thinking how very much he looked like a teddy bear. He was a black and white bundle of fluff with a white muzzle and paws. However, unlike a teddy bear, this bundle of fluff was laid in a much more undignified manner: on his back. And, the ultimate insult Jess considered was that he had the cheek to be snoring. Not unlike Brandon, but not so attractive.

'I don't bloody well believe it, I went to all that trouble of making a lovely bed in the kitchen out of the spare duvet and in return I was kept awake half the night with your chuffing whining. And so it would seem that whilst you were quiet and I was sleeping, you came up with this little plan. If I wasn't so annoyed I'd be impressed.'

Jess just laid there for a few minutes taking in the scene. It was odd to say the least; she had become accustomed to having her bed to herself. It had been getting for the best part of a year now since her split from Brandon and the first time she did share her bed, it was with a dog!

Jess had been up and about for half an hour getting ready for the busy day that lie ahead and still Elvis was sleeping. *This is ridiculous, what does it take to wake that animal? "I know what should work,"* Jess told herself and left the flat.

It was just too convenient having a sandwich shop right next door. She considered it an added bonus that the shop catered for workmen wanting to consume a calorie loaded, big dirty breakfast before heading off to negotiate the local motorway network to earn a day's wage and as such, it sold the biggest breakfast baps in miles. Jess had vowed only to go there once a week in order to lose the few pounds she had had gained since coming home, the pounds she had gained due to her frequent visits next door. The understated little sandwich shop had the unusual name of Route 66 and Jess had previously asked Joanne the owner why she had chosen this as the name for her business, considering that they were situated near Junction twenty-six of the motorways in Yorkshire Jess could not identify a correlation. Joanne had gone on to relay tales of her time travelling the American route 66 which had both intrigued Jess and left her feeling a little sad that she had never fulfilled the travelling ambitions she had planned just before meeting Brandon.

Ten minutes later Jess returned to the flat in possession of two mega breakfasts in bread rolls, ingenious.

"Well Elvis I believe back in the day, the real king was partial to a bit of junk food so if it's breakfast good enough for a King then surely it'll work on you and if it doesn't, I give up you'll have to stay in bed all day, which I believe is another trait of your namesake – maybe Gran was on to something when she named you."

However, it worked. One waft of the delicious aroma in front of Elvis's nose and he was awake and excitedly jumping up and down. Too excitedly it would seem, as it soon became evident to Jess that there was a small wet patch on her bed linen. Not the best start to her day.

Picking up the young Elvis, whilst holding him at arm's length, Jess placed him on the floor and gave him half of the mega breakfast bap. This she concluded was enough for a puppy (albeit a huge one) and so the rest she wrapped up and popped in her bag for later. Realising she was beginning to run late, Jess quickly stripped the sheets from the duvet and then opening the cupboard on the corridor which stored the laundry basket, she threw both items in, taking stock once again, of how much washing needed to be done. Jess could not determine whether she was incredibly clean, hence all the changes of clothes or incredibly dirty, hence the need for the changes in clothes. Jess determined to consider that notion at a time much more convenient than now.

Feeling tired, grumpy and a little stiff, most likely she reasoned, being due to the fact that she had shared her bed with a dog, Jess picked up the very heavy Elvis. *Crikey! I think Gran must have had the King of Rock in his curvier stage in mind when she named you Elvis*, Jess muttered, as she carried him down the back stairs that adjoined the shop. She wasn't sure of his capacity for understanding the logistics of steps and decided that now was not the time to find out. Unlocking the door, Jess encouraged Elvis into the back yard, and in truth was mightily impressed when he immediately did a wee, albeit that he did so like a girl Jess noted.

Having ensured that the gate was securely fastened, Jess turned to make her way into the back room and into the shop. Her intention had been to leave Elvis in the yard, however as soon as she entered the premises, he was immediately behind her again. *Honestly Elvis, you need to stop with this clinginess it's not an attractive quality in a guy*, Jess muttered as she entered the shop and began busying herself with the jobs in hand. Namely release the shutters, put the open sign on the door and put the kettle on, as without fail every morning since Jess had taken ownership of the shop, Mrs Jacobs would be there to offer 'guidance'. Since moving out of the flat above the shop, Mrs Jacobs and her husband had moved into a little bungalow just a couple of streets away. It was much better for the both of them as with each passing year the climb of the stairs to the flat had become progressively more difficult. Jess had become used to this early morning intrusion. At first she had felt a little inadequate, however, in time she had realised that although Mrs Jacobs came across as a bit scary she had in fact, Jess's best interests at heart. She had helped Jess on numerous occasions, be it with advice, a large order or watching the shop whilst Jess popped out (usually next door to the sandwich shop) or just making a brew. One thing was sure, Mrs Jacobs had become invaluable, and very reliable. Usually she arrived at about nine thirty in time to help with the days delivery and left around two in the afternoon, following the lunch time busy period when Jess had made any deliveries. However, this morning Jess rang Mrs Jacobs straight away, immediately apologising for the early intrusion of her phone call and asked if she could do Jess a big favour and watch the shop for the afternoon. Jess then went on to explain the tale of what had happened in the last twenty-four hours and that she wanted to go and visit her Gran in hospital that afternoon and that on her way home, she wanted to call at the shops to get some essential items, namely essential items required for a dog. Jess had already anticipated that she would have to keep him for at least a few days until her parents were back from their holidays in Benidorm. And although she hadn't had much to do with dogs, even she knew that bacon sandwiches wouldn't fill him up. Jess also decided that a basket was definitely required, because one thing was for sure, the young Elvis was not sleeping with Jess again tonight.

Having organised for Mrs Jacobs to stay on a little while longer, she got straight on the telephone to her parents. The international dialling tone rang and just when Jess was about to think that a continental breakfast took priority over answering the mobile phone to their only daughter, her mum picked up. Jess fully expected it to be her mother who answered the phone because for some reason her Dad was just not fond of the *'contraptions',* as he called them.

"Morning Jess."

Not sweetie or love or precious Jess noted. Jess's mum had never been one for shows of sentimentality which is why Jess had chosen to go and stop with her Gran when her marriage had collapsed, but just for once it would be nice.

"I can't talk for long Jess, we're just about to go down for breakfast."

"Well I won't keep you long because this call will cost me a fortune, but Mum I thought you should know, Gran had an accident yesterday. Before you start to panic, she's fine now. She is in hospital though, with a broken ankle but honestly she seems fine and in good spirits. I didn't call you last night because it was late by the time I got home and Gran told me not to worry you and to wait until today. There's something else though that I think you might be a bit surprised at actually."

Jess then went on to explain the story of Elvis and how she had had to step in to look after him.

"So you see Mum when you get back, I'm going to need you to look after him."

"But I can't Jess," came the quick reply.

"What do you mean you can't?" Jess sighed.

"Sid wouldn't like it, he's not young any more you know and he certainly can't move as fast as he used to. No it just wouldn't be right."

"For Christ's sake Mum, he's a bloody rabbit! I don't really see how he can have much say in the matter. Can't you just put him in a cage in the shed like everyone else does or leave him at that fancy bunny retreat you've sent him to while you're on your hols?"

"Well, when you're as old as Sid is I think the last thing you'd want is a puppy pestering you and no, I can't put him in the shed he'd be traumatised plus we've just had the new carpet in the hallway fitted. Sid has been house trained for years but a puppy wouldn't be. So I'm sorry Jess but the answer has got to be no, you're just going to have manage, and you never know you might become an animal lover in the process. Now I really do have to go so pass my love onto your Gran and tell her she must come to stop with your Dad and me when we get back."

And with that the call was over. "Well I had better keep that little snippet of information from Gran, I wouldn't want to depress her," Jess smirked as she put the receiver down.

Mrs Jacobs arrived a little earlier as Jess had requested. Jess was in the store room at the back of the house when she arrived, but she knew instantly it was her. The robust woman moved remarkably fast for an elderly person and she filled any space which she occupied in a confident and charismatic way. Unlike her Gran, Mrs Jacobs had the appearance of a more traditional pensioner. She had thick white hair that she wore pinned securely into a bun most days and her choice of clothing was generally loose fitting blouses and skirts which were predominantly hidden under the floral pinafore that she wore whilst working in the shop. However, for a woman of her age, Mrs Jacobs possessed a fabulous complexion and she had the most beautiful pale blue eyes that twinkled when she laughed or told a dirty joke which she was fond of doing. Jess was intrigued by the multi-faceted Mrs Jacobs whom she considered to be somewhat of a chameleon. Not long after Jess had returned home, she had gone for an Italian meal one Friday evening with Kate and had been shocked to see one very elegantly dressed Mrs Jacobs with one very proud looking Mr Jacobs.

Mrs Jacobs stopped in the doorway between the shop and the store room, "so where is the furry assassin then?"

"Sleeping, again," replied Jess, as she pointed to the furry bundle asleep on some cardboard under the work shelf in the store room "in fact he's been asleep since I gave him the rest of the mega bap I bought him for breakfast."

"In truth though, love I've been inclined to nod off myself after one of those," laughed Mrs Jacobs as she took a step closer to observe the new addition.

Jess stopped herself from pointing out that Elvis was in fact almost seventy-five years younger and therefore had no excuse to sleep so much, however her in- built manners-police stepped up to stop her.

"To be honest," Jess continued, "I'm not over fond of dogs, well any animals really as you know but I must admit, I'm getting a little bit worried because he's either poorly or he is the laziest dog in the world."

"I wouldn't worry love, he's just a baby and that's what babies do, sleep all the time, I'd make the most of it if I were you."

Elvis didn't seem poorly, although he slept most of the morning and as such didn't get in the way of any of the chores she and Mrs Jacobs accomplished. In fact, the only time he had made a noise was when they had both been in the store room working on a delivery and he had started whining, so Jess (thinking it must be time for him to go for another tinkle) took him in the back yard. As Jess had anticipated, he produced another puddle and when he came back in he sat down in the store room by the entrance to the shop.

"He's a remarkably well behaved puppy," Mrs Jacobs praised as she bent down to stroke him.

"Ermm...., we'll see, I bet they all seem great at first," Jess had replied looking at Elvis with misgivings.

"Who you talking about love, dogs or people?" Mrs Jacobs asked as she went back to the delivery she was working on.

"Both," Jess laughed, and then they both quietly concentrated on getting the order completed.

It was two o' clock and Jess had returned from her deliveries.

"Right I'd best go. I want to have a word with the Doctor if I can. The visiting finishes at four and I'm going to bob into that pet superstore on my way back. You know the big one on the ring road, 'We Love Pets' or something else ridiculous along those lines. Anyway, I shall be back in good time to close up, there isn't a great deal to do so I've put some magazines behind the counter and with regard to Elvis -,"

"Elvis!" Mrs Jacobs interrupted with a laugh."

"Yes, Elvis. Not my choice of name," giggled Jess in response, "Hopefully he'll sleep all afternoon for you." And with that Jess was out of the door.

It was half past two when she finally made her way onto Ward Three, the orthopaedic fracture ward, to find her Gran in fine spirits, remarkably fine spirits for someone who had just had an ankle bones reset. There was also a slight bruise to her Gran's forehead and a couple of scratches – *most likely when you landed on the dog I wouldn't wonder,* Jess mused. Nevertheless, her Gran seemed to have come through the experience like a trooper and went on to excitedly tell Jess about her surprise visitor. The surprise visitor turned out to be the very attractive paramedic who had called in especially to see how she was getting on.

"Not that attractive Gran or I would have noticed" Jess intervened. "And no disrespect to you or royalty, but you did say last month that Camilla had got herself quite a catch with Prince Charles and you were talking about his looks not his money or status before you say anything," she added as an afterthought.

"Well Charles is a bit of a catch and so is that nice paramedic," her Gran had chastised, though with good humour.

An hour and half later, having eaten half of the chocolates Jess had bought at the little shop in the hospital entrance and having listened to her Gran report on the variety of illnesses bestowed upon the unfortunate patients, Jess gave her Gran a kiss and left with the promise to return as soon as possible.

Jess arrived back to Funky Flowers, the shop that had become her home, at four fifteen, earlier than she had planned. Her Gran had insisted that her precious Elvis should have his staple diet of the best quality food and his favourite toys and so upon these instructions, she had left an half an hour before the end of visiting time. Jess had decided not to go back to her Gran's until later that evening to pick up the pooch provisions Gran had at her house and though she had not intended to do so, she ended up investing in practically all new products. The priority of these being a new dog basket, this Jess decided was a good investment in order to not spend another night of Elvis sharing hers.

"Am I glad to see you!" was the first thing Mrs Jacobs said as Jess struggled through the door and dumped the seventy pounds worth of products in the middle of the shop floor.

"Why, has it been busy?"

"Well it was steady, which is a good job if you're going to plan on spending on the dog like that on a regular basis; you're going to have to sell a whole load of flowers that's for sure. But that isn't why I'm glad to see you. No, the reason I'm glad to see you is because, this little rascal did nothing but whine for the first hour you were gone. He escaped from that box you put him in straight away, I mean he was going to, wasn't he – a dog that size could do with a lion cage not a cardboard box. And then having escaped he went and stood behind the door for the next twenty minutes, and when Mrs Tyler came for that order for the church hall, she very nearly became his next victim. Tripped over him she did, because he was trying to get out, the little rascal. In the end, up I popped upstairs and brought down one of those cushions off my old sofa and he's been asleep in the back room for about an hour now, I've kept checking on him though. I've changed my mind; I reckon you've got yourself quite a handful there Miss." And with that Mrs Jacobs opened the door that held the very excited Elvis captive and out he came bouncing towards Jess.

"Right then I'll be off and do you know for the first time in years I will actually be glad to get home for some peace and quiet," and on that final note Mrs Jacobs scuttled out of the shop.

"Look, you've upset Bettie now, you little monster. I hope you haven't scared her off completely."

It was supposed to be a chastisement, however it failed miserably as Jess found herself kneeling down to reciprocate the attention being lavished on her.

"So you like your tummy tickling do you? Well then you'd best learn to be good for Bettie or you will be on the transfer list again, I couldn't do this without her you know, so be good in future."

It was just after five so Jess decided to shut the shop early. Picking up Elvis she carried him up the stairs to the flat and left him by the entrance to the door as she hurried back down the stairs to collect her purchases, and balancing all the items inside the dog basket, she made her way back to the stairs to find Elvis sat on the top step whimpering.

"Oh for god's sakes I've only been gone a minute! I see you've managed the first step though." Jess manoeuvred into the living room and threw the items down onto the sofa before throwing herself down next to them.

26

"Great!, One day as the owner of a pet and I've started on the slippery slope to becoming a crazy old spinster who spends all day talking to the animals." Taking in a deep sigh of self-pity Jess stood up "Well I'd best get busy, still lots to do before bed."

Jess made do with soup for tea while Elvis wolfed down his pedigree chum. It wasn't until she was on the ring road headed towards her Gran's house with Elvis strapped into the passenger seat that she had considered whether a puppy might get car sick so soon after eating (though he didn't which secretly impressed her). Jess left him in the car whilst she popped into her Gran's to check everything was ok.

When she came back out, Jess found the next door neighbour chatting to the dog through the window in that annoying, high pitched way people usually communicate to babies. Jess knew it was supposed to have scientific benefit to babies however she seriously doubted that it would have that effect on a dog.

Jess had decided to leave the spare key with the next door neighbour Barbara who had agreed to watch the house for a couple of days until her parents got home, whom she had decided she would then delegate that task to. It felt strange giving the keys of a house that was not her own to a third party, however Jess made the executive decision that fifty years of neighbouring qualified someone to be a key holder. Added to this, Jess knew that Barbara had become a good friend to her Gran, especially since the death of her Granddad. Plus she had consistently sent chocolates round for Jess to cheer her up when she was heartbroken over Brandon. Jess waved to Barbara as she drove the car out of the cul-de-sac and out onto the main road and then started to giggle to herself before talking out loud to Elvis, again!

"In all honesty Elvis if squatters lived next door to Gran, I'd of most likely have been tempted to leave the keys with them if they'd bribed me with chocolate" and then she giggled again, at the realisation that she was having such a ridiculous conversation with a dog. *I'm either really tired or I'm going mad,* she mused to herself, as she made her way home.

When she did arrive home, Jess made a cup of tea and made a quick phone call to Kate, updating her of the crazy events of the last couple of days and then crawled into bed at ten o' clock. She had actually tried bunking down at nine thirty with Elvis in the basket in the kitchen but he whined non-stop. So even though Jess knew she was asking for trouble she had relented and put the basket at the side of the bed next to the window.

It had worked a treat though, and when the alarm went off at seven thirty the next morning, Jess felt refreshed and for once she hadn't been bothered about being dragged from her sleep, predominantly because the recurrent dream of being married to Gerard Butler had been replaced with one of Elvis the dog wearing a jumpsuit and shades singing 'Hound Dog'. Jess hoped it was a one off, she had always enjoyed her sleep and those fantastic dreams but if that most recent dream was going to become recurrent, she considered it would be worth staying up and watching 'Super Casino' or some other late night dodgy TV show.

Jess peeked over the edge of the bed to find Elvis sleeping on his back with his back paws resting on the edge of the basket and once again a soft snore could be heard. *Strange way for a dog to sleep* Jess considered again, and with that she pulled back the covers and grabbed a pair of fluffy socks, one red and one blue out of the bedside drawers. This was a routine she had developed since moving into the flat, purely because the flat was cold in the morning. Jess headed into the kitchen and switched on the kettle, then headed down into the shop to switch on the heater behind the counter to begin warming up the little space. The rest of the shop was cold, and had to be in order that the flowers didn't wilt. She had learnt this lesson previously when autumn had set in – as always the shop had been freezing, and having identified that the thermostat on the radiators had been turned down she had turned them up. She had left the heating on all night, and when she had gone down the next morning, she had found that most of the stock had wilted, which had cost Jess quite a lot to replace. On the positive side, it was the only time the flat had ever felt warm. She hadn't made a profit that month though and so she had implemented some strategies, the socks being one of them.

Running back up the stairs to her flat Jess could hear a scratching and whining noise. As she opened the door to the kitchen she was met by an excited Elvis – who seemed to be a bit too excited, and left another little puddle.

"Oh honestly Elvis! I've only been gone two minutes. Do you know if you were a guy you would have serious issues?"

Jess gave the puddle a quick once over with the mop which had become a permanent fixture over the last couple of days, and then quickly got dressed and headed back down the stairs to the shop with the float for the till in one hand and Elvis in the other.

By nine thirty, Jess had finished her usual routine of unpacking the deliveries putting the 'Open For Business' sign the right way round on the door, checking any orders and popping the kettle on for when Mrs Jacobs would arrive. Then Jess made herself busy ensuring that the flower displays in the window looked fresh and enticing. This task didn't generally take Jess long unless she decided to give the window display a whole new look which she normally did about once a week. However, this morning what should have been a simple routine was being hampered, as every time Jess went to step back or turn around she kept tripping over Elvis. In the end she relented and fetched some stronger cardboard boxes which had arrived with yesterday's delivery, and made a makeshift holding area at either side of the till, with a bucket of flowers at either side holding them in place. It worked – Jess knew that had Elvis been inclined to do so, he could have easily have used his superior puppy power and knocked them down. However, he didn't seem to have the time to work this out due to all the whining he was doing. Never-the-less Jess was pleased with her makeshift kennel and busied herself with freshening and replenishing the window display.

Jess was in the storeroom adding milk to the two mugs of tea when she heard the doorbell chime and Mrs Jacobs made her punctual appearance. Mrs Jacobs had her own routine whereby she headed straight into the storeroom where she would hang her coat. She would then generally make a comment about the weather and then accept the mug of tea offered. Next she would have a couple of minutes moan about Mr Jacobs. They would then both head back into the shop and go over what was on the agenda for the day. Mrs Jacobs was so entrenched in the daily ritual that she had not noticed the subtle changes to the till area. Therefore, she nearly jumped out of her skin (making tea spill onto her fingerless gloves which she always wore at this time of the year in the shop) in response to Elvis springing up from behind the counter. In doing so the make-shift kennel of cardboard went flying, as did the contents of the bucket of flowers, spilling water all over the shop floor.

"Sweet Mary mother of god, I forgot about that little handful! "

Jess didn't reply to Bettie, instead she found herself once again talking to the dog. "Didn't take you long to escape after all did it? Maybe you're not as daft as I took you for."

"Oh so you knew it was there then and didn't think on to warn me. A woman my age, it could have given me a heart attack."

"I'm sorry Mrs Jacobs, it's the first time he's been quiet and I was unpacking those deliveries that I had put in the fridge yesterday, for two minutes I completely forgot about him."

Mrs Jacobs, having regained her composure placed her cup on the glass counter and then studied Elvis as though she had never seen a dog before in her life.

"Jess that has got to be one of the cutest puppies I have ever seen but what on earth possessed your Gran to get one that size? And to be honest, I'm surprised that you seem to be coping with the little guy, I never had you down as being the sort of lass that were keen on pets."

"You would be right Mrs Jacobs, because I'm not all that keen on them as you know, but it's been a bizarre weekend and I'm only dog minding for a short while so I can cope with that."

For the next hour they busied themselves with a large order that the chairwomen of the Women's Institute was collecting before lunch for a charity event they were holding. Jess worked in the back room in order to keep Elvis out of the shop, and the whole time he remained by her side.

"I was thinking, why don't you take Elvis down to the park, we've nearly finished that order now? He might like to get out of the shop for a while."

"I'm not sure Bettie."

Jess still found it difficult to call Mrs Jacobs by her Christian name. It had taken a whole year before Jess had found out her name and she had only done so after Mr Jacobs had let it slip one day upon calling into the shop to inform Bettie that he was off down to the bookies and that he wouldn't be long.

"Oh go on, I can hold the fort for a while. It can't be much fun for the little fella cooped up in there and he has been good and slept for the last hour and he'll be ready for a tinkle by now I reckon. It's not like it's out of the way, I mean you don't even have to cross a road. If you're going to have a dog then you couldn't be better located for the park."

"I'm not going to have a dog, I'm just dog sitting, but yes I will take him out for ten minutes, treat him to some grass instead of the back yard. I'll just pop upstairs and grab my coat and his lead."

"It's pretty cold out there love so I'd wrap up warm," Bettie shouted as Jess headed up the stairs to her flat.

Two minutes later and Jess was back downstairs and found that she mocked other people for it she had already turned into one of those people that talk to a dog as they would a baby. However she still found she could not stop herself from saying, "Are we going for a walkies then? Yes we are, we're going for a walkies," in a ridiculous voice.

"Bloody hell that was quick, I've only had him a couple of days and it's started already!" Jess laughed out loud.

"What's already started?" asked Bettie, looking somewhat bemused.

"Talking to the animals Bettie. I never thought I would turn into one of them people who talks to animals in the manner reserved for babies, but for some reason I just don't seem to be able to stop myself, it's very odd," replied Jess as she bent down to attach the lead to Elvis, patting the top of his head in the process.

Bettie observed the scene with a grin on her face, the kind of grin of someone who knows something you don't.

"For someone who reckons not to be fond of dogs, you could have fooled me."

"I don't usually but I used to say the same about curries and now I love them, so we'll have to wait and see – and you can't deny Bettie that Elvis is incredibly handsome." And with that Jess scooped him up and headed out of the shop.

Being located literally at the end of the high street, it should have taken just a few minutes. However what with Elvis refusing to walk and just about everybody stopping to fuss over him, it had already taken Jess fifteen minutes just to get to the gates of the park. Still carrying Elvis, Jess pushed open the iron gates and made her way in.

As a child Jess had spent hours in this park. It was where she had learnt to ride her bike, where she and best friend Kate had hung out on a night with the boys from high school. It was also where she had had her first kiss believing then, that she and her first high school crush would be together forever.

She had thought that it was the kiss that made her feel dizzy. However now as she stood remembering the moment as if it was yesterday, she smiled to herself with the realisation that it was obviously because they were on the roundabout at the time. It wasn't what you would call a pretty park, there was no boating lake or tea rooms, just a functional space that was well used. The swings and slides had been replaced, Jess noted, with a modern space age looking monstrosity, and skate ramps had been installed. Other than that, it was still just a large green space that the local rugby club competed on every Saturday. Jess hadn't realised until now that the reason she hadn't wanted to come back here since she had returned home was because it held so many mixed emotions.

"Well we're here now, you can't stay in the shop and yard indefinitely," Jess said to Elvis as she gently placed him down on the ground still securely attached to his lead. Jess decided it was too soon to chance how he would react to freedom.

Unlike every other time, he didn't immediately sit down. Instead he actively sniffed a route over to the grass where he immediately did a tinkle.

"Who's a clever boy then, yes you are," Jess heard herself saying, again in that ridiculous voice she seemed fast to be adopting when conversing with this dog.

Jess shivered and pulled the collar of her emerald green fake fur coat up around her neck acknowledging to herself the obsession for fake fur that she and her Gran seemed to share. Because she wasn't moving, Jess was beginning to feel incredibly cold. Her feet were freezing even though she was wearing her favourite cowboy boots, and she had forgotten her gloves so her fingers were frozen. *Gran had sense dressing like an Eskimo, next time I think I'll consider it myself if it keeps me warm*, she mused to herself.

Deciding to keep this first outing short and having been out for much longer than she had anticipated, Jess scooped up Elvis and turned to head out of the park. Up until now she and Elvis had been the only people in there, but as she turned to leave, an elderly man with a Jack Russell entered the park and headed towards her.

'*He looks just like the character Delboy out of only Fools and Horses* Jess noted', with his flat cap pulled low over his eyes, a tan coloured jacket and a paisley scarf fastened round his neck and tucked down the front of his jacket – 'Del Boy' was smart and stylish for a pensioner.

"Morning" Jess chirped up as they passed one another.

Nothing came back in reply, in fact he didn't even acknowledge her.

"How ignorant," Jess grumbled to herself. "There goes the notion that dog walkers are friendly – and old people, come to think of it."

Back in the shop Jess was finishing the flowers for the Women's Institute, which were due to be collected any time now. Jess was still a little peeved that the elderly man had ignored her. She considered herself to be a naturally sociable person, and the lack of acknowledgment from the elderly man had really bugged her.

"Do you know who the man in the park with the Jack Russell could be Bettie? I couldn't believe how ignorant he was; he completely ignored me like he hadn't even seen me."

"I can't think who you mean love, but I wouldn't let it upset you, maybe he didn't see you after all."

"Ermm... maybe Bettie, though I don't really believe that."

In actual fact James had not seen either Jess or Elvis or had he? He really could not be sure. These days he didn't seem to notice much of anything or anyone. The days just didn't seem to have meaning anymore. At first he hadn't wanted to do anything at all and the neighbours had rallied round to shop for him and walk Max. However, little by little, they had reduced this so that James had to go out and since then, walking the dog had ensured he got out of the house. Shopping could be completed once a week but a dog had to be walked every day. And it wasn't that he was ignorant (he had always been known as the life and soul of any party), it was just that now it took so much effort.

It had been six months since his beloved Rita had passed away after a short illness. She had complained of back pain for a long time. However, with her distrust of Doctors she had refused to get checked out, right until the time the pain had become too much to cope with. By then, it was too late and the cancer that had been situated beneath her spine her spread to her other organs and within weeks she was gone from his life.

He hadn't had time to prepare for her not being there and he had not accepted it six months later. In fact tomorrow would officially be six months since she had passed away and he would take some flowers up to the cemetery, he had only been there once as he just couldn't face it, but he knew he couldn't put it off forever. He would call in to the flower shop on the high street tomorrow as he had spotted a beautiful display in the window that he knew Rita would have loved.

Chapter Three

It was 7pm and Jess was sat in the comfy chair next to her Gran's bed, yawning as she listened to her Gran updating her again on the ailments of each of the patients on the ward. She had relayed her own day's events and passed on the phone message from her parents who had called earlier. They had reminded Jess they would be back from their holiday on Friday and could she pick them up from the airport. They had also insisted that Jess talk her Gran into stopping with them for a couple of weeks upon her discharge from hospital. It had not been well received by Gran. Better received were the stories of what little Elvis had been up to and how they had been for a walk, albeit a somewhat short one. Jess was just about to leave. She had thrown on her coat, hooped her favourite scarf around her neck, the one which looked like the kind Dr. Who would wear and had given her Gran a kiss. She was just scrabbling around in her bag to find the car keys when her Gran who had been muttering something to herself chirped up. "That's it, I knew there was something I hadn't told you. That nice paramedic called in again to see me. He said to say hi."

Jess looked up from routing around in her hand bag to see her Gran with a silly smirk on her face. "Is there some kind of message that I'm supposed to glean from that considering the silly look on your face, because I'm sure he was just being friendly? I think being friendly is on the job description if you work for the NHS, unless you're a consultant, although *your* consultant is quite nice."

"Well I think he wants to be friendly with you if you ask me."

"Well I didn't ask you and I'm not sure that I'm going to listen to your dating advice ever again after you told me the postman had a thing for me and that he was drop dead gorgeous. And who did he actually look like Gran?"

Gran did not answer this question, instead she merely started giggling so Jess continued.

"That's right, he looked like a young Prince Charles dressed as a postman didn't he Gran? So forgive me if I don't believe you this time and seriously, what is this crush you have on the future King all about? Anyway, thanks but although I know you mean well, I'm quite happy on my own and anyway for the time being I have Elvis in my life. You know the one you've offloaded on me, the lazy King of the canines who is fond of snoring."

The old lady in the bed next to her Gran had started giggling now. Jess's Gran turned towards Mavis, "I told you she always had an answer for everything!"

"Aye, you did that Jean, you weren't kidding were you?" And then in a more serious tone the old lady turned to Jess, "I think this time lass you should listen to your Gran. I tell you that is one fine looking young man. In fact he reminds of that actor off the telly...what's his name again?"

"Oh for heaven's sake, don't encourage her," Jess replied with a warm hearted smile that was in keeping with the casual banter. And with that Jess planted a kiss on her Gran's cheek and headed home.

As soon as Jess opened the door, Elvis was there excitedly jumping up and down as if separated for weeks and not hours. Jess noted that it was the first time that anyone had actually been so excited for her return home in a long time. Not that a dog was the same as returning home to Gerard Butler or some equally attractive example of the male species, but still it was surprisingly nice to not return to an empty flat. "I suppose you need to go out to the toilet don't you?" Jess asked the excited puppy as she picked him up and headed down the stairs and out into the yard, stopping off to pick up a piece of pretend grass from the store room and placing it in the corner of the yard. Whereby Elvis immediately went to the toilet which in turn spurred Jess into doing the baby talk again. She did try incredibly hard to resist, however she found herself continuing to have a conversation with Elvis in the same stupid voice as before, finishing off by saying, "Right, I think it's time for bed," which Jess was aware sounded equally wrong.

Seven-thirty, fifteen minutes earlier than usual and the alarm was going off. As usual the flat was freezing so Jess went through her usual routine in double quick time and by 8am she was heading out of the door. Elvis had had his breakfast in the time that Jess was getting dressed, though he left some of his Pedigree Chum, clearly not finding the dried biscuits as appetising as a breakfast mega bap from next door. Popping a piece of toast into her mouth, Jess picked up Elvis and headed down the stairs to the shop, stopping to put the heater on. It was a change to her usual routine though one she thought she would try in order to get more work completed by the time Bettie arrived. It was going to be a busy day in the shop and Jess's business head was driving her to be organised. Jess had hoped that at this time of the morning the high street would be a little quieter, however her hopes that it would be a quick walk for Elvis were immediately dashed when three workmen about to enter the sandwich shop spotted Elvis in Jess's arms. She smiled as she watched the burly men fuss over Elvis, stating how cute he was and how you didn't see so many Old English Sheepdogs around anymore. Now, running ten minutes behind schedule, Jess arrived at the park and as she pushed open the iron gates she stopped for a moment before putting Elvis down. The reason for her moment of hesitation was that this time on entering the park she had been struck by how magical it looked, and for the first time since being a child, she appreciated the simplistic beauty of it.

The park was encased with an old stone wall, which this morning appeared to have a silver tint covering it and the abundant expanse of grass glistened with its coating of frost on the early January morning. Jess had not realised, but she had for a moment not taken a breath. Not for a long time had the park held so much magic for her and when she did let out her breath it was tangible in the crisp morning air. "Wow!" Jess said out loud to Elvis and then the moment for Jess was gone. "Come on Elvis let's get you walked and then get back to the real world."

Jess had been so preoccupied observing the understated prettiness of the park that she had not noticed that it was really quite busy for early in the morning, well busier than yesterday. In the distance, she could make out someone jogging, and a number of people were also out walking their dogs. Unlike yesterday, Elvis seemed happy to explore a little further and so they slowly made their way along the path that led to the top of the park. It didn't take long before a woman whom Jess surmised looked about thirty came towards them. She was wearing sensible walking boots and clearly a practical all weather snow, wind and rain coat. "Oh what a gorgeous puppy!" she said as she bent down to stroke Elvis, who, on cue, was behaving like the ultimate puppy. Friendly and attentive, not unlike her ex-husband had behaved when in the company of new people, Jess observed with mixed thoughts.

Hidden behind the end of the world clothing, Jess noted was an attractive woman. True, it was hard to make her out with the hood of her waterproof coat pulled up almost covering her eyes. However, bits of what seemed to be long blonde hair were escaping from the all elements hood. And Jess noted that she had sparkling blue eyes that seemed to dance when she said that, "Elvis was truly the most gorgeous puppy, except of course for Copper, her Golden Cocker Spaniel." She had dashed off then, without really finishing the conversation mumbling something about having to finish breakfast and a late shift. And with that Jess checked the time on her phone and chided herself that tomorrow she would have to be a bit more organised as it was already nearly time to open the shop. She then scooped Elvis up and decided to carry him home, she still had not had the chance to spend the time introducing Elvis to walking on a lead with noise and traffic to adjust to and she decided that she did not have the time to do it now.

11am and Jess had been busy from what seemed liked the moment she had opened the shop doors. In between this, she was attempting to organise some accounts. Betty was in the store room sorting out the delivery and had just put the kettle on for them to take a five minute break to warm up, as it seemed colder than usual in the shop this morning. They had both agreed it did seem much colder than previously and Jess was busy telling Bettie that she might pop down to the hardware shop later if she got chance and invest in a new heater, when the doorbell chimed.

Jess looked up to observe an elderly gentlemen enter the shop. She welcomed him in with her usual 'good morning and if you need any help comment' and then continued with her work on the new window display. Jess could hear Elvis begin to stir from his sleep and seemed to make some strange noise, not quite barking or yelping but a mixture of both. Distracted for the moment, she hadn't noticed the elderly customer come and stand beside her and Jess was slightly embarrassed as she jumped slightly, in the way that you do when your personal space has been entered without you knowing. Composing herself, Jess stepped into professional mode and put on her best smile. She looked at the elderly customer who for some reason seemed familiar, though she didn't think he had been in the shop before. "I'm sorry, I was miles away for a moment there, anyway how can I help you?"

For a moment the gentleman didn't seem to notice that she had spoken, then with a shake of his head he replied, "I need flowers."

"Well you have come to the right place, what did you have in mind." Jess spoke the words in her usual chirpy manner, similar to the way sales' people adopt in order to ensure a sale; however in Jess's case it came naturally to her.

The elderly customer seemed a little more composed now. "Well I drove past the shop yesterday and saw a beautiful bouquet of roses, just there they were, and I wondered if you still had them available? ," he asked, whilst pointing to the area where Jess was currently working on the new display, before turning back to look at Jess.

"I'm afraid I don't have that particular bouquet still, however if you can wait ten minutes I can have one just like it ready for you," Jess answered enthusiastically.

"If you could that would be much appreciated," smiled the elderly gentleman, though the smile did not reach his eyes. He then wandered off to have a look around the shop.

In the time they had been speaking, Jess had been trying to place the individual. He was not one of her regular customers but she could not shake off the feeling that she had met him somewhere before.

James had been wondering the exact same thing. There seemed to be something familiar about this girl and yet he couldn't place it. He was all too well aware that he had not met many people over the last few months except for his family and neighbours and he had not ventured out of the house except for walking Max. At that moment, Elvis woke up and jumped up at Jess for attention. The man stared down at Elvis for a moment and then looked up at Jess.

"I think I owe you any apology," came the unexpected remark, spoken in a calm yet confident manner. "I do believe you spoke to me yesterday and I think I may have ignored you."

Jess recognised him then. Medium height, about sixtyish in age and dressed in a dark suit, smart yet understated. Yes, this was definitely the same elderly man that she had encountered in the park yesterday and had written off as being incredibly ignorant.

For two reasons Jess decided to forget about yesterday's unfortunate introduction. The first being that it was not really in her nature to hold a grudge, in fact she could not think off hand of anyone she had held a grudge against. She had even remained best friends with her ex-husband and his lover. And secondly, Jess respected honesty. At the time, her ex had broken her heart, however he was at least being honest, and it was apparent that this gentleman was being sincere in his apology. Jess decided he had no need to, he could have not acknowledged the event and she would have been none the wiser.

Jess smiled, picked the increasingly restless Elvis up from his makeshift prison and began conversation. "Oh, hello again! Yes, I believe we may have met in the park yesterday.

"Well as I said I apologise, I am not usually ignorant however I have not been my usual self for some time now."

"Really there's no need to apologise" and Jess meant it. Because as the elderly man had been speaking, it had dawned on Jess that in the early days of her relationship breakdown, she had spent considerable time in her own little world, a safe place where the real world ceased to exist, daydreaming had been her saviour. Jess realised at that moment that she knew why he was here in her shop.

Eager to change the subject, Jess smiled her biggest smile. "Well I'm Jess and very pleased to meet you and I dare say that if you walk your dog in the park regularly then I'm sure that we'll bump into each other again."

The man smiled and seemed relieved the conversation was moving on. "So you would like a bouquet of roses?" Jess had asked the question for two reasons, obviously the first to clarify the order and the second being that she had anticipated he may provide a little more information. Jess was right and she received the information she had suspected. That it was six months since the love of his life had passed away, not that he had said the words 'love of his life" but she knew by the faraway look in his eyes as he spoke and, his request for a dozen roses in keeping with a lifetime's tradition.

Jess quickly got to work and in no time had created a beautiful arrangement. Having completed this she then stepped away and busied herself re-arranging some flower displays which stood framing the counter. This she did in order to provide people with the space to write something that was quite often, very emotive. Jess was initially surprised at how quickly he wrote his note, however on reflection, she considered that he had most likely been rehearsing the words ever since they had been parted. When he finished, he passed the sealed envelope back to Jess and she secured it firmly into the dark green velvet ribbon that secured the roses in the crepe paper they were encased in. Happy with the finished product which Jess considered looked beautiful, yet classy, she handed them over.

"They're perfect," he said, "just perfect." He then paid Jess and turned and headed towards the door. Before he opened it, he turned to Jess and smiled. "Thank you again, Rita would have loved these," and with that he left the shop.

Chapter Four

Tuesday morning and Jess was out in the back yard when she heard the doorbell chime and Bettie made her way into the store room with two mega breakfasts.

"I so needed this Bettie," Jess enthused, as she bit into the delicious calorie saturated delight. I got up at a ridiculous hour to take Elvis out; I figured he needs more than the back yard to keep him quiet for a while."

"I agree, a dog that size needs plenty of exercise, I really have no idea what your Gran was thinking you know."

"Me neither and I don't think realistically she is going to be in a position to look after him for a few weeks yet, so I guess I'm going to have to get myself a bit of a dog walking plan going."

"We'll do it now love while we're on our break, you know I'm happy to help you any way I can, well except for walking the little devil!"

It was two o' clock in the afternoon and Jess had just got off the phone to the wholesalers. Having placed an order for more roses, it reminded Jess off her meeting with the elderly man.

"Hey Bettie, you know yesterday when I was telling you about that ignorant old chap in the park, well he came in the shop yesterday. I think you missed him, he came in when you were out the back sorting out the delivery and getting the order ready."

"Why didn't you shout me, I'm curious who you're on about?"

"Well I could hardly say, '*can you just hold on one moment while I tell the nosey lady in the back to come out and have a gander at the miserable old sod I was telling her about!*'"

"Less of the old and the swear words young lady!"

"Sorry Bettie, anyway he was ever so apologetic. It turns out that his wife died six months ago and he said he's been in a bit of a world of his own ever since. He bought a dozen red roses, he was clearly heartbroken.

"I can't think who you mean Jess, and I know just about everyone."

"Well I'm sure I'll come across him again if I'm going to be dog sitting for a few weeks. There aren't that many places around here you can walk a dog except for the park."

"You could take him down the woods," suggested Bettie as she began tidying up.

"I wouldn't dream of it, you're not getting me in those woods on my own. People get up to all sorts of strange things in woods these days. Well maybe not those woods, but I'm not prepared to find out either way."

"What strange things?" asked Bettie, with a look of intrigue.

Jess decided a discussion about dogging as opposed to dog *walking* was not appropriate with a pensioner so decided to change the subject. "Oh it was just something I saw on television, and I only caught the last ten minutes so I'm really not sure," Jess lied in order to not have to expand further. "I wouldn't go in them anyway; somehow I don't see Elvis as a guard dog. Anyway, shall I just pop out with him for ten minutes before you leave and then we'll start the new routine tomorrow?" mumbled Jess as she made her way to collect her coat and Elvis's lead, eager to distance herself from the somewhat embarrassing conversation.

"Go ahead Jess, I'll hold the fort."

As before, Jess headed down the street carrying Elvis in order to save some time, and as they got through the gates she was slightly out of breath. "Wow! I've got really unfit, that's crazy being out of breath in such a short distance," she concluded miserably, as she placed Elvis down. She conceded however, it was inevitable considering that the most exercise she got these days was up and down the flat stairs. Then followed that by a brief notion to maybe join a gym and work off some of the damage being done to her body, most likely as a result of all those breakfast baps.

Elvis was clearly pleased to be back in the park and set off happily exploring. Jess watched with amusement as Elvis excitedly chased after some leaves that were blowing along the grass. Then her excitement turned to despair as she watched Elvis roll enthusiastically in something unpleasant. Jess dashed over and snatched Elvis up off the ground, thankful that he had missed his target of rolling in poo. *A chubby little fella, aren't you Elvis*, Jess noted, *in fact not unlike me at the moment. I think I will ask Kate to check out the gym with me after all,* Jess decided, feeling suddenly inspired.

Her sudden burst of inspiration didn't last long. As is always the case, when you're not feeling or looking your best, or at least something like acceptable, you would either meet Mr Fabulous, or worse still, you would meet a female who personified perfection. In this case, for Jess, it was the latter.

Jess studied the women for a moment as she walked down the side of the park, and came along the path towards her. She wished she had applied some make up or at least combed her hair, which she realised now she had forgotten to do due to rushing to walk the dog this morning. Not that she often combed her hair. Jess's chestnut coloured hair was long and naturally wavy and so generally a bit of a fluff up sufficed, so she couldn't really blame Elvis. *Maybe in future though*, she considered, *a bit of lippy on a morning might not go amiss.*

The paths in the park were icy, as were the streets and the roads, in fact the weather had forecast to snow sometime soon. However, clearly that was not something that would stop the image of perfection trotting around the park in high heeled boots, which were accompanied by an expensive stylish outfit. Even the scarf and hat from which beautifully long blonde hair was strategically placed looked expensive, and finishing the look, she carried one of those overly large hand bags.

I wonder if that's to carry her dog, Jess pondered. However, at present, it seemed more than happy to be skipping around the park. The dog was incredibly cute though, beige, and very fluffy fur and very tiny accompanied by a fierce look on its tiny face. It turned out this was not in keeping with its friendly nature. Upon acknowledging that she was admiring the cute little pooch, Jess wondered if this was the start of her becoming a fully-fledged dog loving citizen. The little fur ball was not on a lead and as it got close to Elvis, (who must have looked like a cow in comparison), it bounced up to him and started running in and out of his legs. In return Elvis whimpered and scampered back to the side of Jess's legs.

"Honestly Elvis that's not very macho of you," Jess giggled as she bent down to stroke him.

"Leave him alone Treacle" laughed the image of perfection, as she caught up with the trio. "Oh, what a lovely looking puppy!" the women enthusiastically continued, as she too bent down to pat Elvis. "Just look at the size of his paws! He's going to be enormous! So cute though. You don't see many of them about anymore do you?"

Jess was about to reply that she hadn't really thought about it until recently. She could see a pattern emerging as this was the fourth time it had been mentioned to her, and it was only their second time out to the park. Coming to think of it, she hadn't seen many herself, having said that she hadn't really been looking. She hadn't even bothered to check out any hot guys since her divorce, though she reckoned maybe there hadn't been any to check. Anyway, one thing she hadn't been checking out for was the diminishing number of Old English sheep dogs. But then Jess considered that she didn't really frequent parks that often so wouldn't have noticed.

However before she could reply, the bubbly and clearly chatty and friendly woman continued. "Elvis, that's an unusual name for a dog, mind you he's a handsome little guy aren't you, just like the King of Rock." Standing up again, the woman smiled at Jess and shook her hand, "I'm Suzie by the way."

In return Jess introduced herself and then seized the opportunity to explain her ownership of Elvis. She was keen to ensure that she was not being misconstrued as a female that would be wearing an Elvis tea shirt under her coat, and stay in on a weekend listening to the Elvis back catalogue even though, she did stay in most weekends, just not listening to the Elvis back catalogue. At that moment, Jess realised that she was on the verge of turning into her mother if she didn't get herself a social life soon, considering her mother did stay at home on a weekend while her Dad went to the golf club. Returning her attention back to the immaculately presented female, Jess quickly fired off the story of how she had inherited the dog along with his silly name and that she had tried to change it by trying different anagrams. They had come out all wrong and made no sense at all, Eli was the nearest she could get but he wouldn't respond to it and so she had relented and decided to run with Elvis.

"Well he is lovely and the name is quirky, something a bit different suits both him and you. Anyway, I'd best be off, I have a three thirty spray tan booked in."

The two women were just about to part company when Suzie stopped. "Oh Hun, you'd best clean that up because I can assure you there are some people doing laps of this park that I'm sure are the Poop Police." Seeing the look on Jess's face of absolute shock and an element of disgust, Suzie quickly went on.

"Don't worry sweetie it's really not as bad as you might think. I'm sure it's not as bad as cleaning a baby's bum, though I reckon these little darlings are like are our babies so I guess the same applies. "Here," she said obligingly as she passed Jess the poo bags. "I guess you haven't brought any with you, though I think pretty soon for that big fella, you're going to need to get a bigger bag!"

"Thanks," was all that Jess could manage to say because the thought of picking up poo with you bare hands, (well not quite with her bare hands but almost) was making her feel physically sick.

"Anyway, I'd best be off, it was lovely meeting you and I'm sure I'll see you about soon." With that Suzie left with Treacle strutting along behind her.

"Likewise." mumbled Jess as they parted company.

At that point she was tempted to pretend that in fact Elvis was not with her and that the offending item was absolutely not her responsibility. The trouble was that she had always had trouble with doing anything that was in any way dishonest. Of course, she had phoned in sick in order to spend the day in bed with Brandon in the early days, clearly before he had become infatuated with someone else. However, other than that she had trouble leaving the car park of the local supermarket the wrong way, even on a night when it was practically empty. It was no good; she was going to have to brave this disgusting inconvenience of being a responsible dog owner. It wasn't as though she could pretend she had not seen 'it' because on this frosty winter's day, the offending item was steaming. She was glad no one could see her gipping as she went to pick it up, and even more so that no one saw her physically retch as her finger nail went through the bag in her overzealous eagerness to be done with the episode.

"I never knew it before, but this is definitely a reason to add to the list of why I never wanted pets," Jess complained to herself as she headed over to the nearest bin in order to dispose of the offending item. Following this, they headed back to the gates where she then had to try and negotiate picking Elvis up without the offending finger getting near the dog or anywhere near her sense of smell.

It was only when, as she breathlessly carried the heavy inconvenience down the high street making sure that her poo encrusted index finger got nowhere near her, her coat or Elvis that she considered the comment Suzie had made, that being different suited her. She was certain of one thing though, that whatever she had meant, it wasn't underpinned with malice, because it was clear to Jess that Suzie was genuinely nice.

Practically throwing herself and Elvis into the shop, Jess went straight through to the back room and scrubbed her hands thoroughly.

"You're going to have to get that little fella used to walking near traffic. If it rains he'll be covered in mud and mud is a devil to get out of anything, and if you sponge that fake fur coat Jess, it'll mark – especially with it being green," Bettie casually remarked as she watched Jess scrubbing her fingers.

"Never mind walking. He's going to have to get used to using a litter tray. I had to clean up after it in the park earlier, and when I got poo down my finger nail I was very nearly sick."

"The joys of owning a dog, love! They are really strict these days though Jess. In my day a dog used to eat the family left over's and go do its business wherever it wanted to. In case you hadn't noticed, these days, pets get as much rights as people, and the owners have almost as much responsibility as they do for their kids. To be honest though, I don't think it's a bad thing, I for one have seen many a stray dog out on the streets starving in all weathers."

"I agree with you," Jess shouted from the store room still scrubbing her fingernails. "I'm not saying it's a bad thing, I just don't want poo in my fingernails and have to be scooping it up with my bare hands."

"Stop exaggerating young lady, just wait until you have your own family and then you'll stop being so squeamish," Bettie laughed as she made her way to the door. "Anyway, I'll be off now love, we had a couple of customers while you were gone and I swept and mopped the floor so I don't think it's going to need doing again today so I'll get going."

"Thanks as ever Bettie, I'll see you in the morning, though I think tomorrow I might give the mega breakfast a miss. Honestly, I could hardly breathe by the time I got to the end of the road!"

"Right you are petal; I'll get you something healthy."

Jess was about to reply 'not too healthy' but it was too late Bettie was out of the door. *I hope she doesn't bring a box of muesli in for the laugh,* Jess mused, as she poured herself a cup of tea and then went and sat on the stool behind the counter so she could warm up.

Chapter Five

The week had passed remarkably quickly, quicker she noted, than before she had been enlisted to dog sit. She had found herself becoming a little bit more organised primarily Jess considered, due to the new regime she and Bettie had implemented. Each day now incorporated three scheduled walks with Elvis, one in the morning before work, a quick trip to the park after the midday rush and another once the shop had closed for the day. In between these walks, Jess was beginning to organise the shop with military precision.

She had been and visited Gran a couple of times in hospital. Each time Gran had complained repeatedly about having to stop with her son and over fussy daughter-in-law who she had likened to Mrs Bouquet with the exception of Sid the rabbit. With her parents now back from their holidays, her Gran seemed to be becoming increasingly anxious with regard to her impending change of address, albeit a temporary one. Jess had tried to allay her fears by some well- intended lying. "She's not that bad Gran," Jess had said, whilst trying to sound convincing. However she had then relented and admitted that actually yes, it was that bad but it was only for a short while. She had visited last night and as it had been a busy day in the shop she couldn't stop herself from yawning. It was so warm on the ward, the heat was putting her to sleep.

"I'll tell you what will perk you up a bit. That nice young man came to visit me again at lunchtime. I tell you that boy has a thing for you. He was asking how you were getting on with dog sitting and I said you seemed to be managing just fine considering you have the business to run. It turns out he lives in the next village to us dear. Amazing, isn't it, how you can live so near to someone and never cross paths."

"Gran tell me you didn't tell him where my shop was!"

"Of course I did pet."

"Well he'd best not turn out to be a mad stalker because I can't see Elvis as much of a guard dog."

"Oh stop being dramatic Jess, he's a lovely lad, I don't think he's as old as you though."

"Thanks Gran! I rescued you and looked after that pesky dog of yours and you thank me with insults!" Jess replied, trying to sound offended but with a smile whilst she was saying it.

"You know I think you're gorgeous and everyone on this ward has told me what a beautiful granddaughter I have, and it seems so does that nice young man."

"Well let's hope that nice young man doesn't end up being the next Ted Bundy shall we," Jess giggled as she stood up to put on her coat.

"Now you're being ridiculous!"

"I know, I'm teasing you, but stop trying to fix me up." And with that she kissed her Gran and had left.

It was Sunday and Jess and Elvis were in the park again. They had already done one circuit and Jess had decided on another one in a bid to tire Elvis so that she could chill for the afternoon in front of the fire and watch television. She wasn't particularly bothered what she watched as long as it wasn't sport, she just wanted to relax. Jess cherished her Sundays as they were the only day of the week she did not have to work. Prior to becoming the temporary guardian of Elvis, she often found herself spending the entire day in her pyjamas. She could happily spend hours in front of the fire, sprawled on her battered old sofa reading a good book. However with the demands of caring for a puppy, Jess found that that luxury was gone. Replacing this luxury, she now found herself meandering around the park. She wasn't complaining about it though, in fact she was actually enjoying being out in the cool, crisp fresh air. Jess had dressed appropriately to ward off the freezing elements, in an ankle length fur jacket, military boots and her favourite multi coloured Dr. Who scarf in which, wrapped around her neck until it reached her knees, she felt lovely and warm.

The park was unusually quiet. Jess generally encountered a number of people walking their dogs and she had noted that everyone had been incredibly friendly. Well, all except one guy walking a Siberian husky. Not that the dog was aggressive, but the owner definitely was. Jess had let Elvis off the lead for a few minutes and the guy had muttered in a hostile voice something about keeping her dog on a lead or else his dog would eat Elvis. Jess, who had always been feisty when she had to be, responded that he had 'best do it quick then' because very shortly her dog would be the size of a bear. Jess had noted two things from this encounter. Firstly, she had called Elvis *her* dog, and secondly she could never imagine Elvis turning into a fierce grizzly bear, he was more likely to be a Yogi Bear kind of a dog. Other than that, everyone else was bizarrely friendly.

As Jess strolled slowly along watching Elvis, she contemplated whether being friendly came with the territory of being a dog owner. Definitely, the customers who had come into the shop and had noticed Elvis had all gone on to tell her about their own four-legged friends and they did seem to be more friendly than some of her other customers. She was still considering this notion when she spotted the elderly man whom she had met earlier in the week enter the park from the far side. This time, as they headed towards each other, he stopped to chat. Jess noted that he seemed more relaxed, and when he stopped he had smiled and observed, 'What a lovely day it is! Though it's so very cold, it might snow later.'

Jess had noted that for a pensioner, he was actually quite attractive. Not that she fancied him, though she considered if he was thirty years younger or likely forty, she may have. At that moment, she considered he would be perfect for her Gran, given Prince Charles' lack of availability, before immediately dismissing the idea as clearly the man was still grieving.

Elvis seemed to be quite fond of the man's Jack Russell and was bounding around behind it. Everywhere the Jack Russell went so did Elvis, in the same way a young child follows an older child. Jess laughed, "Well that should tire him out trying to keep up with- sorry what's your dog called?"

"His name is Max and he's good with other dogs, even puppies which I know some dogs get a bit fed up with," James replied.

"Well he's being very tolerant with Elvis."

"I tell you what, I'll walk the same way round as you and that way the little chap will get some exercise," suggested James.

"Yeah I think he would like that if you don't mind. Sounds like a great idea."

And bizarrely, Jess noted, that it did seem like a good idea to go for a walk with a complete stranger. Jess observed with interest, that having a dog meant you immediately had a common ground in which to make light conversation. Under normal circumstances, stopping to talk to strangers and then wandering off with them would be '*odd to say the least, even dangerous*,' she mused. But accompanied by a couple of pooches, the situation seemed completely acceptable. Later, Jess would recognise this unremarkable event as being when her unexpected venture began.

Half an hour had passed very quickly. And within that half hour they had amiably discussed everything to do with being the owner of a dog, before moving on to some information about themselves. Jess had learnt that James had owned a business down south for many years in which his beloved wife had worked alongside him, and that he had sold up and returned back to the area he grew up in shortly before she had passed away. They had no family of their own;

however up north they had nephews and nieces who had rallied round him for the last six months.

Jess in return had outlined that she too had returned to the area following the breakup of her marriage. However, she left out the bit about her husband running off with his male fitness instructor. Before she knew it, they were back at the far side of the park where James had parked his car, "Right I think that's your lot for this afternoon Max," James had fondly said to Max as he clipped him back on the lead.

At least I'm not the only one who talks to a canine in public, Jess mused.

"Well thanks for walking round with me and Elvis, he looks exhausted now so I should get some peace and quiet for a while this afternoon. Plus it's been a nice change to not do laps of the park on my own. The residents in those houses must think I'm the new neighbourhood watch!" Jess giggled looking in the direction of the houses on the periphery of the park. "It's a lovely park but I'm already getting bored of doing endless laps around it and I've only had Elvis a week. I'm sure I'll be bonkers by the time I've finished looking after him but there isn't really anywhere else to go especially this time of year," Jess added.

"Why don't you take him for a walk in the woods? I've started taking Max down there on a Sunday now that I've started getting out a bit more again, although I decided against it today seeing as my nephew and his wife are calling round shortly."

"Oh, I wouldn't take Elvis in the woods on my own even if it were summer, which I know is silly because I'm sure I'd be fine."

"No Lass, you can't be too careful, I think you're being wise. I tell you what, I normally take Max for a walk in the woods before lunch, your more than welcome to join us, I'm sure Elvis would like a change of scenery. I'll be at the woods next Sunday at eleven thirtyish; I'll wait by the gates on the station road entrance for a few minutes in case you decide to bring him along."

"They've given snow out though," replied Jess, sounding less enthusiastic than she had hoped given that clearly James was attempting to be helpful.

"It's only a five minute walk from your shop in the other direction; if it snows you could leave the car at home and walk the short distance to the woods."

Jess laughed at herself for sounding like such a wimp at the thought of venturing out in a little snow, aware she must have seemed like the vast majority of the country that panicked at the first fall of the dreaded white lifestyle demon.

"You're right, ok then, well just so long as I don't encounter another crisis, me and Elvis shall meet you there." With that, Jess headed back to the flat, and this time Elvis walked down the high street without her having to carry him.

Elvis was exhausted and slept the rest of the afternoon and Jess chilled out on the sofa in front of the fire flicking between one film and another. She ate a hot chicken sandwich, which she considered was a single person's substitute for a Sunday dinner and for three hours, Jess did nothing at all except relax. Curled up on the sofa in front of the fire Jess had slipped into a light sleep, when once again the sound of her phone ringing entered her subconscious. Though this time the intrusion was compounded further when Jess forced herself to answer and realised it was her mother.

Jess had long ago given up on trying to have a meaningful relationship with her mother. She had attempted, as a child she had tried to be the best student and as a young adult she had encouraged mother daughter shopping trips with lunch. However it was all to no avail because what her mother really wanted was the son she had lost to meningitis shortly after Jess was born. Her dad had tried to reassure Jess that her mother loved her just as much as the brother she only knew through photographs but it did not dispel Jess's deep rooted theory that she could never be good enough for her mother.

Jess took a deep breath and then in the most pleasant voice she could muster she answered, "Hi Mum, how was the holiday?" before listening as her mother outlined without stopping for breath, every last detail. When she did stop for breath, Jess seized the opportunity to ask whether she and Dad had visited Gran in hospital to make the arrangements for Gran leaving hospital.

"Of course we went to visit her! She's being discharged from hospital tomorrow and is happy to stop with me and your dad for a few weeks."

Jess seriously doubted this. In fact she knew it not to be the case, though decided not to have that conversation. Because, in truth, Gran did need looking after for a while and with Jess having the shop, and the flat with the steps, and now the dog, it would be impossible for Jess to look after her.

"So I know you won't like it but you will have to look after that animal that your Gran has got herself for a while longer.

"It's ok mum I've got a bit of a routine going now, so I can cope a little while longer. Pass on my love to dad won't you?" And with that they hung up. Two minutes later the phone rang again, this time with a more welcome caller.

"Hi Jess, it's me, how do you fancy a night of wine and Chinese food? And I can't wait to meet Elvis. Who would have thought that you Jess, would be babysitting the 'King of canines' does he have his own jewel encrusted pooch suit?"

Jess was giggling as she listened to the ramblings of her best friend. "Funny aren't you Kate? Now shut up, go get the food and wine and I'll see you in a little while."

Chapter Six

Later that evening Jess was recounting the week's events to Kate. They had devoured the Chinese as if it were their last feast and now they were doing the same with the wine. "I hope that sweet and sour chicken ball doesn't upset Elvis's tummy, I'm not sure he's old enough for junk food," Jess giggled as she polished off her second glass of wine.

"Oh don't worry Jess, its chicken isn't it," Kate replied as she topped up their glasses once again.

Kate took a sip of wine and then without any provocation began chuckling to herself.

"What's so funny?" giggled Jess, without knowing the cause, though not being able to stop herself.

"You are!" Kate hastily replied.

"Why? For once I haven't done anything."

"Haven't done anything? You've only gone and arranged to meet a strange man in the woods! It doesn't sound right to me."

"Well put like that it does sound wrong, but I am merely taking Elvis for a walk with a pensioner," giggled Jess as she sipped her glass of Shiraz.

"Well I think it's wrong," continued Kate, although it was clear that whilst she was trying to make a point, she was also trying not to laugh again.

"Well come with me if you're that worried," reasoned Jess, whilst simultaneously throwing a chip at Kate, this being a childish habit carried over from their youth. Kate had played a pivotal part in Jess's life for as long as she could remember. Their friendship had evolved from skipping in the school yard to skipping lessons and kissing boys behind the bike shed. And when the time had come to move on to higher education, it seemed only natural to choose the same University and even the same psychology course. And now here they were throwing chips at each other, just as they had done in their youths.

"Nah, I don't think so Hun, it would mean wearing terrible dog walking clothes. Wellington boots and anoraks aren't really my thing. Besides, I don't have a dog."

"I know, why don't you bring that stuffed one that you used to push around on a stick when we were kids, I know for a fact you still have it stored in your bedroom. If James is anything like the rest of the British population he won't even comment, he'll just think your special," giggled Jess.

"I am special cheeky, and yes I still have Ruffles but I can't bring myself to part with him," retaliated Kate whilst throwing another chip in the direction of Jess.

"I know you're special hun and you know I'm only joking, Jess replied fondly before excitedly adding, "I know, why don't you borrow your mums. Your Mitzie hasn't seen past that garden in years. I'll bet it'll need therapy after it's experienced a taste of freedom! To my knowledge she hasn't left the garden since the day your mum brought it home in her handbag."

"Borrowing a dog! Honestly, have you heard yourself? You'll be starting the next bizarre craze in accessories, and can you imagine the adverts on television? The ultimate accessory for the discerning dog lover.....a co-ordinated dog!" At this point the alcohol was beginning to take affect and they both began giggling uncontrollably. Though now they were on a roll and in-between polishing off more wine, they continued along the theme.

"The Chihuahua. A girl's best friend, available for photo shoots in particular handbag shoots." Kate was doubling up with laughter now, a mix of the wine and the silly conversation.

"What about a Staffie?" Jess asked with some difficulty as she had snorted some of the wine back up her nose whilst giggling, and as such was choking a little.

Kate may have had a couple of glasses of wine but she was now thoroughly on a roll. "I've got it! Yes a Staffie, the perfect companion for the discerning criminal, on hire for two hours between midnight and 2am, to be returned unharmed."

"I'm not sure that's a fair sales pitch Kate, because I met a lovely middle-aged woman in the park the other day with a gorgeous grey Staffie which was incredibly well behaved."

"Oh come on Jess, I don't mean it literally, although as we both know, people do make assumptions when they meet someone for a variety of reasons and that counts for dogs too," reasoned Kate as she helped herself to some left over prawn crackers. In return Jess helped herself to the last remaining sweet and sour chicken ball which Elvis had been eyeing up for a while and took a bite, followed by a swig of wine.

For a moment they were both quiet before Jess broke the silence. "It's funny, we spent all that time at uni and here we are, profiling dogs, strange old world ain it."

"Well it is, but such is life and it is funny. Now, where were we? What about a Chihuahua."

"We've already done that one," Jess protested.

Immediately Kate had an answer," A girl's best friend or maybe gay."

"You're crazy!" Jess topped up their glasses and then continued. "How about a spaniel? I met a really nice woman in the park with a spaniel. Granted she was dressed like the ultimate dog walker but she was really nice."

"Well what kind of spaniel was it?" Kate shot back.

Jess was impressed; she had forgotten just how quick Kate could be even when under the influence of alcohol. "Well it was a Cocker spaniel," Jess provided the information with an element of intrigue.

"Well there you go then. Nice middle class family dog. Sociable and sociably acceptable. You could take one of them anywhere and not one person would argue how wonderful it was. Whereas, a King Charles and you're talking handbag territory again."

"You're funny!" giggled Jess, starting on her third glass of wine, completely getting into the Guess Who of the dog ownership world. "What about a German Shepherd then?"

"Confident and assertive with a good job."

"What about a Labradoodle?" Having studied with Kate, Jess knew exactly how Kate was character profiling individuals based upon the breed of pooches though Jess was enjoying trying to skew Kate's theories. Though, in truth, even with alcohol as a factor, it seemed not to be working.

"Well anything that doesn't conform to the norm indicates a diverse personality. Come on Jess you know this, it's not rocket science, we did study psychology together."

"We didn't study Animal Psychology, Silly. And I never thought we would be dissecting the characters of dog owners or discussing renting a dog. All those thousands in student fees and this is what it's come to."

Jess took another sip of her wine. "Your right though. It does make sense. I mean if you had cream carpets everywhere in your house you wouldn't want a big hairy dog moulting and leaving footprints everywhere would you?

"Your Gran did," said Kate with a smirk on her face, the look of someone who had just dispelled a new ground breaking theory.

"Well everyone knows she's bonkers, in the nicest possible way of course," laughed Jess. "Though don't hold back will you?"

"You know me Jess, say it as it is, always have and always will."

"True," replied Jess, "And I love you for it."

Kate leant over, picked up the second bottle of wine and topped their glasses up again. Then with a devilish look on her face she continued. "Hey never mind the lifestyle dog, what about the theory that owners look like their dogs, because if that the case you're going to have to stock up on the Immac." At this point Kate had to place her glass on the table beside her as she was laughing that much now, the contents were spilling down her.

"Cheeky Mare! And anyway, I don't believe that nonsense. I'll tell you what I am going to pay attention to in future though, I'm going to see if our dog and owner theory works."

"What do you mean?" asked Kate looking at Jess as intensely as someone who has consumed lots of wine can look.

"What I mean is that whilst I'm walking Elvis, I'm going to see if our drunken theory works or whether it's a whole load of nonsense. It might make walking the dog a little more interesting."

"It's funny though Jess. You've always hated animals, and here you are trudging around the park in all weathers and arranging to meet strange old men in the woods. Next thing you know you'll be wearing green welly boots instead of those rather bling cowboy boots you had imported, and wearing your Mum's anorak." Then, whilst trying to sound as responsible as possible whilst being slightly drunk, Kate relented. "Seriously though Jess, I might have to borrow Mum's dog if it means you're not meeting strangers in woods on your own."

"He's not a stranger, silly, well he is kind of, but I'm sure he's not a serial killer. I know what you mean about what to wear though, it is a problem. I've got away with it so far seeing as it's only been frosty and cold but trudging round in mud or snow is not something I'm looking forward to, though I'm sure I'll think of something."

"Well when you do, let me know so I can bring my camera. I never thought I would see the day when I saw you in welly boots and a sou'wester!" Kate was stopped from saying more as Jess threw a cushion at her, which skimmed past her and nearly knocked the wine glass out of her hand.

"Hey careful, that was three pound from Super Saver I'll have you know," Kate giggled, and then they changed the subject to one in which Kate updated Jess about the latest guy that she was seeing.

Chapter Seven

Throughout the next few days every time Jess took Elvis for a walk she found herself inadvertently profiling the people she encountered. She felt strangely guilty as she constructed jobs, homes and lifestyles around complete strangers based upon the dog they owned but she did it anyway as she justified it as being a bit of fun. For the most part, she kept to the schedule she and Bettie had developed to incorporate busy times in the shop and deliveries, and for that reason she often met the same people each day.

On the early morning walk, she nearly always crossed paths with the women with the Cocker Spaniel who always smiled and greeted her, whilst the dogs stopped to say 'hello' in the way that came most naturally to them. Initially Jess had been somewhat embarrassed by this. However after such a short time, she had become completely at ease with the concept that the sniffing of select areas of a dog's anatomy was clearly a kind of initiation. Every morning, the woman with the Cocker Spaniel wore the same suitable cold weather jacket with the hood pulled down low which Jess thought a bit odd because, as yet, it had not snowed, and the same sensible walking boots. Whilst Jess considered her to be genuinely friendly the woman would make brief talk, usually about the weather and then make the same comment that she and Copper had to get back to prepare breakfast for her husband and that the 'time was ticking.' Jess decided that the friendly woman were most likely a stay-at-home wife whose husband had a good job. The house would be cleaned to within an inch of its life and most likely be a semi and when they holidayed, it would be in the Cotswolds. The lifestyle wouldn't suit Jess now however, except for the stay at home bit; she had pretty much lived the exact same life with Brandon. Jess considered that the woman most likely did not have children, as the only comments she ever made were in relation to her husband. Another notion Jess had reflected upon was that maybe she was on sick leave from work because she always seemed jumpy and anxious. Of course, Jess recognised that maybe she was completely wrong in her profile of the woman and that they could possibly live in a caravan in a field but somehow Jess didn't think so.

When Jess walked Elvis after lunch she nearly always bumped into Suzie with Treacle. She hadn't meant to do it but Jess had surmised that considering that she was always so beautifully presented, she most likely didn't work and that she was married to a wealthy man who drove an Audi. According to her theories, they lived in one of those expensive houses on the edge of the village in the more affluent area that was popular with commuters. It turned out on this occasion that Jess was wrong, very wrong, in regards to Suzie's present circumstances. In Suzie's previous lifestyle, Jess's profile would have been practically perfect. However, Suzie was now single and was working many hours in order to regain her financial stability. She had previously owned an apartment in the city with her fiancé and had been the owner of two businesses, one being a designer boutique and the other a hair dressers cum tanning shop, plus nail parlour, and by all accounts they were both hugely successful. Jess didn't doubt this as Suzie was pleasant and bubbly and a real people person, perfect qualities for building a customer base. As far as Suzie was concerned her world was perfect, a successful business and a doting and gorgeous fiancé who looked like a walking, talking version of Ken, "as in Barbie's Ken," Suzie had giggled. She had continued to outline that the only thing she had to really worry about was organising the wedding.

Her doting betrothed dealt with all the financial affairs. The church had been booked and the invites sent out, she had bought herself a beautiful couture wedding dress and the honeymoon had been booked for the Seychelles. And then eight weeks before what was supposed to be the most wonderful day of her life and the beginning of a new chapter within it, her world had fallen apart. "At least," she said, it had seemed it at the time.

It turned out that the perfect fiancé was not so perfect after all and he had gambled their savings away, which was mostly the money Suzie had saved, as her partner had lost his job in the financial sector when the recession hit. And then to console himself, he had taken a lover who was ten years younger than Suzie. And whilst initially, it was supposed to be a bit of fun, he had become infatuated with the stunning young beautician and set her up in a penthouse apartment in Leeds, paid for in part out of the money he had borrowed from re-mortgaging their apartment and the businesses. It had also sustained his gambling addiction. "And would you believe," Suzie had said, really quite perturbed, "I actually took that little witch on as a trainee. I remember her turning up at the shop with pieces of blonde extensions pinned in her hair, her nose pierced and chewing gum, and she asked as bold as brass if she could have a job."

"She was pleasant though," Suzie added, "And I admired the fact that she came in, asked for a job, so I gave her a chance and to be honest, she turned out to be a good worker and really turned herself around. She never missed her college sessions and she really refined her image, she even started talking like a lady. A real Eliza Doolittle I thought she was, and to be honest, I was really proud of her. I even considered her to be like a sister and then she went and did that. I think I was more upset that she had betrayed me than that shmuck of a fiancé. That's probably the reason that whilst I'm bankrupt now it didn't take me long to get over him. I mean yeah, it was a bit embarrassing at the time having to let everyone know the wedding was off , but to be honest everyone was really good and it turned out they never really liked him anyway, so here I am starting all over again."

The small 'here I am' turned out to be a small rented house not far from Jess's shop. Suzie had started providing all the same services that customers could get in the shop, though now provided a small mobile service. And those same customers who had remained faithful to her now received the same quality service from Suzie in their own homes. Although she was not as financially stable as before, she was managing and slowly she had rebuilt her life. "To be honest," she had said in the same upbeat way that Jess had become used to. "It's the best thing that ever happened to me. And guess what? She had added, "Twelve months later, they were finished. I heard that she managed to somehow keep the flat and he's back with his parents and to be honest I hope they can sort him out, their nice people his parents. He called me a bit after and tried the whole, 'but I love you thing and I made a mistake.' But I stood fast and told him 'good luck with your life and I hope you get the help you need.' Funny old life isn't it?" Suzie added.

"It certainly is," Jess had agreed, and in return Jess had relayed her own story about the breakdown of her marriage and the only difference was that her bloke had gone off with a male. As an afterthought Jess had added that Brandon's fitness instructor was gorgeous and that she was probably more annoyed that he had fancied her husband than her, at which they had both giggled. They had shared a commonality though, that it was hard, really hard at the beginning to get over betrayal. However, they had both agreed that it was true that time proved to be a great healer.

Jess found herself continuing with her pooch profiling theory frequently whenever she took Elvis for his walks. On a late afternoon walk she generally crossed paths (literally as the path was not that wide) with a middle-aged guy walking a male dog aged four, that was crossed with a Labrador – Spaniel cross breed. It was a lovely natured dog and very placid. She had gleaned this information out of a ten minute conversation. The conversation had begun with a simple hello, then followed by, "cold isn't it?" before the conversation moved on to how nice it was when ones dog was well socialised. This then lead to Jess receiving a rundown of all the unsociable dogs and owners to look out for. Jess deduced that both Spaniels and Labradors were friendly natured dogs, though inclined to be giddy as puppies. From this she decided that the gentleman would have lots of patience and have a home that was furnished to accommodate a canine of that size and character. He would therefore most likely live in a semi-detached property with a large garden. Jess struggled with what kind of a career he may possibly hold, as he was too young to be retired, though she had not ruled out the possibility of early retirement. With regard to his profession she considered maybe Police Officer, as he did have his dog very well trained.

She also met a very friendly middle-aged woman called Sylvia, who owned a cream labradoodle puppy called Thomas; the two dogs had become firm friends immediately. Sylvia had opened up the conversation by stating the flowers Jess created were fabulous and everyone in the village thought so. Jess in return had felt both guilty and flattered. Guilty for not remembering that this very friendly woman had made a purchase from her shop and flattered that people were talking about her shop in a positive manner. They had let both Elvis and Thomas off their leads and the puppies had quickly exhausted themselves due to their larger than average frames. Not unlike herself at the moment, Jess had mused. More often than not, Jess would come away from an encounter knowing someone's name without even realising how that snippet of information had come about.

What she had also found out in a short space of time was that Sylvia and her husband were separated. Sylvia had outlined the same relationship issues that she heard no matter what generation they embedded. He did not understand her; he treated her disrespectfully and spends lots of time with his friends – in this case, at the golf course. Finally, they had swapped dog walking schedules and discussed that they didn't think that it was good to be walking round the park in the dark on their own, during these winter months and that, if possible, they would try and synchronise the time they walked Elvis and Thomas.

Another observation Jess had made whilst walking Elvis was that no matter what time of day she was in the park, there always seemed to be someone walking a Shiatsu. She had considered initially that they seemed to be the ultimate canine of choice for the over sixty-five, although she was aware that her Gran was the exception to this rule, and at some point she would analyse this. However, for the most part, elderly men and women could be found meandering around the park at whatever time of day with their Shiatsu obediently following along. Although, as the week progressed she noticed that her original observation that only older people owned them, was not in fact the case. Both young and old could be found doing a lap of the park with their faithful friend in tow. Jess considered that statistically this meant that there was one heck of a lot of Shiatsu's. "I wonder if they're planning on taking over the village," she had thought to herself on one of her late afternoon walks after observing that the cute little fur ball coming towards them was the fifth she had seen in one day.

What Jess had observed in regard to these cute little fur balls, was that for the most part they were all sociable, both owners and dogs. It seemed to be a somewhat compulsory ritual, primarily because even if the owners had not wanted to chat the dogs always stopped to make their own introductions. Two people standing without acknowledging one another is practically impossible and so small talk would always ensue. It became clear to Jess that both Shiatsu's and their owners were vibrant and friendly with lots of character. As yet, she had not met one owner of these personality packed miniature impersonators of an Old English sheep dog that Jess didn't find interesting and sociable. Even those that didn't stop to talk which were few, always smiled and said hello. In-keeping with her new found inclination to profile people, Jess deduced

70

that for the most part these individuals would be financially secure. They would most likely have well maintained properties that were quite orderly; hence this would be an element that over spilled into their everyday lifestyles. Finally, Jess concluded that for whatever reason, trekking through miles of mountainous terrain was not something likely to be a frequent pastime for these people based upon their individual circumstances, be this time or choice.

Jess had to admit that walking Elvis was fun. In the short time she been looking after him, Jess had not only found a way to deploy some of her psychological knowledge, albeit in a non- constructive way. She had also met so many lovely people. And not only had she met them but found out all kinds of random information about them. Sandra with the beige and white Shiatsu had a daughter named Mollie who was due to have a baby. Robert with the black and white Collie named whiskey after his favourite tipple had told Jess all about the operation he was waiting for on his back. In fact, more people than ever before were latching on to her when she popped out to the Post Office or any of the other shops in the village. In fact it had taken her half an hour to get out of the Co-Op the other day when she had bumped into Sandra who went on to tell her that her daughter had had the baby and then went on to relay every gory detail of the poor women's labour. Jess only got away when she managed to get a word in edgeways and tell Sandra that Elvis was waiting in the car and she didn't want to leave him too long in case he ate bits of it. *Yep,* Jess considered as they headed back from another walk, *all things considered it was quite nice having a dog. And so far he hadn't even been too much trouble in the shop or flat.*

Chapter Eight

It was Sunday. Jess had not set her alarm although she woke up early anyway. The first thing she knew even before she opened the curtains was, that it had snowed. The flat was even colder than usual and the bedroom seemed brighter than normal for a cold winter's morning, primarily due to the sky being white with further unshed snow. "Great," Jess mumbled as she ran across the bedroom to locate a sweater with her feet feeling the excessively cold bedroom floorboards even with her favourite bed socks on. At the time she had considered bed socks a strange present from her parents who had just returned from a holiday in Jamaica. *Who'd have thought they would have found bed socks in Jamaica*, she had mused. They were pretty cool though, hand knitted in the colours of the Jamaican flag, and now with the flat being so cold, she wished that they had brought her more pairs back.

Locating the sweater, she ran into the living room and put the fire on at full and then went to boil the kettle. Whilst the kettle was boiling she threw on her jacket and boots and carried Elvis down the stairs and out into the back yard. She had hoped he would go do his business quickly with the hope they could hot foot it back up to the flat which would have warmed up slightly with the fire on at full. However when Elvis stepped out into the snow he clearly was not impressed and hot footed it back inside and up the stairs. "You little devil!" Jess cried after him as she locked the back door and headed up the stairs behind him. "I wonder how long you were planning on keeping the fact that you could get up the stairs from me, you'd have had me carry you up those stairs forever if you hadn't been traumatised by a bit of snow," Jess chided as she made her way back into the flat where she slipped on a little puddle Elvis had left by the door.

Jess was eating her porridge whilst observing Elvis who sat close to the fire as he could get without actually being on fire. She was deciding whether to go and meet James for the walk in the woods as they had planned. *'Maybe he wouldn't be there'* she considered, *he is quite old after all.* On the other hand, the dog would still want a walk and if he lived as near to the woods as she did, then he would most likely still go for a walk. Although how would she get there. Elvis clearly did not want to put his paws in the snow and she didn't fancy getting the car out without knowing how bad the roads were. Worse still, she was going to have to wear those hideous wellington boots she had purchased from the hardware shop. She hadn't expected there to be much of a choice but had still been disappointed to find that the only pair in her size were those in that hideous gardener green colour. She had bought them anyway because everyone knew that snow was coming.

Still observing Elvis, she noticed now how big he had become in just two weeks. "Honestly Elvis if you carry on growing at this rate you'll be able to borrow my wellington boots soon if you're that bothered about snow," Jess said out loud. Jess jumped to her feet, "That's it, I've got it!" she said to herself (a habit that seemed to be becoming entrenched since becoming the guardian of Elvis), she then quickly headed down to the store room. At eleven o' clock they left the flat and made their way towards the woods. In good weather it was only a five minute walk but with Jess wearing layers of clothes and carrying the very large Elvis it seemed to take an age to get there. She had decided that the best way to encourage him to sample the snow was to see if he would be tempted not to show himself up in the company of another dog. She was pleased when they finally arrived at the entrance to the woods having had to stop a few times to get her breath back, each time acting as a reminder that a trip to the gym really was needed. Jess did console herself with the notion that in reality the only time most people carried something so heavy, was if they were moving house or carrying their suitcase out of the taxi and to the entrance of an airport. And, as she had seen most people struggle with both these events, she considered that most of the country was as unfit as her.

Jess felt a little demoralised. It looked like her new dog walking buddy had let her down. She wondered if she looked rather odd considering that she was stood holding an overly large dog at the entrance to the woods in the freezing cold.

"No, we don't look odd do we Elvis? I'm sure coordinated clothing with your pooch will catch on sometime soon." Then she giggled to herself as she knew full well that they most likely did look a bit odd considering they were now wearing coordinated boots. The ribbon that was holding Elvis's make shift booties onto his paws was the exact same as the one she has used to bling up her own boots a little in an attempt to make them look less conventional. In doing so, they had inadvertently ended up with matching footwear. Jess had only realised once they had arrived at the woods and immediately saw the funny side of the oversight. She just hoped that her unlikely new dog walking companion would not think her a little odd. That was if he even turned up as the due to the cold, the few minutes she had been waiting seemed much longer. She was just considering the notion of whether it would be possible to call for a taxi to take them home as it appeared James and Max were a no show and she was not relishing walking back up the hill to her flat, when Jess was spared from the dilemma with the arrival of a rather sporty black car.

"Morning! I didn't think you would be here considering the weather, I was just about to go home seeing as Elvis here doesn't want to get his paws in the snow." Elvis already seemed to have forgotten his issues with the weather and was eager to meet his new buddy.

"No, it just took a little longer to get the car onto the main road." James replied.

"You're very brave driving in fresh snow, I'm not overly keen on driving in it myself." I try and get my dad to do the deliveries when the weather is like this; he doesn't mind driving in the snow either."

"I don't mind a bit of snow lass," James replied. "Many years back I lived up the top of Scotland. Now they really do get snow so after a while you get used to it. Anyway, shall we get moving before we freeze? I think that little chap of yours is eager to try out those fancy boots. Were they buy one get one free?" James remarked jovially with a slight grin forming.

"We do look a bit silly don't we," Jess laughed back as she looked down at her wellington boots which she had felt the need to customise with the red velvet ribbon that she used to secure her bouquets of flowers. They no longer looked like the dull green boots she had bought from the hardware shop. For Elvis, she had made little bootees made of green plastic and she had fastened them around his paws with the same ribbon. Jess was aware they looked silly but so far they had stayed on his paws.

"Next year if you need a sideline, I'm sure you could both secure a role as Santa's helpers with footwear like that," James added with a little chuckle as they made their way towards the gate to the woods.

James led the way and was just in the process of pushing open the creaky old iron gate that formed one of the entrances to the woods when a voice could be heard in the distance.

"Hey wait for me!" Jess turned around to see Kate rushing towards them with her mum's poodle in tow.

Jess smile to herself. She knew Kate would be worried for Jess's safety and wellbeing and though traipsing out in the cold and wet was not Kate's favourite thing either, here she was and she too was wearing wellington boots. However, with her figure hugging jeans tucked into them and a long cream jumper evident beneath a fitted green jacket, she looked smart yet casual.

Although Kate was not an overly tactile person, Jess could not refrain from giving her friend a big hug as she came to join her at the entrance to the woods. "I'm so glad you could make it Kate, I tried calling you earlier but your phone went straight to the answering machine."

"Oh I misplaced my charger," Kate replied with a subtle wink, which Jess knew meant she had left the charger at a guy's house. Then she turned to James and shook his hand firmly "I'm Kate, I've heard a lot about you and I hope you don't mind but I thought I would tag along."

James smiled at the vibrant young woman and was impressed in the knowledge that she had clearly decided to ensure her friends' safety. "The more the merrier my dear," he replied fondly, and with that, the unlikely trio headed into the woods.

"You didn't think I was going to let you go walking in the woods with some strange guy," Kate whispered into Jess's ear as she followed Jess through the gates. "Granted he doesn't look crazy but you never know." Jess just laughed.

An hour later and Jess and Kate were bidding farewell to James as he loaded Max (who had been given a quick once over with a towel to dry him off) into the back of a sleek looking Renault.

"Are you sure I can't give you two ladies a lift back."

"No we're fine thanks, it's literally five minutes up the road and it will well and truly tire Elvis out, I reckon I'll be able to chill all afternoon."

"Yeah, me too, it's not far for me either- but thanks all the same, it's made a real change," Kate chirped up.

"Ok, well I'll call into the shop either sometime this week or next and we'll arrange our next outing. Thanks again for today ladies, it's been a real pleasure," and with that James slowly drove steadily away.

"Well that sounded so wrong! I hope nobody heard him or else they'll think we provide a niche escort service," Kate giggled.

"You really are crazy," Jess replied jovially as she linked up with her best friend.

"Yep, that's why we're friends, because you are as crazy as me. I've got to admit it's been fun though. Even if I am freezing and can't feel my feet," laughed Kate.

"I agree, now let's get a move on and I'll make us a hot chocolate back at mine, I left the heating on so it might even be warm."

"I'll tell you what Jess I was surprised at how many people were down the woods in this weather."

"I know, I was a bit surprised too, but I guess it's the ideal Sunday activity. Go out in the freezing cold, get wet through, tire your dog out and then go home and get warm and have a lovely lunch," Jess reasoned.

"Yeah I guess you're right and it was funny watching Mitzi and Elvis following Max everywhere, although I thought you'd killed them when you threw that stick and it went down the bank with all three of them in pursuit. I can't believe you forgot about the stream below, I mean we spent enough time down there with the gang as kids," giggled Kate.

"Honestly, it wasn't intentional, and I really did forget, I mean I haven't been down those woods in years. I know dogs, or animals in general aren't really my thing, but even I wouldn't do a thing like trying to drown them."

"Don't give me that Jess – that you don't like dogs! You almost threw yourself over the edge after them and you've been clucking over that fur ball all day. Seems to me like you've turned into a born again dog lover."

"I wouldn't go that far Kate, though I must admit even I'm surprised, I think it's because he's really not that much work."

"I wouldn't speak too soon Hun, he'll be lulling you into a false sense of security and as soon as you think he's the perfect house guest, he'll show his true colours, not unlike my last fella actually."

"Sorry I forgot to ask how it was going, I've just been so busy."

"Don't be daft. If I'd have needed a shoulder to cry on I'd have asked, and lets be fair Jess, it was really more of a casual fling. Although it was fine until I let him stop last weekend and I popped out to get fish and chips for lunch and left him supposedly watching football. I was only gone ten minutes and when I got back he'd tidied up and got two plates out for the fish and chips. Well that just did it! Firstly, as I pointed out to him, the flat didn't need tidying and, I didn't appreciate him moving my things. He told me he thought I'd appreciate it because the flat was in a state of chaos, so I told him straight that it was my chaos and besides, who eats fish and chips off a plate? Everybody knows they taste better in the paper. Anyway, thank god that was the last I've seen or heard from him; he was dull anyway, although the sex wasn't too bad!"

Jess stood up and went to see if the pizza was nearly ready and then cursed to herself as she burnt her fingers on the baking tray, "Kate, you're my best friend and I wouldn't let you settle for anyone but the best, you'll have to start walking Mitzi with me more often. You never know you might meet the love of your life in the park! Although in fairness I haven't come across any Gerard Butlers yet- but one can live in hope," she added as she passed Kate the stuffed crust 'Meat Feast' pizza which had always been their favourite.

"You and your obsession with Gerard Butler! You know at some point, you're going to have to get yourself a real man."

"Gerard Butler personifies a real man," Jess replied with a deep sigh as she came back to join Kate on the sofa in front of the fire.

"You know what I mean smart arse."

"Well then, we're going to have to hope both Johnny Depp and Gerard Butler have moved into the area and have dogs that they have to walk around the local park or the woods. That way I can bag myself a date with Gerard Butler and you can bag yourself a date with Johnny Depp, who I know for a fact you still have a crush on because I saw the calendar on your kitchen wall." Jess was giggling now as she leant over to reach her cup of hot chocolate and took a big gulp before continuing. "You never know hun dating with your dog might become the new dating phenomenon."

Kate had just bitten into a huge mouthful of pizza and was trying to mumble something at the same time as laughing uncontrollably.

"That's not a good look Kate!"

Finally she finished the mouthful of pizza. "That's the craziest thing I've ever heard you say, well maybe not the craziest. I think the time you came to mine and as cool as cucumber went on to tell me how you forgot to put the hand brake on your car and the thing had taken itself on a trip down the hill and into the car park of the Police Station, where it collided with a patrol car and instead of getting into trouble, you actually got asked out on a date. I mean, let's face it Jess – you are just one of those people that random things happen to, but dating with your dog, I've heard it all now! I'm sure if you'd spotted any talent in that park you'd have been straight on the phone and the nearest you've come to a single man is an elderly widower and as nice as he is, he ain't no Johnny Depp." They were both laughing uncontrollably now which is what almost always happened when they got together.

"Well you just never know Kate, strange things do happen."

"To you they do. So I take it back, you just never know."

Chapter Nine

By the end of the following week, Jess was despairing of having to walk Elvis. The snow had continued all week and very few people were venturing out unless they were forced to. Of course 'very few' did not include those die hard dog walkers who could be found wrapped up to the nines doing laps of the park, following the well-trodden paths made by those foolhardy dog owners who had ventured before them. The cold and bleak conditions didn't stop people being courteous to each other, although no-one wanted to stop and chat.

Even the consistently friendly Suzie kept moving as she passed by, "Hi Jess, horrible isn't it! I won't stop as I'm sure I can feel a cold coming on." She slipped as she negotiated past Jess, whilst trying to keep in the snow trodden path of others. Jess grabbed her by both arms and managed to save her from falling. "Thanks hun, see you soon and keep warm," and then she bent down and picked up Treacle who was wearing a pink hoodie with 'Princess' embedded on the back in glittery writing. "Come here baby. This was a silly idea of mummy to bring you out, let's go home."

The weather was so unpleasant that even when Jess bumped into Sylvia with Thomas they decided not to stop and let the little guys play. "I feel really bad," they both said almost simultaneously.

"I'm sure the guys would be just fine with their new coats on, though even with all the layers I'm wearing I'm still frozen," Sylvia had reasoned, somewhat guiltily.

"And I can't feel my toes," Jess had added, every word spoken being tangible in the frosty cold. Instead they had decided to walk back towards the exit of the park together in order that the pooches could play for a few minutes. They headed back to the top gates walking as quickly as possible in the deep snow and after a few minutes of small talk, predominantly about the weather, they left the park.

"Damn it, I've missed her again!" Jake said out loud to himself as spotted who he was sure was Jess leaving the park. Even from where he was stood, he knew it was her, granted the red fur coat was a bit of a giveaway because he'd never actually met another female inclined to wear such bizarre clothing.

Jake looked down at Chico the Chihuahua, his sister's dog. He had eagerly offered to look after the little fella until his sister was well enough to return home, having identified this scenario as being the ideal opportunity to accidently bump into the vivacious Jessica Wainwright. He had gleaned enough information from her Gran to know that she was looking after her dog whilst the old lady recuperated. Of course, he knew that the old lady had worked out his ulterior motive for checking to see if she was ok, after dropping into conversation how nice her granddaughter seemed. In return, she had offered up information. How her lovely granddaughter was dog sitting Elvis and that it was a bit of a struggle to manage the flower shop in the high street at the same time. However she also mentioned that Jess had been enjoying meeting new people whilst walking the dog in the park.

So here he was again, doing laps of the park in the freezing cold, walking the most girly dog on the planet. And he realised he wasn't doing his image any favours by putting that ridiculous coat on Chico that had 'hard as nails' written on the back, which had been his Mums' input. His mother had pointed out to Jake that his sister would be devastated if her precious pooch caught a cold. He had of course argued that it was more than his image could bear to be seen out with that. Of course, his mother had won the argument and he had planned on taking the offending item off the dog before he got out of the car. However, in keeping with their reputation, Chico the Chihuahua was temperamental and had tried to bite him as he struggled to remove the offending item. "Well, we've missed her again so we're heading back. You'll have to make do with the ride in the new wheels as your trip out today."

He bent down and picked Chico up, holding him securely around his tummy so he couldn't try and bite him again as he headed back to his new car. He stopped just for a moment to admire the shiny black finish and alloy wheels of his VW Golf. He didn't stand and admire it for long though because he had an idea that if he were quick, he might just catch a glimpse of Jess on the high street. So he jumped in the car and put Chico on the floor of the passenger side. However, by the time they had got to the top of the road that ran alongside the park and turned left down the high street, Chico was already sat on the passenger seat. Jake was too preoccupied to pay much attention to Chico's antics as he spotted Jess chatting to a young woman with a pram. As he drove past them, Jess smiled at the woman and turned to enter the shop.

"Bloody hell I'm turning into some kind of stalker, what the hell has gotten into me? What do you reckon eh?" he asked the bemused looking dog. "Great, love struck and talking to a dog." It's all downhill from here my friend," he laughed to himself and then headed home.

It continued to be freezing cold for the rest of the week with intermittent snow. There were very few people venturing out, especially to buy flowers, and Jess had told Bettie that she might as well go home as the shop was incredibly cold and Jess didn't want Bettie to become unwell. Granted, Bettie seemed healthier than a lot of people half her age but all things considered, a freezing cold flower shop was not the most desirable place to be. Plus, the only warm place to be found was behind the counter which had proved to be a bit snug for her, Bettie and Elvis all together.

It was Friday afternoon and Jess was bored. She had taken to entertaining herself by teaching Elvis some tricks with some plain digestive biscuits that she had brought down from the flat to have with a cup of tea to warm herself. She was quite impressed that he seemed to catch on pretty quickly. By the time she had finished the cup of tea, Elvis could sit down on command and shake hands/paws. The essentials she had considered in relation to being the guardian of a pooch were to teach it a party trick or two. Jess could recount many a home she had visited over the years where obliging pooches would be called upon to demonstrate their variety of talents. Jess recalled shaking hands seemed to be a favourite, along with rolling over on demand and decided that once Elvis had mastered these, he might move on to something a little more advanced like singing or dancing. Then she stopped herself from fantasising about turning Elvis into the next big thing by reminding herself that she wouldn't be looking after him for very much longer. Having shared another digestive with Elvis and deciding that shaking hands twenty times with a dog held about as much entertainment as she could take, Jess was bored.

The shop was incredibly quiet, not that she was overly worried about the dip in business as she considered that people only really bothered about essentials when the weather was like this. She had already prepared some bouquets for an engagement party which fortunately was being held at the social club just a mile down the road. Her Dad had kindly offered to deliver them for her, so she had nothing much to do. She decided that she would shut the shop up early, relax for a while and have something to eat before her dad came to do the delivery. *Good old Dad,* she thought to herself and then locked up the shop and went up to the flat.

Jess had left the flat's heating on all day though you wouldn't have thought so. However, it wasn't cold either and a whole lot warmer than the shop. The previous day Jess had called into her parents to both check on her Gran's progress and secretly assess how long she would be continuing to be the guardian of Elvis, which she considered would be for some considerable time given how uncomfortable her Gran looked. As she had been about to leave, her mother had insisted upon sending Jess home with a large meat and potato pie. Jess's protest that she was trying to diet had fallen upon death ears.

Nonsense! Was the reply she had received. 'There's a time and a place for dieting and this isn't it', her mother had argued.

Sprawled on the old battered sofa, watching TV in front of the fire, whilst tucking into a huge portion of pie was pure bliss and Jess reflected that she was glad her mum had insisted on forcing the calorie laden treat on her. She felt fit to burst when she had finished it, though totally contented and rather drowsy. So Jess decided that rather than get up and put the plate in the sink she would just pop it on the side table and put her feet up for ten minutes. Wrapping herself in the throw that she kept on the sofa to disguise its battered appearance, Jess was in a deep sleep within minutes, her subconscious once again contented to be in the company of the fabulous Mr Butler.

Jess's mobile woke her yet again, once again getting in the way of her wonderful make-believe relationship. However, this time it didn't take her quite as long to wake. "Hello," she answered half-heartedly.

"Jess its Mum. Listen, you're going to have to make that delivery yourself I'm afraid. Your dad has had a bit of an accident getting the car out of the drive."

"Bloody hell Mum, is he alright?"

"He's fine, though the car's looking a bit worse for wear. It just slipped down the drive and straight out onto the road. Then Mr Williams from number fourteen went straight into him. He was only going slowly but it's still damaged all the back end of the car. I'm afraid it's not safe to drive. So I know its short notice, but just this once you're going to have to do the delivery in the snow yourself."

It's ok Mum. I wouldn't expect him to come and do the delivery after that."

"You're going to have to get a move on though Jess, because with all the kerfuffle I forgot to ring you and your Dad's just told me they were supposed to be delivered by seven o' clock."

"Why, what time is?"

"Six thirty."

"Bloody hell Mum! I need to go now."

Jess jumped up and ran straight to locate her wellington boots which she reluctantly had to admit were proving invaluable. She had planned on leaving Elvis behind in the flat. However, as always when she went to pick up her keys and bag, he was already at front of the door. "Oh, come on then. I haven't got the time to mess about."

Jess had prepared the three bouquets earlier and placed them in the cold store room. She was struggling to open the back door that led out onto the lane when she remembered the bottle of champagne that she had also prepared earlier.

"Damn, I nearly forgot the champers Elvis!"

If she hadn't been in such a rush she would have thought to do one thing at a time. However, her common sense had gone completely out of the window. So, still carrying the flowers and handbag, plus keys, she opened the adjoining door to the shop. The moment the door opened, Elvis shot through the door before her and jumped straight up at the counter to get to the half-empty packet of biscuits which Jess had left on the counter earlier. He was already big enough standing on his hind legs to reach the desired objects. However, in his overzealous action, the bottle of champagne which Jess had lovingly finished in a beautiful gift bag with tissue, glitter and ribbon, began to wobble. Jess seemed to be moving in slow motion as she tried to catch it before it hit the floor. Wrestling with flowers, handbag and keys it was impossible. Her initial hope that the bottle wouldn't have broken was shattered when she saw the liquid seeping out from the seam of the bag.

"For God's sake Elvis, you choose now to turn into a devil dog?" she shouted at the cowering puppy who had left the biscuits and instinctively moved away from the offending, noisy item.

Seeing that he was clearly shocked by the incident, Jess put the flowers down on the counter and went to pick him up. "Come on silly, it's not that bad and I didn't mean to shout, I'm just stressed and running late," Jess began to explain to Elvis without stopping to consider that a dog could not possibly understand. Elvis just looked up at her with his sad puppy dog eyes. "Come on little guy, I'll just put you in the car where you can't get into any more trouble."

Rushing out of the back yard, she zapped the car key and put Elvis on the passenger seat before running back into the shop to collect the flowers. She then quickly picked up another bag of accessories and left the shop, putting the flowers in the boot, well out of the way of Elvis. Jess then placed herself in the driver's seat and faffed about trying to buckle the seat belt which was not cooperating with her need to make up time. Having finally secured herself, Jess leant over and buckled Elvis into the passenger seat before starting the ignition. "Right then little man, let's nip down to the local shop and pick up a replacement bottle."

Jess was nervous of driving in the deep snow, although the roads were not as bad to drive on as she had feared. Even so, the clock was ticking to make the delivery on time. She pulled into the car park near the front of the shop, quickly hopped out of the car and zapped the key fob to lock it. Jess knew the shop well and went straight to the alcohol section, a particularly well known area, immediately zoning in on the bottles of champagne that the mini supermarket had in stock.

Quickly making her choice, Jess made her way to the checkout which of course had a massive queue and only two people serving. *Typical!* She grumbled to herself. *There would have to be every man and his dog wanting to pay their bills, buy mobile phone top ups and hoping to be the next winner of the Euro lottery roll over, when I'm running late.*

Twenty minutes later and Jess was finally out of the shop and feeling incredibly stressed. Not looking where she was going, she very nearly smashed the new bottle of champers as she slipped on some slush on her way back to the car. She was distracted by trying to put her purse back in her bag with her spare hand and zapping the car key to unlock the car whilst balancing the bottle of champagne.

Having reached her car she negotiated herself into the driver's seat and then turned to pick up the spare gift bag and ribbon she had placed on the floor of the passenger seat. Many things happened in the moment that followed, as Jess's stressed out brain tried to make sense of the situation.

"Hang on a minute, where the hell is Elvis?" she asked herself. At the same time, it began to dawn on her that the car didn't feel right. It was at that point that Jess turned and looked at the car situated alongside hers. In doing so, she found herself looking directly at Elvis who was sat watching her from its passenger seat. Jess stared bewildered for a moment before realisation began to dawn. She then looked back the other way.

It was then that Jess saw her. An old lady with short, tightly permed, snowy white hair sitting in the rear of the car, laughing. Jess jumped out of her skin and very nearly swore, "Oh dear God, you scared me!"

"It's ok dear. It's the funniest thing I've seen in a long time. I saw you go in looking frazzled and come back out looking the same. Your face is a picture my dear."

Jess was acutely embarrassed, "I'm so sorry, you must think I'm bonkers. In fact I think I must be."

"I'm sure you're not dear, we all do silly things when we're rushing. Though in truth I don't think I've come across anyone getting in the wrong car before. I can't wait to tell the girls at bridge club tomorrow." The old woman was clearly trying to reassure Jess, although as she finished her sentence she began giggling again. She looked over in the direction of Jess's car. "That's a very cute dog you have by the way, though he looks like he's getting a bit upset."

Jess looked back towards her real car, where indeed Elvis was trying to eat the window, presumably wanting to find a way out. "I'd best get back to the little monster before he destroys my car. It's his fault I've just made a complete twit of myself; I'm supposed to be delivering some flowers with champagne to Bakers Lane. And now I'm going to be really late because that beast went and smashed the champagne and I'm not even sure where I'm supposed to be going. My dad generally does deliveries for me when it's weather like this."

The old lady smiled, "It wouldn't be the Reynolds house would it? I know they are having an engagement party for their daughter Tilly."

"Yes that's the one."

"Well you'll be there in two minutes so I wouldn't panic. Go straight down the main road, left at the lights and left again into the cul-de-sac. They happen to be my next-door-neighbours so it looks like your dog might have brought you a bit of luck after all."

Jess turned to look once again at Elvis, who was clearly quite distressed now. She opened the car door and stepped once again into the cold evening air before bobbing her head back into the car.

"Thanks ever so much for not thinking I'm crazy and trying to abduct you and for giving me the directions, it's been a pleasure meeting you."

"You too, dear. You've given me the best laugh I've had in ages."

Jess giggled to herself as she made the short journey to the Reynolds' house, finding it straight away thanks to the clear directions. She composed herself before handing over the delivery and then giggled to herself again on the short journey home. "I don't know whether you did me a favour or not you, you little devil," Jess was saying to Elvis as she fed him some of the remains of the meat and potato pie she was greedily finishing off. "I never even had the time to worry about driving in the snow because I was in such a rush. On the other hand I'm going to get a reputation as being that crazy florist who lives on her own with that big dog and gets in strangers cars if I'm not careful." Elvis just sat by Jess's feet watching carefully as she finished the last of the food. Jess looked down at the cute little puppy that had been the cause of so much change in her life over the last couple of weeks and reflected upon how possibly the change was for the better.

"It's no good giving me those puppy dog eyes little man. Mum made this pie for me, plus you don't deserve any more considering you made a twit out of me today. Anyway, I'm doing you a favour. All those calories won't do you a bit of good so you can stop drooling. Though I think Elvis, it's me that's putting on the pounds to be honest." As a result of this observation, Jess shared the last of her supper between them, Elvis' tail gently tapping on the floor as he chewed.

Chapter Ten

The following Sunday, Jess, Kate and James were joined by James's nephew, a tall, good looking guy of around thirty. "I hope you don't mind the extra company ladies, it's just that Luke called in just as I was about to leave the house," James explained.

"Yes, I hope you don't mind. It's just I was at a bit of a loose end and when Uncle James told me that he had an arrangement to meet two lovely young ladies I was intrigued."

"We don't mind at all!" Jess and Kate chorused together, "in fact the more the merrier."

They took a different route through the woods this time and found a shallow stream where the unlikely group stopped to let the dogs paddle in the water for a few minutes. They simultaneously laughed when Elvis slipped on some ice and his long legs went from under him, which ultimately led to Elvis slipping and sliding across the ice until he came to a stop, head first in shallow water.

Luke had not known what to expect from this unscheduled outing. However he was thoroughly enjoying being out in the fresh air and being in such good company. "I might join you guys another time if it's ok with you? It's not bad this dog walking, is it? I'd be tempted to get a dog of my own I think if it wasn't for the amount of time I'm out of the house with work."

James immediately spotted an opportunity, "You're more than welcome to borrow Max any time Luke. In fact you'd be doing me a favour, especially until the weather warms up."

"Actually Luke, you'd be doing me a big favour too, if you walked Max during the week," Jess joined in. "I stay away from the park on an evening because I don't like going in there on my own when it's dark, so if you do decide to take Max out let me know and I'll meet you. In fact, I'll let my friend Suzie know too, because I know she's not fond of going in the park either in the evening."

"Now I'm feeling left out," Kate chirped up. "I might have to borrow Mitzi more often. I don't want to miss out if you're having a social gathering."

"It's hardly a social gathering Kate," laughed Jess.

"Well what else do you call a group of people getting together? It's like 'Come Dine with Me' with dinner being replaced by pooches."

"Talking of dining," Luke interrupted, "Why don't we head back and take the dogs home. I think they've had enough now anyway. Then if you're up for it, we could meet at Harry's Carvery in about an hour and get something to eat."

"Sounds like a plan," they all agreed.

An hour later and the group were sat around a table near to the open fire at Harry's, chatting animatedly as they waited for the queue for the food to die down. Jess had initially been horrified to see the length of the queue which was snaking its way around the entire periphery of the premises and had tried to persuade the others to reconvene elsewhere. However, unlike Jess, Kate, Luke and James were blessed with a degree of patience. Plus the delightful aroma of the renowned carvery had already worked its magic on them hence they were more than happy to be patient.

Jess was glad she had agreed with the consensus because now she was laughing along with the others as James relayed to Luke how the unlikely event had come into fruition. With a slight smirk forming, Luke had interrupted his uncle to ask whether meeting strangers in the woods was a past time James had kept quiet about. In response, James laughed and stated that he knew exactly what his nephew was implying and that, whilst on reflection it probably did sound a bit wrong, he was glad he had suggested the walk to Jess because he had thoroughly enjoyed himself. Both Luke and Kate supported this last statement as each agreed that they were glad Jessica and James were daft enough to arrange something like that in the first place as they had enjoyed the day. Jess took a moment to observe the group as they chatted and pondered for a moment about how random and changeable life can be. Then the moment was lost as she spotted that there was no longer a queue for the carvery.

"Everyone quickly, now's our chance!" Jess exclaimed to the others. And without waiting for a response she was on her feet and walking determinedly towards her target, spurred on by the rumblings in her stomach she had suddenly become conscious of. An hour or so later and they had parted company with arrangements in place to meet in the park at 7 pm on Wednesday evening.

Later that evening, Jess was looking through the orders for the following day and deciding what she needed to purchase from the wholesalers accompanied by her music on full blast. This, she justified to herself, was the only way to listen to the Arctic Monkeys. And besides, no one lived in the adjoining flats. The music began to distract Jess and she placed the papers down beside her. The lyrics to 'I bet you look good on the dance floor' were belting out and for a moment Jess was transported back to a time before she and Brandon had separated.

Kate had come down to London for the weekend to attend a house party Jess and Brandon were throwing to celebrate yet another of his promotions. It had been a fun and drink fuelled party, one of their happier times. With that memory it brought alive a plan that maybe Jess should throw a house warming party in her flat. After all she had been here a while now with no official acknowledgement.

"I might have to throw a party soon, invite some of our new dog walking friends. What do you think Elvis? Like the idea?" Elvis generally looked up whenever his name was mentioned but on this occasion was busy chewing on the rawhide treat Jess had bought him in a bid to stop him from chewing any more of Jess's possessions, which now included her underwear, a pair of shoes, two hairbrushes and even some of her make-up.

The flashing of her mobile caught Jess's attention, the music so loud she didn't have a hope in hell of hearing it. "Hiya. Sorry, hang on I can't hear you. Oh hi Gran, how are you surviving living with mum?"

"It's driving me mad love, although if I'd have had to listen to that racket, I think I may be better off here. You can't call that music. Not a patch on Elvis is it?"

"You and your obsession with Elvis, Gran! Don't you think it's about time you got over it? I mean the guy's been dead for years now."

"You don't move on from perfection dear. Talking of Elvis how is he?"

"He's fine Gran. In fact we've had a lovely day." Jess then went on to tell her Gran about her day and how a bizarre social group was in the making.

"As soon as you're better it'll be you meeting the dog walking fraternity. They're nice – you'll like them."

"I'm not so sure about that love."

"What do you mean? You've always loved meeting new people."

"No, not that, I'm sure they're lovely. It's just that I'm not sure that I'm going to be able to look after Elvis. It's going to be a long time before I'm fully recovered."

"Gran you'll be fine, and he can stay with me until you're back on your feet, literally speaking."

"We'll see love."

They chatted some more and Jess promised she would take Elvis to visit her Gran again the following Saturday after work. She couldn't help but be concerned though. Her Gran had sounded resigned to the idea of not being able to cope. Jess threw herself back down onto the comfy old sofa, now mentally distracted from her party planning. Immediately Elvis jumped up on to the sofa beside her and, although Jess knew better than to encourage him, she found herself cuddling the affectionate fur ball. Jess momentarily mused over the notion that her Gran could part with the new family addition. However, Jess was convinced that once her Gran was reunited with the gorgeous Elvis she would not possibly be able to part with him again.

"Let's not worry yet little guy. I'm sure once she's seen you on Saturday she won't be able to bring herself to part with you."

Chapter Eleven

It was 7 pm on Wednesday evening and Jess, Luke and Kate stood freezing in the park, intermittently rubbing their gloved hands together whilst breathing onto them.

"This is crazy!" Luke was the first to utter his protests.

"I must admit I don't think I can stand here much longer. I'm afraid I'm not going to be able to move if we don't call it a night soon," mumbled Jess in agreement.

"Me too," Kate chorused. "Plus we must look like a right bunch of saddos and I don't even have to be here. Stood in the park freezing my arse off and I don't even own a dog!"

"Nobody forced you Missy," Jess snapped back.

"Hey, I won't bring Max again if you're going to start arguing. I thought this was going to be fun."

"We're not arguing. Spend any more time with us and you'll soon see this is just us." They giggled, elbowing each other like school kids.

Luke gave them both a sideways look and smirked before whistling into the darkness in order to locate Max in a manner more in keeping with a builder than an accountant."

"Hey guys!" They all turned at the same time to see Suzie coming towards them carrying Treacle. "Watch out for –!"

Jess didn't get the chance to hear the rest of the sentence as her legs went from under her and although she tried her best to reach out for help from Luke and Kate who were simultaneously trying to catch her, she ended up in the snow on her bottom, with the culprit, Elvis, excitedly licking her face.

"Here, give us your hands," offered Luke and Kate as they pulled Jess to her feet.

"The Furry Assassin strikes again," Jess laughed.

"Are you alright?" Suzie asked, dusting snow off Jess's red fake fur coat.

"Yeah, I'm good, embarrassed but good. Though I think I might call time on the Assassins walk tonight."

"But I've only just got here," Suzie protested.

"Oh ok, I'll do one lap and then that's it I think, cause I'm wet through. Plus the neighbours really must be beginning to think we're the new Neighbourhood Watch!"

"I have a suggestion," intervened Luke. "Why don't we do just one circuit of the park and then retreat and meet up in the Pear Tree, dog free. It's quiz night and I'm told they do a great curry supper."

By 9 pm the group had all convened around a table in the corner of the Pear Tree. They were all drinking pints except for Suzie who sipped a glass of white wine.

"Do you know Jess, I think you might be on to something with this dog walking thing? Jess! You're not listening to me," Kate was saying in a slightly raised voice.

"Sorry, I was miles away." In reality Jess had not been miles away, she had been watching Suzie and Luke chatting amiably with Suzie giggling intermittently. *Perfect,* she thought to herself. It was Kate that disturbed her silent match-making.

"Honestly Jess, I'd love to know what planet you're on sometimes. I was saying I think you might be on to something with this dog walking thing."

"But I haven't got any dog walking thing. It was by chance that I got chatting to James and Suzie and then Luke."

Hearing their names, Luke and Suzie were now paying attention. "Did we hear our names being mentioned?"

Kate repeated herself again. "To be honest, I think Kate has a point," both Luke and Suzie agreed.

"I mean if it hadn't been for you Jess, none of us would be here tonight. And it is nice getting out and meeting new people without having to get glammed up and head into town, where generally you only get letches and creepy old men chatting you up," Suzie added.

"Can't say I get chatted up by creepy old men though, you do get the odd letchy female I suppose," laughed Luke.

"They are right though Jess. I mean, you've mentioned loads of people you've been chatting to and I'll bet most of them were on their own. It's well known people get themselves a dog so they can get out and about or to feel less lonely."

"Exactly. Why on earth would anyone want to walk their dogs with strangers? And why, if it's such a good idea, do I have to do it. If hanging out with strangers to walk your dog is a new social phenomenon why doesn't one of you do it?"

"Well, we were strangers a couple of weeks ago," the listening trio chirped up in unison.

It was Kate who then put forward an argument for Jess to be the facilitator of the fast emerging new group. "I'll tell you why, because you're the one who talks to everyone. Plus you could easily stick a poster in your shop window. Come on Jess, I think it could be fun."

"Well after the weekend I might not be looking after Elvis anyway. Gran's decided she doesn't think she's going to be able to look after him, so I don't know what's going to happen."

In between trying to answer the pub quiz questions, downing more drinks and tucking into the curry supper, which they all agreed was incredibly good, the group spent the rest of the evening trying to persuade Jess that she couldn't possibly part with the adorable Elvis.

Chapter Twelve

Jess looked at her reflection in the bathroom mirror of her Mum's house and took a deep breath. She was outnumbered and losing the argument, and she knew it. Heading downstairs again, she pushed open the kitchen door before heading straight over to the cookie jar and taking out one of her Mum's home baked golden oat cookies. Jess had continued to contemplate joining the gym to lose the few pounds she was aware she had put on. However, at that moment she was in the need for comfort food. As soon as she entered the kitchen Elvis came to stand beside her.

"You see what I mean? That dog has stood by the door the whole time you were upstairs. It's obvious to everyone that he's already totally devoted to you."

"But Gran, he'd be totally devoted to you if you just gave him the chance. He's really friendly. I'm sure he'd adjust again and I'm sure he remembers you."

"I'm sure he does too love, but it doesn't alter the fact that I can't look after him and I have to admit I might have been a bit of a silly old fool rushing into getting a dog that size. It's just not going to work love."

Jess looked at her Gran who was at the kitchen table on one of the sturdy dining table chairs she had chosen to sit on as it was easier to get up from. With her pot on her leg and intermittently shuffling in her seat, it was clear to Jess that her Gran was right. She really wasn't in any fit state to look after

Elvis at the moment, and in truth Jess knew it would be a considerable time before she was.

Jess gave a loud sigh and bent down to pick up the now incredibly large and heavy Elvis who immediately started licking her face. "But dogs are so annoying. They need feeding and walking and I haven't had a lie in since I began looking after him. Plus he's chewed the heel on my cowboy boots. He's used that favourite red coat of mine as a rug and the second time I caught him with it, I think he was wanting to get to know it better!"

"They weren't the blue boots?" Even her Gran seemed to find it difficult to justify keeping him if it meant he had eaten the fabulous blue cowboy boots she had acquired off eBay and loved from the minute she had unwrapped them.

"No Gran, they weren't that pair, but even so it's still a bit annoying."

"Annoying it might be, but just think of how much fun you've had since you got him, plus all the nice people you've met and I'm sure he wasn't getting friendly with your best coat. The breeder said he wouldn't possibly be interested in that kind of behaviour until he was *much* older."

"Did she have her hands behind her back when she said it because I think you'll find she may have had her fingers crossed?"

Jess's Gran laughed. "You're very funny, young Miss Wainwright."

With the mention of Elvis's previous owner providing a personality profile for him, Jess's interested was piqued. "So what else did the breeder say about him, other than that he wouldn't try and hump inanimate furry objects?"

"Well she said he was very lazy and laid back and that as he got older he would be very loyal and protective."

Jess studied Elvis. She couldn't deny he was incredibly lazy and chilled out, and the loyalty she could understand because he was never more than a few feet away from her, although she struggled to see that such a lazy, chilled out dog would be protective. However, what her Gran had pointed out about her new social life was true. In the time she had been looking after Elvis she had met some interesting people and made new friends. In fact she had not chatted to so many random people in such a short space of time since her last holiday with Brandon. On that occasion they had spent a great deal of time apart, at the time she had not understood why Brandon seemed sullen and distant towards her. However, upon their return home the reason became all too apparent as he had left shortly afterwards. As a result of her enforced isolation from her husband, Jess had done what came naturally to her and that was to talk to anyone else who entered the vicinity.

With the brief thought of holidays, came her last defence. "I'll never get another holiday if I own a dog."

"Now you're just being daft. You never go on holiday anyway and if you do decide to go somewhere I'll look after him for you."

Jess knew this battle was lost, she couldn't part with him and she knew it. Looking into Elvis's eyes, she kissed him on the end of his nose, "Well Elvis, it looks like I've got myself a dog."

She then placed Elvis back on the kitchen floor before heading over to the wine rack that was neatly hidden away at the far end of the kitchen. Having located one of her favourite bottles of Chardonnay, she poured herself a glass before heading back over to join her Gran at the kitchen table, very nearly spilling the contents of the glass over her Gran as she tripped over Sid the rabbit.

"That bloody rabbit! Honestly Mum, Gran is supposed to be recuperating. If she can trip over something the size of Elvis then I'm sure she's definitely going to trip over that thing."

"You're right dear, I keep forgetting and letting him out of his cage on a morning, me and your Dad are so used to him that he never gets under our feet."

Jess looked in the direction of her dad and found a familiar exasperated look upon his face. The one she had witnessed often and it usually acted as a ten minute warning for him leaving for the golf course, whatever the weather. For what seemed like the millionth time Jess contemplated what on odd couple her parents made. It seemed to Jess that they were as different as two people could possibly be. Her Dad presented an easy going nature, generous, helpful and fond of a pint with his friends. As Jess watched her dad kneel down in order to fuss Elvis, she noted that he was still a smart man. He possessed a full shock of wavy hair, albeit slightly greying now and with his casual attire, he could definitely have been mistaken for a good ten years younger than his fifty nine years of age.

Whereas her Mother presented as someone who preferred to stay at home and cook and clean. She was constantly anxious and worrying over something or another and always seemed a little uncomfortable in social settings. Other than when they holidayed, Jess could not remember a time when they went out together socially. Jess was aware that her dad had encouraged her Mother to join him at some of the many social gatherings that took place at the golf club. She also knew that her mother could not be persuaded, instead choosing to stay in and watch her soaps. Jess still considered her mother to be an attractive woman and was aware that her somewhat staid dress attire of traditional skirts and blouses had the effect of making her look much older than her years. Jess wondered if maybe she should buy her mother something a little more glamorous to wear for her birthday because beneath the staid exterior was a woman with very few wrinkles, sparkling green eyes and thick hair that was cut into a short manageable style.

However, as Jess observed the look of affection pass between them as her father joined them at the table and made some silly joke, she resigned herself to the notion that maybe she should refrain from meddling in her parents' relationship. Jess considered that in the case of her parents it seemed that not only do opposites attract, they continue to do so for thirty-three years of marriage.

Jess stayed and ate dinner with her parents and Gran and actually quite enjoyed herself. Over dinner she relayed to her family the story of how she had nearly kidnapped a pensioner whilst purchasing the replacement champagne. At which they had each laughed and observed that a situation like that didn't surprise then in regards to Jess. "Talking of alcohol, I think I might just leave Elvis here while I pop to the shop and treat myself to a bottle of Shiraz. I think taking on a new responsibility warrants a treat and I need a few other bits."

Rising from her chair, Jess grabbed her bag and headed to the front door, car keys in hand. She quickly slammed the door shut, headed down the path, closed the garden gate behind her and got into her car. She was just in the process of putting her bag on the passenger seat when there was a scraping at her window. Jess turned and nearly jumped out of her skin as she was greeted by the image of Elvis, on hind legs against the driver's door, peeking in through the window.

"Holy shit, you crazy dog, you nearly scared me to death!" Jess took a deep breath to regain her composure. Getting back out of the car and scooping up Elvis in the process, she headed to the garden gate, only to find it closed. While she paused there for a moment, trying to make sense of the scenario, her Dad walked down the garden path towards her.

"Well in all my days, I've never seen anything like that! The door didn't slam shut properly behind you and that their puppy shot down the path after you, scaling the gate in one."

"But Dad, that gate must be four foot high and he's just a baby! Do you think he's hurt himself?"

"It doesn't look like it Sweetheart," her dad replied, giving Elvis the once over. "I have to agree with your Gran though, Jess. For whatever reason it looks like you've got yourself one very devoted friend for life."

Chapter Thirteen

Jess's official initiation into dog ownership did not go well. The very next day that ownership had been transferred to Jess, Elvis became poorly. She didn't initially pay much attention to the fact that he was not his sociable, excitable self either in the flat or out on a walk. Neither did she pay much attention to the fact that he had not eaten much and not even bothered to chew any of her items. However, she did pay attention to the fact that he kept her awake much of the first night and almost all of the second. It wasn't that he was whining or whimpering, he just would not settle down and kept pacing round the bedroom and scratching at the door. After choosing the snooze option of her alarm for an extra thirty minutes, Jess managed to drag herself out of bed and headed to the bathroom in the hope a shower might revive her little. As she went to turn on the shower to let the water warm up she caught sight of herself in the bathroom mirror and was not pleased with the image that reflected back at her. Faint dark shadows were present beneath puffy and bloodshot eyes and her hair although naturally given to being a bit wild looked like she had been dragged through a hedge. "Great start to pet ownership!" she mumbled to herself as she splashed water onto her face in a bid to rectify some of the damage caused by sleep deprivation.

Although she knew what the answer would be she rang her Gran for advice anyway, only to have it confirmed a trip to the vets was required. Fortunately for Jess, the ever loyal

Bettie was there to manage the shop whilst Jess and Elvis headed out for his trip to the vets.

An hour and half later they were back and Jess immediately went in to the back room where she threw off her coat and dumped her bag on the work top before rummaging about in the bottom of it.

"So how did you get on then," Bettie asked as she made her way over to the sink to fill up the kettle.

"Well this is what my fifty seven quid's worth of consultation got me or Elvis should I say," Jess replied holding out two small items, one of them being a small bottle of antihistamines and the other a small white bottle of ear drops. "It seems young Elvis has got a dodgy ear as a result of eczema, most likely the result of an allergy," Jess grumbled as she unscrewed the lip of the ear drops and popped a couple of drops into Elvis's left ear.

"I've never heard of a dog with allergies before," Bettie giggled. "How do they treat that," she enquired, genuinely curious as she made her way towards Jess carrying the two cups of tea.

"With these drops," grumbled Jess. "And Piriton, would you believe, which I'm sure I could have got a lot cheaper at the chemist over the road. Almost sixty pound it cost me to be completely humiliated," she continued to grumble before taking a sip of the much needed cup of tea.

Observing the somewhat peeved look upon Jess face, Bettie was keen to know what could have upset Jess with just a simple trip to the vets. "What do you mean humiliated?"

Jess took a sip of her tea and then let out a sigh of exasperation as she said, Bettie do you think I'm fat?"

Bettie nearly choked on the sip of tea she had just taken, however she managed to say "absolutely not Jess," before beginning to cough. Having regained her composure she added, "Why ever would you say that?"

Jess took a further sigh and then began. "Well we waited about half an hour and then the vet came to the door and shouted us." She then deviated from the story for a moment as she described the vet as being a short funny looking man who looked to be in his mid-forties and looked like either a librarian or a tax man. Jess then took another sip of tea and still aggrieved continued with her story. "Anyway, as we made our way to the door he looked at Elvis and said, 'He's a big lad isn't he?' Obviously I didn't think anything of it because Elvis is clearly huge, but I then had to endure ten minutes of a lecture as to how with Elvis being overweight, it could affect his joints both now and when he's older. He even had the cheek to say that dogs like humans are affected by calorie intake and that as '*one!*' gets older it will..."Jess paused, took a deep sigh and another sip of tea, before adding, "Well! It will make you fat."

"I've never heard anything so ridiculous or inappropriate in my life," protested Bettie.

"Honestly Bettie, at first my brain was trying to process who he was talking about, me! Him! Or the dog! So in the end up I just came out with it and said, "Sorry which one of us are you are referring to."

Jess who had initially been staring into her cup of tea now looked over at Bettie as she heard a slight giggle. "It's not funny Bettie. Just how old do you think he thought I was?" though before Bettie could reply Jess continued. "And I know I look a bit rough this morning and maybe I've put on a few pounds but seriously that outing was enough to make a girl really paranoid."

"Have you finished now, can I finally say something?" Bettie quickly added upon Jess stopping from her ranting for a moment. Then deciding to draw closure to the conversation Bettie took a step towards Jess in order that she had her attention and that she meant business when she rather sternly said. "Now listen to me young lady, you are a beautiful, caring and funny young lady, and you take no notice of what that fool said, in fact he most likely wasn't even referring to you. Now go and lie down for an hour and catch up on some sleep, if we get busy I'll shout you."

Jess observed the obstinate look upon Bettie's face and chose not to argue with her. Instead she gave her hug and then made her way upstairs followed by Elvis, though as she did so she was grumbling to herself. "He did mean us didn't he Elvis, well we'll show him won't we, I mean how hard can it be to lose a few pounds."

The next day Jess felt more like her usual self thanks to a good night's sleep and Elvis seemed much happier as a result of treatment. Mrs Jacobs had just left for the day when the shop bell tinkled and Luke walked in, grinning like a Cheshire cat. "I hear you're officially the proud owner of an incredibly large puppy." Luke stopped at the shop counter and bent down to fuss Elvis who clearly recognised him. "I swear that dog has doubled in size in a week!"

Jess, who had been in the process of strategically sorting fake flower petals into colours for her Valentine's Day display, left the task and headed over to Luke and Elvis. "Him and me both it would seem," she mumbled to herself as she headed over to them.

"Sorry I didn't catch what you said," Luke stated in a matter of fact manner.

Not wanting to open up this dialogue Jess casually altered the sentence to, "I said, so it would seem and thanks for pointing that out Luke!" she continued jovially. "I had noticed, if he carries on like this I'm going to have to find a bigger place to live. Do you think I made the right decision?"

"I'm joking with you! And yes, I think you made the right decision," laughed Luke. "You won't need to move house because he'll be that tired from all the exercise he'll get as part of your new dog walking group, all he'll do is sleep."

Jess was silenced momentarily as Luke held up a poster. It was clearly homemade but a lot of effort had gone into it. Across the top of the A4 paper written in bold in order to attract as much attention as possible were the words '*The K9 & Co Club*'. Underneath that it read.

'Bored of walking your dog on your own?

Are you limited in the places you can walk your beloved pooch?

Then why not come along to the new and exciting way to walk your dog and meet new people?'

Below that the poster explained that the K9 & Co Club would meet at 1pm each Sunday afternoon at the entrance to Judy Woods. Those interested were advised to contact Jess via her shop phone number or by calling into Funky Flowers. Around the edges of the poster were random pictures of different breeds of dogs, including one of an Old English Sheepdog wearing a white jumpsuit and shades.

"Are you mad?" was all that Jess could manage to say.

"Not at all. Kate phoned me to let me know you were keeping Elvis and that she had spoken to Suzie and we all thought it was a great idea. So I thought I'd just give you a prompt."

Jess felt slightly aggrieved that she had not been consulted on the matter. "So let me get this straight, along with running this business and looking after this lump, you want me to spend my spare time standing in the woods waiting for complete strangers to come and strangle me? Are you all insane? And on top of all that I'm not sure that adding that picture of Elvis really reflects what the group is supposed to be about. We'll have strange people joining who believe dressing their pooch up like Dolly Parton is the norm in the hope of marrying them off to an eligible Elvis."

Luke just laughed and picked up some Blu-tack from the counter, before making his way over to the window and sticking the poster in a prominent position next to the door. "We're all going to help you silly, you won't be on your own. As if we'd let you wander around the woods meeting complete strangers. We just think it could be fun. Maybe the fancy dress thing does kind of give out the wrong idea. Neither Suzie nor I actually considered anyone would think anything of it. We certainly didn't, so I'm sure nobody else will either. Anyway, I'll be off, see you tonight." And with that, he left before Jess could say anything else.

Chapter Fourteen

Friday evening and Jess and Kate were pounding the treadmill at Planet Fitness, the gym which they had been promising to attend as part of their New Year's resolution. In all honesty, if left to Jess and Kate they most likely would not have made it over the threshold. However, they had been dragged there by the newest member of the K9 & Co Club, Lucy, who had responded to Luke's advert. So here they were, sweating like kippers, giggling at how unfit they were and how unglamorous they looked.

Jess had been stunned when Lucy, a tall, attractive female with a huge smile and shoulder length red hair that fell in waves to her shoulders had confidently walked in to the shop and enquired over the new social group. Jess had explained that her friends had talked her into it, believing it to be a good idea. Lucy had agreed, adding it sounded an intriguing way to meet new people and that anything fun, and she could be counted in.

Lucy and Harry, her miniature Schnauzer, had joined the group that evening and as Jess had expected, Lucy was chatty and good company. They were on their second lap of the park when the conversation had moved on to fitness. Kate had made a comment that with all this new exercise she would soon lose the extra pounds she had put on over Christmas, and Lucy had excitedly suggested that they join her gym. It turned out that Lucy had recently bought the gym which was situated on a main road about two miles away with some inheritance money and she offered that they could come along for free to check it out. She would even arrange for them to have some personal training. Lucy had been so positive about them coming along that they had felt obliged to attend. And as Jess and Kate chatted on the phone later they had giggled about the possibility that the fitness instructor might be incredibly fit and so for that reason alone it would be worth a visit. They hadn't been disappointed. Paul the PT instructor was tall with blonde hair, blue eyes and muscles to die for. Jess looked to her left to see Kate in full flirt mode with Paul clearly reciprocating, albeit in a subtle and professional way. Yep, Jess was sure that Kate would have secured a date by the time they left.

"I think I might count this next one out if you don't mind," stated Jess as she stopped the treadmill and stepped off, gasping for breath, a combination of acting and reality.

"Are you sure?"

"Yeah, if you don't mind Paul, I think I'll go find Lucy."

"Ok, but don't forget to do your warm down exercises."

"Will do. Right I'll leave you to it then."

While Jess and Kate were creating some feel good endorphins in the gym, Jake was in the Pear Tree staring into his pint despondently. "You're not listening again are you? And I bet I can work out what you were thinking of, you know you really need to move on. Why don't you just have a one night stand? That girl in the far corner keeps giving you the eye. Or what about trying your chances with that Lucy from the gym, she's cute."

Jake and his best mate Tom had been to Planet Fitness after work and arranged to meet for a pint later. After Jake had walked that bloody dog of his sisters' again, of course, just on the off chance he might bump into Jess. "Sorry mate, I'm not much company tonight am I? I was just thinking about that awful road accident we attended this morning. That poor kid."

"Yeah that one was a bad one, but I don't reckon that's what you were thinking of. I reckon it was a beautiful brunette."

Jake laughed, "There's not much I can get past you, is there mate? Maybe you're right. I might just go chat up those birds sat in the corner."

Tom was beginning to lose patience. Jake was his best mate. They'd worked together for years and been through so much. It was a tough job being a paramedic and they had seen some terrible things in their time. Despite this, they had always managed to have a laugh when they were having a wind-down pint. Tom just wanted to see Jake back to his usual self, flirting with the ladies and having his choice of dates. "Oh for God's sake! Right I've had enough of this; tomorrow we're taking that damned girly dog of your sisters' round and round that bloody park until you see her. I don't care if it takes all day, she must be there at some point. But I tell you what Jake, you owe me big time. If anyone sees me walking that thing I'll never pull again."

The following afternoon Jess took Elvis for a quick lap around the park before Mrs Jacobs left for the day. It was unusually quiet, unsurprisingly given that it was mid-February and bitterly cold. As Jess made her way along the path leading to the exit of the park she could make out two males in the distance. They stopped and embraced before continuing in her direction. At first she didn't see the dog as it was so small but as they drew closer she could make out a Chihuahua trotting along behind them.

"Christ Tom, that's her! I don't bloody believe it, it's really her!"

"Alright Mate, calm down, you don't want to act like an excitable puppy! Play it cool. Take some deep breaths and chill out. For Christ's sake, what's the matter with you? If you mess this up I'm not going round this bloody park again, seven times is enough. Just breathe man and act normal, although normal for you used to be a lad about town, pulling a different girl every weekend. Now you're acting like a teenager trying to get laid for the first time. "

"Shut up Tom," Jake hissed furiously.

Elvis went bounding up excitedly to the two guys and Jess belatedly wished that she had put him on his lead. Most people who walked their dogs in the park were friendly but she had observed that some people were a bit precious about their tiny pooches and generally picked them up. The path around the edge of the park was not overly wide and to some extent people had to manoeuvre around one another when passing. Jess had surmised that this was the reason you generally ended up passing pleasantries with one another. It seemed rude not to when in close proximity to another, even a stranger.

Of course not everyone felt the desire to acknowledge a stranger but Jess could tell instantly that these two seemed friendly. Jess stopped as she and the two men crossed paths and as she looked up at them, she had a strange feeling that the taller of the two looked familiar, though for the life of her she could not place him.

As usual the pooches began their own pleasantries, which generally involved something embarrassing. At least Jess considered it cringe-worthy to try and hold a civil conversation whilst one dog was busy sniffing the other's arse. On this occasion it was even more embarrassing as Jess noticed from the corner of her eye that a certain pint sized lothario was humping Elvis's back leg.

"Hi, nice dog," was all that Jake managed to produce, an octave higher than he would have liked. He nearly cursed himself out loud for sounding like such a sap.

"Yeah, he's quite a good puppy most of the time. I haven't had him long."

Jake was about to mention that he already knew this, but stopped himself for fear of sounding like a stalker, which of course he was aware he was becoming to some extent.

Usually known for being a bit of a joker amongst his mates, Jake was now aware he was struggling to find something to say. "Cold today isn't it?" again he cursed himself inwardly.

"Yeah, it certainly is. I can't wait for spring. Though it looks your little guy has found a way to keep warm," Jess replied with a laugh.

"For God's sake Chico, get off him!" Jake had never been more embarrassed. Normally he'd have seen the funny side of it, but his sister's dog fornicating with the dog of the girl he was trying to make an good impression on, and who he had spent ages trying to orchestrate a meeting with, was not what he had intended.

Jess just laughed, "Oh I wouldn't worry. If Elvis was fond of nicotine he looks like he'd be stood there smoking a cigarette after their encounter." Jess hoped her silly comment would ease the tense atmosphere that for some reason she felt. Possibly due to the fact that the conversation seemed a little forced. "Right then Elvis, let's let these nice men get back to their walk. Nice meeting you," and with that she carried on her way.

Just as Jess was about to leave the park she felt compelled to turn around. In the distance she could make out the two guys getting into a nice shiny Mini Cooper. Jess bent down to put Elvis back on his lead. "Well that was awkward wasn't it, for both of us. They seemed nice though, clearly gay, but nice and once again she had the notion that she had crossed paths with the cute guy with sparkling blue eyes before. It's such a shame, that's the first guy I've thought was hot in ages and he happens to be unavailable. What is it with me and gay men? I think I'll ring Brandon later and ask him where I'm going wrong. You seem quite popular with the males of the canine world for that matter Mister. Though you are a good looking young fella so wouldn't they, eh? Oh well. Come on Elvis, let's go and get that order finished for Mrs Roberts."

Safely in the car, Jake let out a deep breath. "So now do you see why I've been trying to track her down? She's gorgeous."

"Yeah, I have to admit I can see why you're trying to take her off the market, but you do realise she thinks we're gay."

"Don't be ridiculous man!" Jake almost shouted at Tom. "Why would she think that?"

"Why do you think?" Jake was quiet while he re-lived the encounter, and then he lent forward and rested his head on the steering wheel. "You're right – she does, doesn't she? She kept looking back from me to you and I bet she saw that bloody man hug and then the chick's dog and this ridiculous car of my sister's. I hope to God she hasn't seen me driving this thing."

Jake's car had been recalled back to the garage due to a technical fault and so with his sister still in Devon with her boyfriend, it was either borrow her Mini Cooper with pink flowers splattered all over its body, or bus it. And with his anti-social shift patterns, the car made more sense. He was man enough to take the jibes off his colleagues. In fact, he saw driving the car as a bit of fun, but he hadn't considered the implications of Jess seeing him in it. Well, why would he worry, the notion that someone would think he was gay had never even entered his head. "For Christ's sake! Now what am I going to do?"

"You're going to do what you should have done all along, which is get yourself down to the shop and ask her on a proper date and if you don't I'm going to bloody well do it for you. Honestly Jake, you need to man up."

Jake knew full well that Tom meant it. He knew better than to call his bluff. Jake had been on too many stag dos to know there wasn't much Tom wouldn't do. In fact, he couldn't think of a time that Tom hadn't completed any dare, bribe or challenge. "Alright, alright, I'll do it! I'll call in the shop this week."

"Well I'll give you until next Friday and if you haven't asked her out by then, then I will."

Chapter Fifteen

It was Sunday lunch time and Jess was walking with her friends as part of the new K9 & Co Club routine. James had decided not to join them and so there was just Luke and Suzie who were chatting animatedly together, giving the remainder of the group – Jess and Kate the ideal opportunity to hold back a little in order to gossip. Kate gave Jess the low down on her date with Paul, the hot personal trainer which had happened the night before.

"Well go on then,"

"Go on then, what?" teased Kate.

"Don't give me that. Spill the gossip about last night!"

Kate gave Jess a sideways glance with a coy smile, "Well, what can I say? It was the best night of my life!"

"Bloody hell Kate, that good! I've never heard you be so enthusiastic about any of your other conquests!"

"Well that's because I didn't have the fun I had last night. I'm telling you Jess, that guy is the full package, hun. He's really good company and funny and generous and the sex was out of this world! Jess, it was like an Olympic event, I ache all over today, I think he might be The One."

"I wondered why you struggled to climb over that fence back there!" giggled Jess, "Though I've never heard you say a guy might be 'The One' before, so he must have done something special."

"Believe me Jess… he did!"

"Alright, alright… I think I've heard enough. You'll put me off my lunch if you go into all the gory details!"

"I wasn't going to, but all I can say is that I think having a date with a personal trainer is something all the single ladies out there should do. Maybe it really should be made an Olympic event."

"Which would mean millions of people watching you and your toy boy having gratuitous sex?"

"Well, okay, maybe not then because I plan to keep this one to myself for a while and anyway there are channels for watching that sort of thing, though I doubt it would be as good!"

"Bloody hell, you really do have it bad." Jess giggled again before they started running to catch up with the others.

Later that day, the human contingent of the K9 & Co Club sat around the corner table of Harry's. The carvery, as ever, was delicious and for a few minutes the group silently savoured each mouthful. Luke was the first one to break the silence. "So you already had one taker on joining your new canine club. I told you it would be popular."

Jess laughed, "It's not *my* canine whatever club you called it. Though, I have to admit you're right. I had two more people enquire after it today and I think Sylvia is going to join us too."

"Really?" the others exclaimed simultaneously.

"Yep, though I told them to join us next Sunday. I know we meet on a Wednesday in the park but I thought that being stood there in the dark together isn't that much fun. At least on Sundays we get to spend a couple of hours walking in the daylight in the woods. Plus the dogs get to have fun too. Once the weather warms up a bit it should all be much more appealing."

"Yeah, I think you're right Jess." Luke clearly had switched his business head on and Jess could see him working out the rationale behind it. "You know, maybe you should have charged a fee if it's going to take off like it is."

"To be honest I'm just a bit shocked that people are even interested in the concept of walking their dogs with strangers."

"Oh come on Jess, we know all about the attraction of being part of a group. Remember we did it at Uni?" interrupted Kate.

"What do you mean did it at Uni?" Suzie had zoned into the comment.

"It's nothing really," Jess began to explain. "It's just that being part of a group gives people a sense of belonging. It's not rocket science! Me and Kate studied psychology together, though in truth our group is a group of dog owners so they already have something in common."

"Hey, you're a pair of dark horses aren't you? I didn't know you were part of the elite, 'I can read your mind' brigade" Luke added jovially.

"That's because we're not. It's just common sense most of it. Anyway, getting back to what we were saying, I think the Sundays are a much better plan. At least they'll think they're part of a group they can see. So don't bail out anytime soon you lot, because it was your idea…. especially you Luke."

I'm not going anywhere," Luke responded enthusiastically, with a subtle glance in Suzie's direction. "My Sundays were a bit boring before I met you guys."

"Ok, so we're agreed then. The next people to enquire, we'll tell them to meet us by the woods. Bloody hell, it really does sound like a group for people looking for an alternative kind of entertainment!" Jess smiled at the image created.

"Except that it's during the day and none of us turn up wearing leather gear," voiced Suzie, stifling a laugh.

"Ok then, so we're all agreed… no kinky leather."

120

Chapter Sixteen

Friday afternoon and Jess had begun looking at her orders for the following day. She couldn't be certain, but it seemed that considering the terrible weather her books were looking a little more optimistic. Sheila, another Shiatsu owner, had called in to buy some flowers for her sister's birthday. And then there was Bob with the medium sized cross breed that she had encountered during an early morning walk, he had purchased flowers for his daughter as a gift. Yes, it seemed that considering the financial climate, Jess would be able to put forward a positive first year tax return. In addition, both customers had enquired after the K9 social group. Jess was pleased that they were both of the same age, and hopefully might have something to chat about on a cold wintery afternoon in the woods.

Jess was in the back room of the shop with her Arctic Monkey's CD playing much louder than would be recommended for a respectable business owner. She was frantically bidding on a pair of red Frye cowboy boots that she had been watching for the last couple of days and with only seconds to go before bidding closed, she was determined to win them. As a result of being immersed in the bidding hell and the music blaring out she completely missed the doorbell's chime.

"Nice choice of music!" Jake shouted above the noise as he leant against the door frame. Jess jumped at the sound of the voice behind her. Then she turned around, once again to be met by the most gorgeous specimen of a male she had ever seen in real life.

"Oh. Hello again!" Jess managed to say in a voice as near to her usual as possible given her flustered state. She was trying her best to step into customer service mode, although Jess was struggling, primarily due for two reasons. The first being that the temperature in the room seemed to have risen and the second being that she knew the gorgeous intruder had cost her precious moments to bid, hence she would have missed her opportunity to own those fabulous boots. Looking up at the very tall man propped against her door frame, she made a note never to play her music so loud again. It was crazy, anyone could have walked in and robbed her, although she had to admit that if anyone was going to rob her of her opportunity to add to her boot collection, then it could be a lot worse. Because, whether he was off limits or not, Jess couldn't dispute that this guy could only be described as male perfection, a hunky six foot two of perfection, perfectly accompanied by dark hair, beautiful ocean blue eyes and a perfectly dazzling smile. Trying to rein herself in, Jess was aware that at any other time she would have either been in über flirt mode, playing it cool or talking utter gibberish. This time though, she knew that the Adonis standing before her was totally not interested in her. Regaining her composure, Jess tried to remain indifferent to his commanding presence and prepared to apply her sales pitch. It was more difficult than usual though, as the shop which always felt cold really did seem now to be uncomfortably warm. It was no good, she had to break the silence. Smiling up into the twinkling eyes, Jess noted again how very tall he was, before asking in the most professional voice she could muster, "How can I help you?"

For a moment Jake just stood there trying to compose his nerves, kicking himself for once again making himself look a fool. He had however, noted that she had recognised him. Although he could have sworn that for a moment she had seemed a bit flustered, he now witnessed her take on a professional demeanour. Tom was right, she clearly did think he was gay. He realised that now was his opportunity to expel Jess's unfounded theory of him. Though how could he just blurt out, *I know what you think and it's not true, I've been borrowing a dog, and yes, I realise it's a girly dog but it was the only thing I could think of to see you again?*

No, he knew how it would sound, *how would it sound*? He would sound desperate and sad, that's what. So he made the split second decision to play along with her unfounded assumption. After all, he had already decided to join the dog walking social group, the concept of which he had initially considered bizarre. If anyone had suggested to him that walking your dog with strangers was something he would ever find himself doing, he would have laughed. However, having walked that bloody dog for hours relentlessly on his own he could now see that it wasn't such a crazy idea. And if it meant spending time with this intriguing girl who was wearing a mismatch of colours, no makeup and hair that had clearly not had a comb through it today or maybe any day recently, yet still so attractive, he was prepared to do it.

Jake dispatched his killer smile, the one that displayed perfect teeth and had previously successfully got him the girl that he wanted, or who wanted him, which was often the case. When he was younger he had been bemused by the full on approach girls used and when he was younger and naive he had thought they really liked him. However, over time he had realised that they had only wanted to be seen out with him, and weren't interested in him as an individual. Not that he had complained, and in truth Jake knew he had used them just as they had used him. And he had been happy to go along with it until the morning he had crossed paths with Jessica Wainwright.

Jess turned the music off and made her way to the store room doorway, squeezing past Jake to stand behind the counter, a place where she felt much more confident. Jake followed her route, noting that her cheeks were now a little flushed. At the same time he also noted that he really was besotted with this girl and it was beginning to drive him a little bit crazy.

"So, can I help you with something?" Jess asked once again, sounding a little sharper in tone this time. Jake noted the slight agitation in her voice and was amused that he was having some kind of effect on Jess. He flashed her that smile again and as calmly as possible, asked for the first thing that came into his head, which in a flower shop was going to be flowers. "Hi yeah, I'd like some flowers." Jake had a sinking feeling the moment he made the request. With Valentine's Day being in a few days' time he guessed she would assume the order would be for his imaginary male partner.

Jess didn't answer for a moment and Jake wasn't sure that she had been paying attention. In fact Jess had been paying attention, but not to his request. Instead, she was busy soaking in the sound of his sexy voice, strong and well-spoken with an element of a Scottish accent, *not dissimilar to her Mr Butler's,* she noted. Jess had always been attracted to guys with an unusual accent. Before she had married Brandon she had struck up a conversation with a guy from a different branch of the car rentals company she was working at over the summer break from Uni. His speaking voice had a similar effect on Jess and in time they had arranged to meet for coffee. In her mind Jess had constructed a profile of what he would look like, an image similar to that of the man standing before her now. Unfortunately, her coffee date had presented as being the complete opposite of her imagination and had talked about fishing for three consecutive hours. From that moment she had never been transfixed by the way someone spoke, up until now.

This is crazy, Jess chided herself, *this man is completely out of bounds.* So once more she smiled up at the customer and enquired if he had any particular ideas, although she had already assumed that he would be making the purchase for his partner. For a moment Jake considered again just coming clean with the real reason for his visit. However, he had to work Valentine's night so he couldn't ask to take her out for a meal. As a result, he decided he would carry on with the facade for a while longer. He was intrigued by this woman and though he was desperate to get to know her better he had waited so long already a bit longer wouldn't hurt. Plus he was working nights all week. Besides, he was curious how long it would take her to work out the real Jake and his true intentions.

"Ermm I'm not sure," and Jake really was not sure. If he ordered roses as part of the charade he knew it would cement her theory and seriously reinforce her already skewed opinion of him. On the other hand, he didn't know anything about flowers; he was out of his depth. Jess could see he was struggling; she was used to this, although generally speaking most people had some idea. Clearly roses were not in the equation or else he would have instantly asked for them and so she considered a bouquet of mixed flowers might be suitable, striking but not too overly romantic. Jess decided a visual prompt might help and taking the photo album from under the counter she fumbled through the pages with fingers that seemed frustratingly uncoordinated until she reached the page with an image of the floral arrangement she had in mind. "What about something like this?" Jess asked without actually looking up at Jake.

"Yes, they'll be fine, maybe a little smaller though." Jake did love his sister and she had been ill so flowers were not out of the question as a gift for her. However, he didn't want to make the gift too ostentatious because he knew his sister would be taking the mickey out of him for years for going to such elaborate lengths to spend time with the object of his affections. Jess began to work her floral magic while Jake watched, quietly impressed at how quickly and skilfully she could create something so beautiful. Beautiful! Bloody hell, soon he'd be writing poetry and love letters for her affections.

"What do you think of this?" Jess asked as she looked down at Jake who was now knelt down stroking Elvis who had his head on Jake's knee revelling in the attention. *Honestly, even the dog seems to have fallen under that man's spell*, she mused. Twice she had to repeat her question as Jake seemed to be in some kind of day dream. "Aww, bless, that's so sweet, he must be thinking of his partner."

Jake had been brought back into the present with the question and he hoped he hadn't looked like a hopeless romantic. He wouldn't tell Tom he'd behaved like a love sick puppy; he knew he was expected to report back with details of an X-rated night of passion given his past record or at least a date secured.

"Thank you, they're perfect," Jake replied, holding her gaze as he got to his feet. As much as he was tempted to just absorb the image of Jess for as long as possible he was aware that she was looking a little unnerved and so he forced himself to look away, focusing instead on the floral arrangement she had created. He wasn't an expert on flowers by any means; however he knew they were good. Jake was impressed. Jess was not only beautiful, she was talented too and whilst she had been working it had given him the opportunity to regain his composure and reinforce his game plan.

"Would you like to write the card? It's a little short notice, but if you'd like them delivering I could try and fit it in," Jess asked as she slid the card over the counter towards Jake in order that she wouldn't have to touch him. She had tried to look away, she really truthfully had, and yet at the last minute she just happened to look. '*To Charlie*'. She didn't see the rest of what Jake wrote as she was aware that he had caught her indiscreet glimpse and so she too bent down to stroke Elvis. Jake finished writing the card, tucking it into the envelope before passing it back to Jess. As he did so their fingers touched, only slightly but enough for Jake to experience what he could only describe as static electricity. He remained calm and seemingly unaffected by the contact. However, as he watched Jess arrange the envelope amongst the flowers he could see her cheeks flush once again.

He paid for his purchase before deliberately turning to give the impression of leaving, then stopped and turned to look directly at Jess. For reasons she could not explain, Jess had felt the need to turn away from him and draw breath. Jake wasn't planning on leaving without bringing up the whole reason he had been talked into entering the shop, and what he knew was going to be his opportunity to spend time with Jess. He had heard about the new social group from Lucy who owned the gym, and though it went against all his male primal instincts, he would do it. He would walk around with, well he didn't know what kind of people spent time together walking their dogs. However, he had always been a determined guy so if nothing else he was prepared to withstand the jokes in the pub.

"By the way, I spotted the notice in the window…"

Oh, what now? Jess almost said the words aloud. She could not seem to think straight and just wanted him to leave. This male, who looked startlingly like Gerard Butler was not only ridiculously attractive, that she could cope with. It was the fact that he made her feel a bit, what was it she felt around him? Odd, yes, she felt really rather odd around him. She also felt like she had met him somewhere before and couldn't place it. She was aware that she had seen him and his partner in the park, but she felt that she had crossed paths with this man before that. Then she chided herself for being silly because any female who had been in this man's company just once would not forget him. At this moment however, she was not in the mood to ask, she just wanted him to leave. Jess recognised the unsettling feeling as being attraction. The irony being that it was the first time in ages that she was attracted to someone, yet she knew he was out of bounds. She made a mental note that she really must call Brandon that night and ask his advice.

Trying her best to look aloof and composed, she smiled up into those dazzling eyes and casually enquired, "Notice in the window?"

Jake was now beginning to have fun with this whole situation. Yes, he desperately wanted to kiss her luscious lips, but he could wait a little longer. *This situation,* he decided, *could be fun.* "Yes, the notice in the window for the dog walking group. I thought I might come along. I was thinking little Chico might like a bit of company." He almost burst out laughing at uttering such a ridiculous statement but instead managed just a slight smirk.

Damn that bloody notice, Jess seethed. It had attracted far more attention than she had anticipated. "Oh, *that* notice. Well, yes there is group of us that walk our dogs together on a Sunday for a couple of hours down the woods. Though I'm sure you wouldn't want to spend your Sundays with a group of dull dog lovers. Yes, it's dull, very dull and cold and wet and I'm sure little Chico wouldn't like it very much."

Jake nearly laughed out loud at her attempt to dissuade him from going along; instead he just gave his killer smile once again. *I must really have ruffled her,* he mused, silently impressed. "Oh I'm sure it can't be that dull and I hear the carvery in Harry's that you have afterwards is well worth enduring the cold for a couple of hours."

Jess realised immediately that he must have been talking to someone about her new social group. Well it wasn't officially hers, though she did seem to be at the helm of the new concept. She would interrogate everyone later, after a much deserved glass or two of Shiraz. Jess knew he was not going to be deterred. "Well you're free to come along if you like. It's not like the Free Masons. There's no secret handshake or ritual you have to go through to join. It's open to anyone, though really I think you'll be disappointed, we don't do anything exciting."

"Really? That's a shame," Jake replied, eyebrow raised, deliberately aiming to make an ambiguous insinuation. "Well dull or not, I think we'll come along and see for ourselves, so I'll see you on Sunday."

Chapter Seventeen

The following Sunday lunchtime and the group had expanded once again. Gathered in the cold at the entrance to the woods stood Jess, Luke, Suzie, Kate and Paul. James and Sylvia, had also decided to join them as the weather was a little milder. They stood together, chatting excitedly and intermittently complaining that they would be glad when the spring weather finally arrived.

As the group prepared to make a move, Jess surveyed her new friends and secretly hoped that Jake would join them, purely because she had a sneaking suspicion that James and Sylvia would get on like a house on fire, which would mean she would become a bit of a gooseberry. "I wonder how much longer we should wait," Jess addressed the rest of group which stopped the varied small talk occurring. "Maybe he won't turn up. He does have a boyfriend when all's said and done, and I wouldn't have thought he'd have needed to join a group like this."

"Why wouldn't he? It kills a few hours on a Sunday. Maybe he's just as bored with Sundays as the rest of us were," Kate argued.

"Yes but we were all sad and single. Well, at least we were in the beginning. It seems I might be the only one who isn't spoken for at the moment," Jess replied quietly, with a grin.

"Eh, I know I've brought Paul along again but you could hardly say we're a couple, I've only spent three weeks with him."

Jess noted the way she was looking at Paul who was chatting with the others a little distance away and out of earshot. "Yeah, whatever! Look again. This time without your blinkers on, silly," Jess prompted by trying to discreetly gesture in the direction of the others.

Kate looked at the group, Paul was heading back to her but the others were slowly beginning to head off in to the woods. Suzie was giggling at something Luke was saying while Sylvia was nodding in response to something that James was saying before laughing too. "Bloody hell, Jess – you're right. How long has that been going on?"

"Well obviously James and Sylvia have just met, but I'm confident that might flourish into something. As for Suzie and Luke, I think something's been going on between them from the beginning. I just haven't seen her to ask, and anyway it's their business. I'm sure they'll tell us when they're ready."

"So in the short time since we got this crazy group together, that's potentially three pairings already, that's mad. I don't know about the K9 & Co club; maybe you should change it to 'Dating with Your Dog.'"

Jess just laughed, "I don't think so. Can you imagine the effort I'd have to put into profiling each individual and anyway it would exclude anyone just wanting to tag along for something to do," Jess reasoned.

"Talking of which Jess, I think this might be our new member now."

Jess turned to the direction in which Kate was looking. Coming to a stop and parking the gaudy Mini Cooper was Jake, who she could see had a big grin on his face as he muttered, "Here we go Chico, let's have some fun."

Jake got out of the car carrying Chico and strode confidently towards Jess. "Morning ladies, lovely day for a stroll around the woods don't you think?" Jake flashed his killer smile once again, the smile which had previously won him the attention of a whole host of broken hearted females. Jess could see from her peripheral vision that Kate was stood open mouthed, clearly stunned.

"I agree, shall we get a move on and catch up with the others," Jess replied calmly, although inwardly she was fighting off the urge to start giggling like a school girl, something she did when she was nervous.

"Alright mate," Paul shook hands with Jake and then put his arm around Kate's waist and pulled her away. "I think we should leave them to it," he whispered in her ear as they headed away with Mitzi excitedly yapping and running to catch up with Max and Thomas.

"Leave them to it?" Kate echoed his words, clearly confused.

"And by the way," he teased, "I hope I had that effect on you the first time we met."

"Well you might have but if I remember rightly you were trying to kill me off in the gym." Kate giggled and elbowed Paul.

"You'll pay for that later," he teased in response, tickling her just under her ribs which he had discovered was one of her sensitive spots. The others, he was looking forward to exploring later.

Jess could have sworn she had seen some message pass between the two guys; maybe she was going mad, she certainly felt strange whenever she was near this man. "Shall we join the others then? It's a bit cold to be standing around."

"Yes, good idea. Let's make tracks." As they made their way into the woods, Jake put Chico down on the floor and the little guy immediately went off to catch up with the other dogs. Elvis as usual was reluctant to leave Jess and was happily plodding along behind her.

131

"Nice outfit," Jess commented, gesturing in the direction of Chico who was wearing a hoodie, albeit a combat style hoodie.

"Yeah, I thought so too. Well I wouldn't want the little guy catching a cold." He almost added that his sister would never let him live it down if he let anything happen to her beloved pooch but managed to stop himself just in time.

Jess was trying to catch glimpses of Jake and deployed the tactic of turning round to urge Elvis to keep up in order to do so. She had that feeling again that she knew him from somewhere and it was beginning to annoy her. She still could not place any encounters and so she resigned herself to thinking it must be because he looked like a film star.

"So what would you normally be doing on a Sunday? Don't you generally spend it with your partner?" Jake was a little taken aback by her direct questioning but merely smiled and responded, "To be honest, I work a lot of Sundays, it depends what shift I'm working."

"Oh, you work shifts. What do you do?"

"I'm a paramedic," Jake replied casually enough although he was waiting to see how long it would take for her to make the connection.

For a moment Jess was quiet as her mind mulled over his last comment. "That's it! I knew I'd seen you before; it's been driving me mad. You're the paramedic that came to my Gran's rescue the morning she fell." Jess had stopped in her tracks and was staring up, directly meeting his gaze. "I knew I'd seen you before somewhere." She would kill her Gran when she saw her. Primarily because he was gorgeous as she had stated and he did seem nice but her Gran had clearly omitted the part of him being gay. Then again, she probably wouldn't know that fact and given her Gran's previous attempts at fixing her up, why would it surprise her that her attempts had once again failed.

"I wouldn't go so far as saying I rescued her, but yes it was me who attended the call. How is she by the way?" Jake

132

tore his gaze from her and began to walk slowly on. If he didn't move away from the intense look she had focused on him then he would be tempted to kiss her and end this whole charade. He was tempted to end it anyway. Although never had he been mistaken for anything other than a hot blooded heterosexual and he was interested to find out why she had made that assumption, although he guessed the car and the dog had a lot to do with it as Tom had wisely pointed out. Plus, he was starting a week of nights and wouldn't be able ask her on a date or spend any time with her which he was desperate to do. So he made the decision that for the interim, being part of this random social group would at least mean he could get to know her better.

"She's doing okay thanks, although she isn't really enjoying having to stay with my parents, well my mum anyway." Jess was still trying to get a look at him as she tried to keep up with his long strides. How could she possibly not have noticed that he was that nice looking when he had rescued her Gran. Although she had been stressed and preoccupied it was no excuse to not identify perfection when it was in your vicinity. Not that it mattered she supposed, after all he was already spoken for.

"Hey, which way should we take do you think?" Suzie was shouting back towards them.

"We could take the longer route. It's not a bad day and the stream's a bit easier for the dogs to access at the far side of the woods. It's up to you guys though."

"Sounds fine to me," the others choroused.

As Jess had expected, the others stayed in their pairs and Jess noted that James and Sylvia seemed to be making easy conversation. Jess was still not her usual relaxed and chatty self; although Jake was easy to talk to and incredibly funny and so over time she began to relax. Any other day Jess would have been taking in the view, which was spectacular, however today she was distracted. They headed towards an area where the trees cleared in density a little. This combined with the sound of the stream ahead and being hypnotised with the sexy speaking voice of Jake ultimately meant that Jess did not hear the herd gathering behind her. She had been distracted enough to not be paying attention to the whereabouts of Elvis and the other dogs, which based on her earlier experiences she knew was a mistake.

Bang! Elvis accompanied by Max and Thomas hit her full force in the back of her legs, once again knocking her off her feet. Only this time she didn't hit the floor and land in the mud and slush. This time she was saved the indignity by a strong pair of arms reaching out and catching her, although Jess wasn't sure which would have been more embarrassing – hitting the floor in some undignified pose or being held like a bride about to be carried over the threshold. *Yep, infinitely more embarrassing*, Jess concluded as she looked into those amazing eyes and managed to smile and say, "Thanks for rescuing me! You seem to be making a habit of saving the female members of my family from that dreaded mutt and his cronies. That's two of us he's nearly taken out now. Furry Assassin certainly suits him."

Jake laughed, "Is that what you call him, the Furry Assassin?"

"Yep and I think he's already justified the title!"

"Well I don't mind rescuing the females of your family one bit." Jake knew he no longer had any valid reason to be holding onto Jess but having been given the opportunity he did not want it to end and for a moment he just looked down at her with the intense urge once again to kiss her.

Jess could see something playing on his mind, and in truth she was quite enjoying being held by this incredibly attractive male who ticked almost all her boxes. She was aware that in any other circumstances it would have been quite a romantic encounter but this male was spoken for. Somewhat reluctantly whilst gazing up at him she mumbled, "I think you can put me down now, and besides we have an audience and I'm beginning to feel a bit daft."

"Of course." Jake carefully ensured Jess's feet were firmly on the ground before stepping into professional mode to enquire if she had sustained any injuries. He was not in the least bothered that they had an audience now as the rest of the group silently watching the scene unfold; his only concern was for Jess.

"I wonder how long he's going wait before he tells her," mumbled Paul to himself.

"Tell her what?" Kate was on to the comment straight away.

Paul was trying to think fast in order to think of a realistic answer. Trust a woman to not miss a thing. Though he didn't have to, because just at that moment the group all chorused, "Watch out!" as the group of Canine Assassins were once again heading their way.

This time Jake put his arm around Jess's waist as they stood close together and moved slightly to the right in order to avoid any impact. Jake was secretly enjoying the second opportunity to be in such close proximity. *Christ, I've waited long enough*, he reasoned.

Jess, on the other hand had had enough. She might have to think of a reason to ban him from the group if it meant that it was she who spent all her time predominantly on her own with him because, although she hated to admit it, she was attracted to him. She would ask Brandon. He and Justin were coming to stop the weekend after next; she would run it by him and find out why she kept falling for inappropriate guys. "I think we should put them on their leads for a bit. They're becoming a bit of a menace. In fact, why don't we head back? I think it's time we headed to the pub." The group all agreed it seemed like a good time to leave the woods now and as usual meet up in an hour at Harry's.

Jess had dried and fed Elvis who was now happily sleeping on the rug near the radiator. Clearly he too considered the flat to be cold and had identified one of the few places any heat could be felt. She had quickly changed into one of her favourite dresses. It was a black, long sleeved dress that was flared from the waist and finished with a blue starched underskirt of which an inch could be seen beneath the bottom of the hem. She combined this with her blue cowboy boots and pale grey fake fur coat. Jess took one last look in the mirror, secretly impressed with what a difference a couple of visits to the gym could achieve. Then she grabbed her keys and headed out of the door, chatting to Kate on her mobile as she made her way down the stairs.

"Bloody hell, Kate! He looks just like Gerard Butler with slightly darker hair, he has got to be one of the best examples of a male I've ever seen. Except for Paul, of course" clearly this last comment was for the benefit of Kate's new boyfriend who was obviously eavesdropping on the conversation. "And would you believe he's gay, it's just typical. It's so true what they say about the best ones being unavailable."

"He never is Jess, I don't believe it."

"He is! He's the guy I was telling you about in the park with his partner and then there were the flowers to 'Charlie' and the floral car."

"Well, I suppose when you put it like that it does sound a bit suspicious, although I swear I thought he was going to hold onto you all day in the woods."

Jess laughed, although she was glad that she hadn't been imagining it. "Anyway, never mind. I'll see you at the pub in about fifteen minutes."

"Might be more like twenty, or twenty-five even," giggled Kate.

"Oh for God's sake. Everyone knows it doesn't take more than fifteen minutes, now hurry up."

"Maybe for you. If so you obviously haven't met the right guy, babe."

"I'd settle for any at the moment, fifteen minutes or not. Now hurry up Kate and stop wasting time, or I'll be the only one in the pub."

In fact Kate was not the only one in the pub; of course the pub was busy as it always was, due to the reputation it had gained for its delicious carvery. With regard to her group of new friends, Jake was the only one there at the moment and he was ordering a drink at the bar. He had changed too and looked just as gorgeous in dark jeans and shirt. Jess took a deep breath and walked confidently towards him. He had seen her as soon as she had walked into the pub, as it seemed had everyone else. She was one of those women that attracted attention, although the interesting thing he noted was that she seemed to be unaware of it and he liked that about her.

"What can I get you?" he asked as she came to stand beside him.

"I'll just have half a lager thanks."

"Are you sure? You can have whatever you like."

Jess noted that he seemed to want to buy her something more than just a standard half of lager and didn't want to disappoint him. "Ok then, I'll have a medium white wine please if that's ok with you?"

"Medium white wine please," he politely asked the girl serving behind the bar, who seemed to be a bit jittery as she picked up the glass and almost dropped it. Jess looked away, amused that he had this effect on not just her; *it must drive his boyfriend mad*, she thought. Jake was aware of her look of amusement knowing full well that she had noticed his effect on the girl trying to act cool whilst serving him. "I managed to keep us that table in the corner. Why don't you go take a seat and I'll be right over."

For some reason the rest of the group seemed to be running later than usual, which meant that Jess had half an hour alone with Jake to find out that he had his own house on the periphery of the village. His parents had moved to the coast and he had one sister, she also found out that Jake had worked as a builder for a few years before training as a paramedic. He was an unusual character she considered, which she liked, particularly because Jake clearly evidenced that gay men can, and do, work in manual trades. He was funny and attentive too and of course attractive. *Such a shame,* she couldn't help but think. *All the best men are unavailable.*

"I wonder how long the others will be," Jess pondered mainly to herself.

"I guess they've got held up," Jake replied, seeming unconcerned.

"Well I know why Kate's held up. She's teaching that new toy boy of hers a trick or two!"

"Magic?" laughed Jake.

"Well if that's what you want to call it," giggled Jess. She was having fun with Jake and was actually glad that the others were running late. However, the curiosity of why he was spending his time with her and not his partner would not go away. And so she could not help but ask, although she wished afterwards she had been a little less blunt when she did. "So where's your partner today?"

Jake nearly choked on his drink. He was having a good time monopolising Jess's attention and had forgotten about his silly facade. Fortunately, he was saved from having to explain or come clean by the arrival of the others, who all arrived at the same time as he had secretly asked them to be a little late.

"Over here," Jess beckoned, waving her arm to draw their attention in the crowded pub. For the next couple hours the group chatted animatedly as if they had all known one another for years as opposed to a few weeks or less.

"So were you run off your feet in the shop this week Jess?" Sylvia enquired as she finished off her delicious dinner.

"It was crazy Sylvia, which I know is good and it's nice to see that most of society still seem to have the love bug, but I have to admit I was glad when I closed the doors on Friday. Poor Elvis hardly got to have a walk and my Dad was run off his feet with deliveries, although I think he was glad to be out of the house from mum for a bit to be honest. I did get extra help in but it was still exhausting. I've never been so ready for a glass of wine in front of the television as I was that night!" Jess could have kicked herself for sounding like a sad lonely female who stayed in with her dog instead of being wined and dined on Valentine's Day, but it was too late. She had said it so she just hoped no one made a comment to this effect and was relieved when no one did. She did however just for a moment, consider telling the group that she had received two dozen red roses. They had arrived at her shop just before lunch with a card attached that simply read 'Happy Valentine's Day' with a question mark underneath. She had of course told Kate, although she had sworn her to keep quiet. After all it could be that they were meant for someone else.

Jake had however noticed the comment of how she had stayed in, and though he hated to admit it, he was glad that she had spent Valentine's evening on her own. He couldn't have taken her out because of his work schedule and he had hoped that some lucky guy hadn't done either, although he knew it wouldn't be long before they did. He had already overheard a couple of guys at the gym talking about her. He would have to come clean about this whole silly misunderstanding before he missed out altogether. But for now it would have to wait, he had work to do and needed to catch up on some sleep. He hated nights anyway, never mind when he was tired, and as much as he hated having to leave the company of Jess and the others he knew he needed to get a couple of hours sleep. "Right everyone, I'd best be off. I'm on a night shift tonight and I need some sleep before I start and I don't think I'll be able to join you next week as I'm starting days, sorry." The others chorused their disappointment, while Jess tried not to stare at Jakes fabulous physique as she watched him put on his jacket.

"Well I'll see you soon then. It's been nice meeting you all, enjoy the rest of your day," and with that, Jake made his way out of the pub, not without attracting the attention of a group of women seated near the door. Jess could see one of the group make a comment as he passed them, leading the other women in the group to start giggling. *It seems everyone is affected by that man,* Jess mused.

Chapter Eighteen

The following Wednesday afternoon Jess closed the shop just after lunch, in keeping with the majority of the businesses in the village. Having lived in a variety of locations throughout the country, Jess knew that this tradition did not transcend to all. She could hardly imagine Harrods closing down for a few hours on a Wednesday afternoon; a point she had debated with Mrs Jacobs in the first week of working in the shop. It had not taken long however, for Jess to mould back into living this alternative life. Now she looked forward to her Wednesday afternoons off work and it did not make any difference to her takings for the week. She had tried keeping the shop open one Wednesday afternoon not long after she took ownership of the business and not one person came through the door. At the time she had wondered where everyone had gone, and what on earth they were doing to make the village look like a ghost town. Now though, she was glad of the time and made use of it for recreational activities, which usually meant either shopping or food. Today was no exception. She was treating her Gran to some respite from her mother and had organised to take her out for lunch.

"Where do you fancy going then Gran?"

"Anywhere pet, it's just nice to be out of the house. I know your mother means well but honestly she's driving me mad with all her fussing."

"I know, we'll go to Howarth, that's not far and they have some nice little cafes."

"Sounds good to me love, but it's entirely up to you."

They drove in silence most of the way. The scenery was beautiful and Jess concluded that her Gran wanted to be quiet and just soak up the view having been stuck in doors for so long. Howarth was as picturesque as ever, even on a cold day like today, however Jess had not considered that parking near their chosen cafe would be impossible. Being situated on the brow of the hill that ran down the narrow cobbled high street it did not lend itself to having a car parked outside. As a result, Jess had to negotiate her Gran out of the car and into the cafe, which took a considerable amount of effort due to her injuries. Having made sure that her Gran was comfortable at a convenient table near to the wood burning stove, Jess left to go and park the car, returning ten minutes later to find her Gran with a ridiculous smirk on her face.

"Sorry I would have been back a few minutes sooner but I got the heel of my boot stuck in the cobbles. It was a bit embarrassing to be honest, although it gave a bus load of kids on a school trip something to giggle at. Talking of which, why do you have that silly smirk on your face?"

Clearly something had amused her Gran but it was apparent that she was not going to share what this may be just yet. "I'm sure I don't know what you mean, now here have a look at the menu that the very spritely waitress brought over for us, I'm sure she'll be back in no time to take our orders."

Jess knew that her Gran was insinuating something, but she had gone without breakfast and was now famished, so decided to instead concentrate on the menu instead of getting to the bottom of what was amusing her. The menu consisted of a selection of traditional, hearty Yorkshire meals and Jess decided that such a miserable day warranted something wholesome and so opted for a steak pie with chips. "What do you fancy Gran?" Jess enquired, looking up from her menu and noticing that her Gran was looking much more like the vibrant women she was before the accident.

"The steak pie does sound lovely but I think I'll go for the traditional dinner love."

"Do I need to go and order, do you know?"

"That won't be necessary Jess, here she comes now," replied her Gran, again with that look on her face.

Jess turned to the focus of her Gran's attention and indeed the waitress was making her way over, which Jess conceded may take a while. She had never seen anyone so old actually working; in fact it was a long time since she had actually seen anyone so old full stop. Jess smiled at the old lady as she shuffled towards them, and then turned back to her Gran, "Bloody hell, she must be ninety if she's a day! I think I should go to her, it isn't fair on the old girl."

"I wouldn't love, you might hurt her feelings and anyway she's made it half way now. Just pretend we're talking so we don't put pressure on her to hurry up."

"Hurry up," Jess repeated, raising an eyebrow, "I don't think so somehow!" And so they pretended to chat and all the time Jess could see in her peripheral vision the women slowly making her way towards them. In fairness, Jess considered being waited on by someone who looked like their previous work experience would have been with Acorn Antiques, did add to the effect of dining in a village steeped in so much history.

Eventually the woman stood beside them at the table, notepad in hand. "What can I get for you?" asked the oldest working woman in the country in a quavering voice that fitted her image perfectly. Having taken the orders, the old lady smiled a smile that reached her watery eyes and made them twinkle before turning and making her way back towards the kitchen.

"Aww bless Gran, she's so cute. I can't imagine why she would want to work at her age though."

"Well I suppose it keeps her young at heart. It gets so boring being stuck in the house all day so it'll give her something to do and she most likely owns the place so she can take a break whenever she wants."

"Yeah I suppose so."

While they waited for their meals, Jess updated her Gran about how the shop was doing. She also explained that the new dog walking group seemed to be quite popular to which her Gran responded that she was not at all surprised. After all, who would want to walk a dog in the woods on their own when they could be in the company of interesting people and, stay safe. Jess suggested that as soon as her Gran was well enough and the weather was a bit nicer, she should join them. At first she seemed a little resistant and Jess wondered whether she had lost a bit of confidence following her recent accident. Thinking of an incentive she added, "Well if you do come along at some point then you'll be able to catch up with Jake."

"Jake?" her Gran echoed with a look of bemusement on her face.

"Yes, Paramedic Jake."

As anticipated, it had worked and a look of realisation now replaced the previous noncommittal one. "Well if it means I get to have a chat with that lovely young man then I might just join you after all. I told you he liked you and I knew he would find a way to meet you. That lovely boy sure does seem to have it bad for you."

Jess had actually been quite exasperated with her Gran. For a woman of her age she was really quite clueless. And so she reiterated that in fact, while Jake was indeed gorgeous and lovely and good company, he was in a relationship – with a male. Her Gran nearly choked on her cup of tea, before exclaiming that she had never heard such a ridiculous thing. They were interrupted at that moment by the old lady making her way tentatively back to their table with a meal in either hand.

"Oh God, I don't think I can look! She can't have the strength to carry two meals, surely."

144

"Leave her be," her Gran had quietly protested, "She's clearly stronger than she looks." Evidently their waitress was, as she successfully placed the meals on the table. The old lady had not asked, and both Jess and her Gran had been so preoccupied whether she would successfully make it, that it had not occurred to them to remind her who was eating what. Before Jess had time to change their meals about, her Gran, obviously impeded by her arm, which was still bruised from her fall had informed the woman that the meals were in fact the wrong way round. For a moment, the woman just looked at her Gran as if trying to decipher what had been said. Then, very slowly, she bent over taking hold of her Gran's plate at either side before slowly turning the plate around so that the contents were facing the other way. Jess was too stunned to say anything and she could tell her Gran was again trying hard not to laugh. Jess just had to bite her lip hard as the woman did the same to her plate. Jess then thanked the woman before she turned and slowly ambled back into the kitchen. As soon as the door had closed Jess quickly swapped plates with her Gran and then they both laughed heartily into their napkins, trying hard not to be heard.

"Well, another eventful day in the company of Jessica Wainwright," her Gran mocked, as Jess helped her into her parents' house.

"I aim to please Gran," Jess laughed. "Right I'd best be off and see to Elvis."

"Ok love, well thanks again. It has truly been a lot of fun. And don't forget to think about what I said about that nice young man." Jess laughed at her Gran's naivety to herself on her way back to her flat.

The following Sunday Jess stood with the usual group waiting for two new members of the club to arrive. "So who have we joining us this time?" enquired Luke.

"A guy and a girl. They're not a couple though. They came into the shop on Tuesday a couple of hours apart. Each of them looked in the window initially, and I assumed they were admiring a new display I'd put there but no, when they came in it was to ask about the K9 Club. They did buy some flowers too though, so all in all it was a good result."

"We told you it would be popular," Kate chirped up.

"Well it's only two more people but they said it was a fab idea. The girl, Donna said she liked the idea because of not wanting to walk somewhere quiet and the guy said he liked the idea of meeting new people. I think he meant of the female variety! Anyway, they both seemed really nice and I have high hopes for them, after all they both own working dogs. I think maybe you crazy people might be right about this bizarre concept. Anyway, let's give them a bit longer, I'm sure they'll turn up because they did seem quite keen." Jess's last comment went under the radar of Luke and the others.

"Aren't you excited about having the local press coming to do a piece for their 'Local Events' section? You seem uncharacteristically calm," chipped in Kate.

Jess, who had been looking down the road for the new members turned slowly towards Kate and calmly asked, "What do you mean the local press?"

Kate could not keep her gaze and instead in a childlike, and very guilty manner simply muttered, "Whoops! I must have forgotten to tell you."

"How could you forget to tell me something like that, you silly mare? When did you organise it anyway?" Jess demanded, hands on hips.

I didn't. Lucy organised it. They were coming to the gym to do a piece on the new classes and special offer membership she's doing and the guy interviewing her noticed the poster. So she told him all about the K9 & Co Club and they both agreed it would make a great piece for the events section, which it will." Kate added, trying to justify herself.

"And how exactly did you manage to forget to tell me this snippet of information?"

"Sorry Jess, I called into the gym to see Paul the same day and Lucy ran by me what she had arranged. I told her you would be cool with it and I'd make sure I told you, but as you now know, I forgot. Can't think why I'm distracted at the moment," she sniggered, nudging Paul.

Jess sighed, resigned to the fact that the oversight hadn't been intentional and that they had had the best intentions when they came up with the silly idea. "Honestly Kate, you are one dippy female at times! It's not that I'm against the idea, although God only knows why they would want to do a piece on our random club. I'm more bothered that if I'd know we were going to have a picture taken, I'd have made more effort to do my hair and makeup."

Before Jess could protest any more, the two new members pulled up, the first of which was Donna who arrived in a blue Ford Focus with her chocolate Labrador Cassie peering out of the boot. Jess went to welcome her as soon as the women got out of her car and was met with a somewhat shy and reserved response. Jess considered this to be completely understandable given the fact she had signed up to enter the woods with a group of strangers. In fact Jess considered it to be rather brave of her.

The second new member, Richard was now getting out of his car and so Jess left Donna to get Cassie on his lead whilst she headed over to Richard who was busy getting his dog Cooper out of the boot of his silver Volvo estate car. Unlike Donna, Richard seemed rather self-assured and shook hands with Jess in a confident manner.

As Jess and Richard made their way towards the rest of the group Jess felt compelled to consider the similarities between the two new members. Not only did they both drive practical cars in understated colours, they were both wearing sensible outdoor clothing which had clearly been worn regularly before. Hence, Jess surmised they would both be outdoorsy types. To top it all off, they both had Labradors. Jess became aware that she had gone quiet for a moment while she considered these facts and so she snapped out of her chain of thought, reminding herself that it was in fact a social group and reverted to her usual sociable self.

Jess escorted the two new members over to the others who had remained at the entrance to the woods and began the introductions and although she wasn't sure how they would react, she decided it was best to let Donna and Richard know straight away that the press was supposed to be here any minute.

"I hope you don't mind but my friend here forgot to mention that the local press has been invited along today to run a feature on the new group," stated Jess while gesturing at Kate. She made the statement with a smile plastered to her face and tried to sound as unfazed by the ensuing event as possible, hoping the potential new members would not be running to the nearest hills.

Both Donna and Richard began laughing, although it was Donna who spoke first. "Well I don't mind at all though before it goes to press I'll have to make sure to tell my friends. I don't want them thinking I've joined a strange group that hang out in the woods getting up to no good."

"Well we do hang out in the woods, although I don't think we're that strange and we don't get up to no good," laughed Jess.

"If I'd have known I was going to have my moment of fame, I'd have made more of an effort with my appearance though," Donna joked.

"Tell me about it! It's all her fault," agreed Jess whilst focussing her attention on Kate.

At which point Kate, who was not known for being overly humble and clearly was not going to spend any more time apologising added in a forthright manner, "Alright, alright I messed up but I'm not apologising again. Anyway it will be good publicity for your club."

"I keep telling you it's not my club," Jess mumbled, predominantly to herself as no one else seemed to be listening. Jess had to admit that she a little surprised by Richard's reaction to the idea of being potentially humiliated in the local press.

His reaction was, "Hell, why not? It'll give the rugby lads something to rib me for."

The jovial banter came to a stop as a car drew up and two people got out. Both looked to be in their early twenties and Jess concluded that they had most likely recently graduated and were trying to work their way up the journalistic ladder by being forced to report on random non-events like this. As the pair came towards the group, flashing perfect white smiles, it was the female of the pair that was the first to speak. "Hi my name is Rachael Richards and this is my colleague Adam Roberts. We're here to do an article on your new social group. I'm guessing that you must be Jessica Wainwright?" the confident woman asked, whilst focusing her attention on Jess.

Jess felt like a rabbit caught in the headlights. She had spent most of her adult life in the shadow of Brandon's light and even though she had launched her own business, she was not comfortable being the centre of attention. *Interesting,* Jess mused to herself, somewhat aggrieved. *The press couldn't be bothered turning up to the opening of my flower shop, but here they are, all excited and enthusiastic to cover a dog walking group.* Perhaps the reporters were simply good at pretending to be interested and although media was not Jess's forte, even she knew there were innuendos aplenty to be made with the concept of dogs, woods and strangers.

As the pair came to a stop in front of the group, Jess noted them quickly assessing the participants. She stepped forward and, with a convincing display of confidence, shook both of their hands. "I'm Jessica, although most people call me Jess. It's nice of you to come and do a piece on our new group," Jess lied.

"Oh it's no bother at all. When we ran it past our editor he loved the idea."

Jess doubted it, but played along with the notion anyway. "Really? Well that's very kind. So what would you like to know? And I'm guessing that as your colleague has got a camera, you would like a picture."

"Just a quick overview of how the group came about and maybe a couple of quotes from the members. It won't take long at all. I'm thinking though, that maybe as there are quite a few dogs, it might be best if we take the pics first in case anyone wants to set off on their walk."

"Yeah, good idea," clearly a pragmatic women, Jess noted.

And so they all huddled into a group which proved a little difficult, trying to get all the dogs in and expecting them to stand or sit calmly. The first attempt went horribly wrong when Cooper squatted down to do his business just as the camera flashed, it had everyone laughing or in Jess's case, retching, whilst the offending object was removed. On the fifth attempt, Adam had got his picture. Kate was the only one of the group that looked like she had made an effort with her appearance. Jess couldn't be envious however, because Kate always looked good and so most likely hadn't bothered to go to any effort. She was also as excited as a child on the first day of the school holidays about the whole thing. As it turned out, they all stayed to chat to the reporters before commencing their walk, each adding their own bit once Jessica had outlined how it all came about.

"It's great isn't it," Kate was enthusiastically adding to the comments made by the others, "and to think that two new couples have already got together because of this new group and it's only been going a few weeks."

"Really?"

This throwaway comment by Kate had immediately caught the attention of the reporter as Jess knew it would as soon as she has said it. "I wouldn't go that far Kate," Jess intervened, trying to play down the comment.

"They have. You've got Suzie and Luke and Kate and Paul and none of them would have got together if it hadn't been for this social group." Lucy was insistent and Jess struggled to think of a reply when the facts were put forward like that.

"Dating with dogs, I like it. Do you think we could get a picture of the new happy couples?" asked the overzealous reporter, who was beginning to act like a dog with a bone now she was on to something.

Jess was about to say she didn't think it was a good idea as it would portray the wrong image of the group when she was overruled by Kate who had always been much more confident than Jess and was comfortable being the centre of attention. Paul didn't look too fond of the idea, obviously not keen on having to explain to the lads at the gym. However, he found he didn't have much choice as the camera snapped before he had time to open his mouth. In fairness, he was so smitten with his vibrant new girlfriend he would have gone along with it anyway.

Shortly afterwards, the aspiring reporters left and the group made their way into the woods. They were each laughing about how the pictures would turn out and discussing how the article might sound. None of them had ever had their fifteen minutes of fame, so it was a bizarre way to get into the papers.

It had been a pleasant walk, except of course for the obvious dislike for each other the newest members of the group had exuded. Jess's initial observations had led her to believe that the similarities between the two would cement a fabulous friendship. "How wrong could a person be?" she had cursed to herself, whilst having to intervene between the two, halfway into the walk.

"Dick by name, dick by nature," Donna had whispered to Jess as she caught up with the bickering pair. It turned out that

Donna worked with the homeless and had quite socialist views with regard to politics. Both she and the charity for which she worked had been hit hard by the austerity measures deployed by the Conservative government of which Richard was a staunch supporter. Jess was sure that they may have quite literally come to blows over their differing opinions on how the country should claw back its financial security. Every time Jess thought that she had managed to encourage an element of compromise between both sides, they started again in a manner that would give the main party leaders a run for their money. In the end it was Paul that saved the day when he steered Richard away with a lads' talk about rugby.

'Well, that dispels that theory' Jess mused to herself as she took a moment to walk by herself with Elvis obediently plodding along behind her. Jess had initially assumed that given that both her new members owned big dogs who were inclined to be silly and get very dirty, they would both exhibit e as predominantly calm individuals who were not fazed by a little bit of chaos. Furthermore, she had derived that they would both be financially stable and for the most part lead structured lives, In fact, Jess had deduced that that a Labrador owner would be thoroughly dependable in an emergency. "I will have to revaluate my theories Elvis," Jess found herself saying, more to herself than her increasingly devoted pooch who was as usual just a few feet away from her.

Later that afternoon the two new members joined the rest of the group for the now obligatory carvery, however they didn't sit near one another and it was clear to Jess that the atmosphere was cool between them.

Jess watched the pair who had unknowingly discredited her theory throughout dinner. However, it was evident to her that neither of them intended to spoil the fun for the others. Each of them chatted animatedly about the afternoon's events with the rest of the group as they enjoyed good food and discussed how they would be portrayed. The consensus being they hoped they had not been portrayed as either sad or odd, although they reasoned that they shouldn't be, as none of them were either of those things.

Chapter Nineteen

It didn't take long before Jess and the rest of the group found out. Jess had forgotten the local paper ran its 'Local Events' section on a Thursday, having been preoccupied putting together a couple of orders. However, the first enquiry with regard to the group began at around 10 am and they continued consistently for the rest of the day. When Jess managed to nip out at lunch time and grab a paper, she could see why the article had created so much interest. As opposed to Jess and the rest of the groups' fears that they would be portrayed as complete freaks or dogging fetishists, it put forward the K9 & Co Club as being simply an alternative way to get out and meet new people. It was accompanied by two pictures, the first being that of the entire group smiling giddily like children having a school photo, due to an element of hysteria at the ridiculous situation imposed upon them at such short notice. The second picture showed a smiling Luke with his arm around Suzie, who was also beaming like a Cheshire cat. It did, as Jess had suspected, have the expression 'dating with dogs' woven cleverly into the narrative as the piece went on, to inform the reader that indeed the two smiling individuals captured for prosperity in the local press, had met due to the new club. Jess hoped this would not be misinterpreted by those who read it, fearing it would alienate anyone who was currently single and with absolutely no interest in finding Mr or Mrs Right but just simply wanted to get out and meet new people. But yes, on the whole, she was quite pleased with the portrayal.

That evening she had convened an emergency meeting at her flat, primarily to discuss the fact that it would not be possible to invite all those who had enquired to walk at the same time. This she had put forward to the others on the grounds that it would be chaos and would scare the living daylights out of any joggers who encountered a pack of dogs approaching them at speed. Jess knew only too well the damage that had caused, and momentarily thought of Jake whom she had not seen or heard from all week. So here they all were, comfortably sat around the fire in Jess's flat. Donna and Richard couldn't make it due to difficulties with work commitments, and James had simply said he would go along with whatever the rest of the group decided. And so, as the rest of the group tucked into yet another Chinese takeaway, they excitedly discussed the review and Jess updated them on the response since going to press.

"So yeah, the response has been crazy," Jess was informing them in between bites of sweet and sour chicken balls, which Elvis who was sat obediently at the side of her, was clearly hoping to get a piece of. "The trouble is," she went on, "I'm not sure we can accommodate them all at the same time. I had seven enquiries today which if you add that to our dogs, it's too many to have running about the woods, scaring small children, pensioners and joggers. I don't want any claims against me for death by dog," she giggled.

"Ermm... I suppose you're right," agreed Luke, who again had his responsible business head on. "It was supposed to be a bit of fun, I don't think any of us thought it would take off like it has."

In between enjoying the Chinese, they all agreed that maybe they had bitten off more than they could chew with regard to it as a concept.

"The trouble is," Jess continued. "The phone rang all day which really got in the way of what I was supposed to be doing, so I just took numbers and names down and said I would call them back with further details tomorrow or

Saturday. There was one funny moment though quite late on in the day. Mrs Jacobs had gone and I was tidying up. Anyway, I saw this smart looking guy in a suit looking in the window and then he came in and just kind of wandered around the shop. So I left him for a few minutes and then asked him if there was anything I could help him with. And. would you believe it?"

The story Jess had been telling had piqued the others' interest and collectively they all stopped devouring their supper and encouraged her to continue.

Jess started giggling, "Well he was a bit sheepish and didn't want to look me in the eye and he mumbled something about the group. I couldn't hear him though, so I asked him to repeat himself and anyway, basically he wanted to know if the group held special events. 'Special' as in going down the woods on a night wearing masks and definitely not with your dog. In fact, I doubt he even had a dog."

"You're kidding!" the others chorused, whilst laughing and beginning to once again spoon Chinese noodles greedily into their mouths.

"So what did you tell him?" Kate asked, dipping her prawn toast into the sauce on Paul's plate.

"Well I told him in no uncertain terms that it was not that kind of a group and he would most likely be best googling what he was looking for."

"Oh god, I hope they don't think that's what the group's all about down at the bridge club. I'll never live it down," sighed Sylvia.

"I'm sure they won't and he's the only one. But honestly guys, if you'd seen him, you would never have believed it. Really respectable he looked. I thought he was buying flowers for his wife or girlfriend."

They all agreed that you could never judge a book by its cover before digressing onto discussing a variety of subjects such as the news which was on the television in the background and Coronation Street which followed it. Finally, they got around to discussing the impending issues the group faced by having too many people attend at the same time. By the end of the evening, Luke had agreed to make a web page that would provide details and a place to register people who wanted to join and for which walks, as they had decided that most likely people would not want to come along every week anyway.

They all agreed that they would need to know who was planning on joining the group for the traditional meal afterwards as it was getting increasingly difficult to get a table with the growing numbers. Luke, who clearly had a head for business and figures, suggested again that maybe a minimal fee should be introduced due to the amount of effort being put into the project now the group was growing, to which they all agreed. Luke then got to his feet and headed to the kitchen to take some of the plates and glasses in with a view to washing them up for Jess as he was aware that she had already had a busy day and did not want to burden her with another task.

He hadn't meant to look, however the title of the group and the scribbling beneath caught his attention. The untidy notes consisted of breeds of dogs with arrows leading from them to adjectives such as tidy, organised, disorganised and laid back. From this were further arrows that had comments such as carpets or laminate and even work schedules and job types.

"Jess, what's this?" Luke shouted from the kitchen.

"What's what?" Jess replied, without actually going to look at the object of interest.

"This," continued Luke, as he came wandering back into the living room wafting the A4 sheet of paper about.

Jess was immediately on her feet, knocking the last of her Chinese off her plate onto the carpet in her haste. "Now look what you've made me do," she protested as she made her way towards Luke, and Elvis quickly gobbled up the last of the

157

chicken balls which had fallen on to the floor. "Give me that Luke, it's nothing but silly scribbling."

Before Jess could reach out and grab the notes, Kate was already beside Luke and had grabbed the sheet out of his hand. "What on earth is all the fuss about," she asked, although more to herself as she scanned the notes. "Yeah, I would agree with that Jess, it makes perfect sense. I mean someone with a small, neat dog is likely to have a tidy house and like some kind of order. And yes, they'll not necessarily want to go trekking for miles, so yeah, on the whole I'd agree."

"What on earth are you two on about?" asked Lucy on behalf of the rest of the group, whose interest was now piqued. For the rest of the evening, the group, laughed, ridiculed and were intrigued by the theories the two amateur psychologists put forward into the psyche of dog ownership, the consensus being that they would watch with interest to see if their theories were upheld.

Chapter Twenty

The following Sunday, four more people joined the group. A portly man in his early fifties with a cute white Bichon Frise which he was quick to point out, had belonged to his wife before she ran off with her boss. He had gone on to say that he was not overly keen on being responsible for looking after the dog. However, having lost one owner, he did not have the heart to re-home the little fella and so he was stuck with Roger.

"Roger?" Jess repeated, somewhat bemused, only to be advised that interestingly, that was also the name of the boss with whom his wife had run off.

Two sisters also joined the group that day. Jess could not work out how old exactly they were because they clearly looked after themselves, but she guessed they would be in their late fifties, maybe sixtyish, and they both owned Springer Spaniels. Just when Jess considered that maybe the group seemed to be catering for a more mature clientele, the fourth new member had turned up. An attractive guy in his early thirties who informed Jess that he worked as a fireman and shared custody of a bearded collie with his ex-wife, which worked out quite well due to his shifts. He told Jess that when he'd commented positively on the article in the paper, the lads at the station had ribbed him a bit, but he thought 'why not?' He usually went for a run with the dog through the woods on his free Sundays and had in fact seen the group before and wondered what the situation was. The fact they all headed to the pub afterwards for food was just a bonus.

It had turned out to be an interesting and somewhat amusing induction to the group. Everything had started off according to plan. Jess had suggested that they all split up and mingle with the new members and so Luke had charmed the two new women, Patricia and Pamela with his easy banter and intelligent conversation. Suzie and Sylvia chatted animatedly to Peter, the member with the unusual name for a dog. It was purely platonic, but Jess considered by the enthusiastic way in which he never stopped talking, that he had maybe been starved of social conversation for a while. Meanwhile, Jess and Paul chatted to Nathen, the fireman with the Collie who kept them all entertained with his funny stories with regard to his job. The walk had been totally civilised until they reached the clearing that lead down to the river. Having kept the dogs on leads, only letting a couple off at a time in order not to cause chaos, it was the turn of Roger and Mitzi to enjoy their turn at freedom and they happily scampered off in the direction of the river. No one in the group was paying attention, so didn't notice that they could not be seen and would not have worried even if they had, as the woods posed little danger to their beloved four- legged friends. And so they continued with their easy conversation as they turned the corner into the clearing.

Luke, Patricia and Pamela were leading the way when Jess suddenly stopped listening to Nathen recount another funny story as she heard Pamela say, "Oh heavens above!" and turn around, briskly covering her eyes with her hands, clearly trying to block out something offending .

This was followed by Patricia doing the same thing whilst commenting, "I think we should give them some privacy," a twinkle in her eyes as she spoke.

Jess stepped ahead from the others to join Luke who was laughing loudly, "Get them a room more like," he whispered.

Jess just stood and stared for a minute. She had never actually seen canine fornication in action and she wished that now was not the time to be initiated into the unpleasant scene. Well, unpleasant for Jess and the rest of the group who were coming to see what the commotion was about.

Peter was the first to speak, a smirk on his face that looked like he was trying really hard not to laugh, he blurted out, "Roger by name, Roger by nature I see!" clearly trying to make light of the situation.

Kate was the last to encounter the scene and Jess was dreading her reaction. As she came to a stop beside the others she casually asked, "What have you all stopped for?" This was followed by silence as she took in the situation before shrieking, "Bloody hell, my mother will kill me!"

Jess tried to rationalise the situation. She won't hun. It's not like it's you that's just got yourself in the family way."

In response to this comment, Jess received a scathing look.

"Can't we stop them? We're all stood here gawping or looking at shoes or phones," the latter was obviously aimed at Jess and Luke who were trying to find a diversionary activity.

"I don't think you're supposed to intervene hun," Paul reasoned, putting his arm around Kate in a protective manner.

Kate started to grin then, her old mischievous self returning, "I wouldn't have thought it was possible, I mean the little guy is half her size."

Suzie who had yet not spoken as tears were running down her face and who had clearly not wanted to let the rest of the group see that she thought the whole thing was hilarious, managed to add, "I think you'll find she's on her knees," before giving into laughter. This comment piqued the interest of most of the group including the more mature new members who Jess could see also turned around for a sneak peek to see if this was possible.

The group spent the next twenty minutes making small talk until a thoroughly contented Mitzi made her way back towards them followed closely by Roger. "Right I think we'll call it a day shall we and reconvene in the pub?" Jess suggested trying to sound as normal as possible. They had all agreed it was time they left and even Elvis seemed pleased to be leaving today. Jess was glad to get back in her car, buckling Elvis into his safety harness and patting his head. "Bloody hell Elvis, what an induction for the new members! I bet we don't see them again."

As it turned out, she did see them again, she saw them an hour later in the pub, laughing and joking. Each of the new members were there, including Lucy, who said she was gutted she had been held up at the gym and missed all the fun. Kate laughingly told the group how Mitzi had seemed thoroughly disappointed on her journey home and even her mum had noticed how depressed the dog seemed. "Honestly, if that dog was a female, she would have been begging for his number," Kate added in between enthusiastic mouthfuls of larger. She then went on to tell the others that she had decided to plead complete ignorance, which they all agreed sounded like a perfect plan.

Chapter Twenty One

The following Wednesday lunch time, Jess was just about to close the shop for the afternoon, with her plan being to take Elvis for a quick walk before chilling out for the rest of the day. She had already put the shutters up at the window and was just cashing up when the doorbell chimed and Jake entered the shop, striding confidently towards her and looking as drop dead gorgeous as ever. "I thought I'd call in and see the local celebrity; I saw the piece in the local Telegraph."

Jess could feel herself blush and cursed herself for doing so. "Oh, I wouldn't go as far as that. Though it has to be said it has attracted quite a lot of attention," she replied trying to act as if she were completely unaffected by him. *Thank God Brandon and Justin are coming up this weekend*, she thought to herself. *I really need to discuss why this totally off limits male is having this effect on me.* "So did you call in just to congratulate me on my new celebrity status or was there something you wanted. Some flowers maybe?"

Jake new that the insinuation had been *did he want flowers for his partner* and found the subtle questioning amusing. He considered that she would find his real reason for being here a little odd and wanted the request to seem as casual as possible. So he walked around the counter and bent down to stroke Elvis, who lapped up the attention. Without looking up and continuing to tickle Elvis behind the ears, leading to him producing an odd moaning noise he casually stated, "Actually I called in to see if you would consider going to dinner with me, tomorrow evening. I hope it's not too late notice."

Jess had been smiling as she had watched the scene unfold of Elvis once again relishing in the attention from Jake, observing that even her dog seemed to be captivated by this man. Now though, the smile slipped from her face and she stood shocked and speechless, trying to make sense of the request. *Surely he would go with his partner,* she was thinking to herself.

Jake, still kneeling down and fussing Elvis, looked up to gauge the reaction from Jess. *God, she's so pretty,* he thought. *Even with a look of bemusement on her face.* Jess still did not speak though and merely caught his gaze as she tried to make sense of the situation and decide what to say.

Still holding her gaze, Jake stood up, "So what do you think? Could I talk you into going to dinner with me?"

"Just the two of us?" she mumbled.

"Yeah," he replied quickly, although his mind was picturing them chatting intimately over a candlelit table.

"Why me though?" this on Jess's part was a genuine question because she reasoned as he was such good company, he must have lots of friends.

The question posed to Jake was easy to answer as it was nice for him to just be able to tell her the truth for once. "Well, as you know my sister is poorly and having to stay with her boyfriend for a little longer and they were her tickets that she won in support of some charity. Anyway, as she isn't able to make it, she suggested I use the tickets, they are for the Waterfront Hotel and she said they should have cost a fortune. And, well I thought I would see if you were free."

Jess tilted her chin slightly, one eyebrow slightly raised, adding to the bemused look which captured how she felt, although she was beginning to regain some of her composure. Obviously his partner must be busy, and she considered that they were friends now in a funny sort of way; it wasn't his fault that she was becoming increasingly attracted to him. Jake could see Jess trying to make sense of his suggestion and considered just telling her the truth now when there was just the two of them together. However, he decided a romantic dinner would be a much better setting to dispel her theory of him, he could wait one more day.

Jess was beginning to think the idea of a nice dinner with good company would make a change from the usual carvery that had become a Sunday routine and was pleased to have a good excuse to get dressed up for a change. One thing was still bugging her though, and she could not help but ask, "So is your partner busy?"

Jake had been anticipating the question and therefore was prepared. The tactic he had already planned was to avoid the question, one more day and then they could stop this silly misunderstanding. "Something like that. Anyway, so is it a yes then?"

Jess relented, "Why not? I've not been there since I returned home, thank you for thinking to ask me Jake."

Thinking of asking you, Jake mused, he had thought of nothing else and in the end it had been his sister Charlie who had given him the courage to ask Jess. Having accomplished what he had set out to do, Jake suddenly felt the need to escape before she changed her mind. "Listen I'm going to have to go. I've lots to do today," he lied. "Shall I pick you up? Seven-thirty good with you?"

"Yep, sounds fine with me. See you tomorrow then."

This is crazy, Jake told himself as he changed into a third set of clothes. Jeans and a black t-shirt it will have to be. He had already spent way longer than the usual twenty minutes it took to get a quick shower and throw something on. Then again, he had never had the need to try and impress the ladies because with very little effort, they were impressed. He had managed successfully to maintain a string of what had recently become referred to as 'friends with benefits' and had been quite happy with his no commitment style of relationships. That was until he had met the vivacious Jessica Wainwright who bizarrely thought he was gay. Tonight he would ensure that Jess found out that he was certainly not. *What a difference one day can make* he considered to himself as locked the door behind him and jumped into the taxi. He wasn't driving tonight; he needed a drink to calm his nerves. *This is ridiculous she's just a girl*, he told himself. A very attractive one though. All long wavy hair and sparking emerald green eyes, and when she laughed as she had done when the ambulance door had fallen off, little dimples formed in her cheeks. Despite the hoodie clearly over her PJs and lack of makeup, the first time they met, she was incredibly pretty, beautiful in fact. A fact that had not changed, even though every time he had seen her since, she had been wearing a bizarre combination of colours and fur.

Jake laughed, his sister Charlie was right, he did have it bad. He would ring her tomorrow and check she was on the mend from the appendicitis that she had been taken so suddenly with whilst visiting her boyfriend in Devon, and update her on how the evening had gone. She would be dying to hear all about his first date with someone he actually wanted to have a second date with. It was Charlie who had given him the courage to ask Jess if she wanted to make use of the tickets to the swanky restaurant in the neighbouring village. Charlie had won the tickets for an all expenses meal for two in a charity raffle and had intended to take Blake her boyfriend but as she was delayed for a while whilst recovering, she insisted Jake make use of them to impress the lovely Jess.

Jake arrived punctually at the restaurant based within the stunning hotel. The original plan to pick Jess up had changed when Lucy had passed on a message to him to say that Jess had forgotten to take his number but wanted him to know that she would meet him at the venue. She was going to be a little bit late and had remembered that Lucy would have his contact details. This had made Jake nervous that she would not turn up, but then he reasoned that she would not have made the

166

effort to contact him if she planned on letting him down. As such, he was reading a sample menu located near to the doorway when he heard a car pulling up. Jake was known as being a talkative guy but if he had been required to speak at that moment he would have been unable to because he was stunned into speechlessness.

It had been a lovely sunny day considering it was still only March and as a result, Jess had not bothered wearing a jacket, deciding that she was not too old to be irresponsible. She had been dying to wear the full length red designer number that she had discovered in a charity shop on a trip to the seaside last year, and had been waiting patiently for the right occasion to wear it. It fitted Jess perfectly, skimming over her curves before tapering out as it reached her ankles. With her dark hair pinned up and a few curls strategically falling loose combined with classical jewellery, the effect was classy. Jess was conscious that she hadn't spent this much effort getting ready in ages. Of course, the extra fifteen minutes it had taken for her eyes to stop smarting from the discomfort of putting Elvis's ear drops into them instead of her eye drop drops she had mistakenly identified them for when rooting around in her handbag for her favourite lipstick, had added to the time it took for her to get ready. However, on the plus side her eyes were now sparkling like she had never seen before. She just hoped this was not because she had inadvertently stripped a valuable protective layer from them. She was fully aware of the irony of the fact that the one occasion that her eyes were sparkly and her hair and makeup looked okay, she'd be spending the evening with the area's most attractive homosexual. , However, she had heard the restaurant was fabulous, so all in all she hoped it would be a good night.

"What's the matter with you? Have you forgotten your wallet or something? You look miles away," Jess blurted out in place of a greeting upon seeing the somewhat vacant expression on Jakes face.

"You look stunning," was all that Jake replied before stepping back to enable Jess to enter the restaurant first. At the reception area Jake handed the tickets over, dimly aware of the receptionist saying something. However, a mixture of adrenaline and testosterone was coursing through his system and so he didn't quite catch her reply. They weaved their way around the busy restaurant, and just as they were about to be seated, Jess suddenly realised that Jake had been guiding her through the crowded room with the palm of his hand on the small of her back. It was a fleeting thought because just at that moment, they arrived at their table. Jake was a little disappointed to see that their seats were part of a larger round table that seated eight. The other diners where made up of couples that seemed to know each and they all looked to be middle aged.

"This restaurant must be as good as they say because for a Thursday evening, it's full," Jake stated whilst attempting not to sound disappointed.

"These evenings are always booked up dearie. It's such a fun evening," interrupted a robust women of about fifty.

"Oh yes, you can't beat a bit of Basil and Cybil," her husband joined in.

Jess leaned in close to Jake and whispered, "I hope that's a fabulous dish and not some bizarre swinging party we've got dressed up for! I'm not getting my keys out because there isn't anyone I like the look of."

Jake laughed, "Relax babe. I'm sure the gossip would have travelled if they held Swingers nights. They're probably talking about something to do with the charity."

The waiter arrived and took everyone's orders, returning promptly with the drinks. While the food arrived, the diners made small talk. Fortunately for Jess they didn't discuss caravanning holidays which, if the rumour were correct, were known to attract swingers. It turned out instead that they were merely neighbours whose children had all grown up together and over the years they had become firm friends. As a collective they were funny and entertaining and Jess was enjoying their banter and ridiculous jokes. The starters had been delicious and the service first class, definitely doing justice to the restaurant's reputation. With the wine flowing, it was clear everyone was relaxed and in good spirits.

The main courses began to arrive in the same efficient manner and Jess who had been busy chatting to Jake looked up as the waiter came and stood at her side. He was short in stature with a Mediterranean look and, Jess noted, quite a bit older than the other serving staff, most likely the head waiter, she thought. He seemed slightly stressed and a little dishevelled, unlike all the other well-presented staff. He began to lower his silver serving dish towards Jess, simultaneously removing its lid and speaking two words, "Ratatouille, Madame."

At that moment, a furry little critter scurried off the serving dish onto Jess's knee and under the table. At which point, she screamed and stood up, knocking the serving dish crashing onto the floor. It was chaos.

"I so sorry," muttered the waiter in a strong Mediterranean accent as he dropped to his knees and scrambled under the table. The table cloth seemed to be tangled up with him and simultaneously the diners around the table reached for their glasses as chinaware and cutlery crashed to the floor.

Jess was stunned and was just about to take the glass of wine that Jake was holding out to her as he too had got to his feet and was asking if she was okay when further chaos ensued. This time it was created by a middle-aged woman dressed in an immaculate lilac two piece, a scarf neatly tied around her neck who came walking towards them.

"Basil!" she shouted in a high pitched, rather posh voice. "Basil, where are you? Come here this minute!"

"Yes dear, I'm coming!" At that moment a tall, gangly man with long limbs and dark hair with a receding hairline, producing the look of having a long face, came ambling towards them. He was carrying a bottle of wine in either hand, randomly splashing some of the contents over other diners as he rushed towards the woman.

As Jess stood, feeling shocked and taking in the scene of mayhem around her, it became apparent to her that rather than the other diners being annoyed at the unprofessional events occurring, everyone in the room was laughing and thoroughly enjoying themselves. Slowly, as was the case sometimes with Jess, it began to dawn on her what was happening. It was not an intimate dinner in a posh restaurant as she had been expecting, the clue being that it was for a charity event. It was rapidly becoming obvious that they had stumbled into one of those themed events evenings that she had seen advertised in the Telegraph sometimes. Even more evidently, tonight was a 'Fawlty Towers' evening. Having worked out what was happening, Jess couldn't help but get caught up with the fun atmosphere of the room and started laughing.

Jess turned to Jake to take the glass of wine he was holding for her, and one look at his face told Jess that he did not know about this, and had not yet worked out what was happening. She leaned in close and whispered, "It's okay Jake. It turns out it's an 'Events' night, although it's quite innocent. I'll put money on it that it's a 'Fawlty Towers' night."

With Jess being so close to him, Jake could smell her perfume and for a moment he didn't take in what she was saying. When she repeated herself, he came to his senses and took the situation in for what it was. He could kick himself for not checking the tickets properly and would have serious words with his sister tomorrow. He knew full well now that his romantic candlelit dinner was not going to happen. Still, all was not lost. He looked at Jess who was trying to take a sip of her wine but struggling as she was laughing so much.

'Manuel' was still scrambling around on the floor. However, at that moment he came up from the floor wrestling with a small furry object, clearly it was not a real rat but it looked quite convincing. "Sorry Madam, I bring you another Ratatouille."

"Oh for heaven's sake Manuel! Get that rat out of here, and Basil – you get the lady a complimentary drink," the faux Sybil chirped up in her high pitched voice, sounding startling like the real thing. Even Basil was incredibly convincing as he tripped over chairs and generally caused further chaos whilst constantly apologising to his wife.

Jess took her seat now that 'Manuel' was no longer scrambling at her feet and sipped her wine, "Jake this is fabulous! I never fancied coming along to one of these events but they really are a lot of fun. Thank you for inviting me, although I have a feeling you didn't know either."

"That obvious, is it?" he laughed.

The rest of the evening went in a blur with a steady mixture of laughter and continued hilarious events and as the evening drew to a finale, they found themselves doing the conga around their restaurant, the adjoining restaurant and the bar area. Jess would have been happy to sit this one out as it really was not her sort of thing. However, Basil had grabbed her hands and strategically placed them on his hips holding them there so she could not refuse to join him. Other diners had been quick to get to their feet and join in, and as Jake watched the object of his affection being led away to the sound of 'Show me the way to Amarillo', he had resigned himself to sit this one out and wait for her return. However, his plan was foiled when Sybil took his hand and dragged him to his feet, insisting they also joined the crazy train of diners.

Oh, what the hell. In for a penny, in for a pound, he thought and just hoped to God that there was no one in the building that he knew.

It was eleven o' clock and Jess felt tipsy and was still giggling as they stood outside waiting for her taxi. They were going in different directions and so Jess had insisted that he did not have to see her home. "I've had a fabulous evening

Jake. Honestly, I can't remember the last time I had so much fun."

Jake was enjoying seeing Jess look so animated, her cheeks a little flushed due to the wine, although he knew he was running out of time to dispel her silly notion of him. The evening had been great, he decided, despite not having been the evening he had anticipated. Most importantly, he had hoped he would have got to kiss this girl. Instead, any minute now she was about to leave and he would miss his opportunity. "Jess listen, there's something I wanted to –" He didn't get a chance to finish his sentence as a few of the guests from their table were leaving the restaurant and stopped to chat to Jess.

"It's been lovely meeting you," they said, giving her Jess a peck on the cheek.

"Likewise she said," And then as her taxi arrived, Jess turned to Jake and said "Right hun, I'd best be off. Thanks again for a lovely evening, see you soon." She gave him a quick peck on the cheek and scampered into the taxi, giggling as she did so.

"Damn!" he said to himself, as he watched her leave.

Chapter Twenty Two

"I've been thinking Bettie," Jess started to say in between mouthfuls of her breakfast bap.

"What was it like" Bettie replied with a smirk on her face which Jess observed when she looked in her direction, confused by her response.

"What was what like?"

"Thinking," Bettie replied in as serious voice as she could conjure.

Jess started giggling, belatedly realising that Bettie was innocently joking with her and she loved her for it. Jess truly loved this woman who had become like a member of family to her.

"Go on lass, I'm only jesting with you."

"I know you are Bettie and I do love our silly banter. But anyway, I was thinking of throwing a party, a kind of celebration of how well both the shop has done and the K9 and Co Club. And I thought it would be a good way for some of the new members of the group to socialise. I mean I know they get the chance to chat when were out walking the dogs and of course the carvery afterwards, but a party is different, it's much more informal."

"I think it's a great idea Jess, you should celebrate what you've achieved and I agree, people are very different when they're relaxed, especially with a few drinks in them. Go for it love, what's the worst that can happen."

As it turned out, quite a lot happened.

Jess had spent the next few days contacting every member of the club and had quickly organised the party to take place the following Saturday. She was not sure whether to find it sad or reassuring that everyone else seemed to have a social diary as uneventful as her own. As soon as Jess closed the shop on the Saturday, she and Kate went shopping and purchased a ridiculous amount of alcohol. Then as they tidied the flat they belatedly realised they had not purchased any food and decided rather than dash back to the shops, they would place an order for a curry to arrive at 10 pm. They then parted company and Jess got ready for the evening. She chose to pin her unruly hair up again and decided upon a figure defining dress. It was black and backless and there was not very much of it. She then chose a couple of pieces of jewellery before applying a modest amount of makeup and by seven thirty she was sat sipping a glass of chardonnay and wondering if anyone would bother to turn up, which they ultimately did.

However, what Jess had not bargained for, was that by 9 pm her flat would not only be full of people, it would also be full of dogs. It was by any standard an understated accommodation and moderate in size, however by 9 pm and with what seemed like every man, women and his dog packed into her flat, it had taken on a very surreal ambience. Jess had not for one movement assumed that her guests would also include their dogs. However, once Nathen arrived with his bearded collie, followed by Donna and Richard who had also arrived with their pooches in tow, it became the norm to Jess that the others would also arrive with their beloved pet. Donna had even tied a ribbon around her Labradors neck, Jess noted. Though she chose not to make a comment, remembering how she had made matching booties and coat for Elvis. The first half hour of the party was bedlam. Jess didn't think her battered old sofa could take much more of numerous pooches jumping on and off it and it was proving impossible to relax so Jess suggested the canine element of the social gathering play in the yard for a while. With the animals vacated from her tiny flat, normality resumed and Jess was able to act as the party hostess, mingling with her guests and ensuring everyone had a plentiful supply of alcohol. An hour later and the party was proving to be a success. There was much laughing, joking and general banter now between the guests and Jess observed that even Donna and Richard were talking. Nathen had invited a friend to come along to the party and they were animatedly chatting to Lucy and her friend from the gym. And even Mrs Jacobs and her husband popped in with a bottle of whiskey to add to the drinks collection.

Just before ten the doorbell rang and Jess went down stairs to collect the curry. For a moment, Jess just stood there as her brain processed the situation as stood before her was not Mo from the Khyber House but Jake holding a bottle of champagne.

"I'm sorry I'm late but I've just got off shift."

For a moment Jess stood riveted to the spot, aware that adrenaline had for some reason started to pump through her veins. However, she reasoned that he seemed to have this effect on most females, so assumed her reaction to him to be beyond her control. On the surface though she was sure she looked completely unaffected by him and she managed to calmly say "I'm so glad you could make it, come on in." Once again Jess did not mean to look at his physique as he walked up the stairs to her flat but she could not help herself.

Jake was met with a warm welcome from the other guests and although he mingled effortlessly, he always seemed to be within arm's reach of Jess. She reasoned the most likely cause for this was the flats' small footprint – it was merely a matter of logistics.

The food arrived and the idea of a curry was well received by most of the guests. The pooches were back in the flat now but had clearly tired themselves out, all but Donna and Richards Labradors' were asleep. Instead, they had chosen to drink red wine from the nozzle of a three litre carton in the kitchen when no one was looking. Jess decided to keep this information from Donna and Richard who were sat next to each other on the sofa, with Donna smiling at something Richard was saying. "I knew them two were perfect for each other, my theory at work again," Jess mumbled out loud.

Jake was immediately upon the comment. "Did you say something about a theory working again?" he asked with a look of intrigue.

"Oh, it was nothing, would you like another drink?"

Jake was feeling a little more confident than usual when in the company of Jess now that he had had a couple of drinks, and took a step towards her suddenly overwhelmed with an urge to kiss her. "I have ways of making you talk you know," he said jovially, although with an intense look.

"Stop messing about Jake," giggled Jess, fully aware that Jake was being a little inappropriate given his situation and once again beginning to question herself. Jess felt like she needed a few minutes on her own, she knew she was falling for this guy or already had and that knowledge plus the alcohol were making her feel a little dizzy so she excused herself for a moment and headed to her bedroom. However, her attempt at solitude was impeded when she opened her bedroom door to find Richard's Labrador Cooper on her bed and humping her favourite fur pillow. Meanwhile, Donna's pooch, Cassie, merely lay at the side of the bed on Jess's rug and looked thoroughly dejected. Which Jess considered understandable given that Cooper clearly considered an inanimate object to be more fun than poor Cassie.

"Cooper get off that," Jess shouted from the doorway.

However, Cooper was clearly not going to take any notice of Jess. Hearing his pooches name mentioned, Richard was already making his way towards Jess, followed by Donna.

"What's the matter," Richard, asked with a noticeable effect of alcohol in his speech.

"I think you'd best take a look for yourself," Jess replied as she stepped back to allow Richard and Donna access to the scene.

"Get down off there, you dirty beast," scolded Richard, as he made his way into Jess's bedroom, followed by Donna. Jess decided she needed another drink and headed back to her kitchen, while Donna and Richard went into Jess's bedroom to recover their pets. Jake, who had in the meantime been chatting with Paul and Kate, immediately made his excuses and made his way back to Jess.

"What's the matter?" he asked, as he poured her another glass of champagne, observing the slight look of exasperation upon her face.

Jess took a large drink and savoured the bubbly liquid for a moment before speaking. Then she sighed and quietly said, "I am wondering how I ever survived university, when this is what we did every night. As much as it's been a fun night, I will be glad when everyone decides to leave."

Then, observing the somewhat dejected look on Jakes face, she quickly added, "Present company obviously excepted."

Thankfully, this last comment seemed to have worked as he had smiled down at her and reassured her that no offence had been taken. Fortunately for Jess, over the course of the next hour, all of the guests had departed, well all except one, and that one was Jake.

As she poured the remains of the champagne into her glass, Jess noted that she had drunk the entire bottle herself. She considered this to be the reason she felt heat rushing through her blood stream and not that she was reacting to the fact that Jake was now stood within arm's reach of her. He stood holding her gaze for a moment before stating that maybe he should leave too." Jess had forgotten what a gorgeous voice Jake possessed along with his many other attributes and she wished now she had not noticed. This man made her feel odd and she wasn't overly comfortable with that knowledge.

So she turned to put her glass on the worktop with the plan being to give Jake a friendly farewell hug. However, her hands were unsteady due to the combination of drink and adrenaline and as such she misjudged the logistics of the simple task with the result being that the glass smashed as it hit the worktop, slicing into Jess's hand as it did so. Jess just looked on as the blood began to seep from her wound whilst her drink-fuddled brain chose to respond. However, Jake immediately acted. He quickly guided Jess towards the sink and held her hand under the cold tap, leaving her stood there for a few moments whilst he raided the cupboards for something to dry the wound. He then came back and stood behind Jess as he once again took hold of the wounded hand, continuing to hold it under the running water a few moments longer. Jess was not aware of any pain from her injury because at that moment, all she could feel was Jakes firm body pressed closely into hers and the heat from his breath upon her neck.

Abruptly the contact was broken as Jake turned off the running water and slowly turned Jess around, keeping pressure upon the wound as he did so. Then having ascertained from a somewhat stunned Jess where she kept her medicine box he wrapped the wound and held the compress in a firm hold for a few moments, before reassessing the injury. Satisfied that it was nothing more than superficial cut, Jake once again relaxed. However, he did not let go of Jess's hand. The contact with her was reminding him of how he had felt with her body pressed into his which even in work mode he had registered. He looked down into her dazzling green eyes and once again held her gaze. He knew what he was about to do was risky but he could not help himself. And so, still holding her gaze he lifted her hand to his mouth and kissed the wound. Jess stood riveted to the spot, relishing the feel of his lips upon her skin and even though she knew it was wrong, she was lavishing in the feel of her skin reacting to his touch. She was battling with her desire for him and the knowledge that he was unattainable. However, as they now stood transfixed staring into each other's eyes, it was as if some unwritten rules were being broken. For a brief moment Jess's brain now improvised with alcohol considered these rules, however as Jake took a step closer all she could think was *'what are rules if not to be broken* ' as he began lavishing Jess with a kiss that began gentle and sensuous before the passion and electricity now pulsing through each of them, took over.

Chapter Twenty Three

The following day Jess felt tired and toxic. Elvis had had to wait until after lunch for a walk. Jess had tried to drag herself out of bed earlier but she literally could not lift her head off the pillow due to the headache from hell. She had woken early, but only stayed awake long enough to grab a glass of water and take some painkillers, she then fell straight back to sleep. She did however have one of her fabulous dreams and this time, she actually kissed the gorgeous Gerard Butler. When Jess finally woke again just before lunch, she lay in bed for a few moments contemplating two things. Firstly how she had ever survived drinking so much alcohol and secondly, how very real her dream had seemed.

Gingerly, Jess began to slowly sit up, and having assessed that her head no longer retaliated every time she moved, she threw back the bed covers and made her way to the bathroom. Half an hour later she felt slightly human, having showered, washed her hair and brushed her teeth. In truth she did not feel human enough to walk Elvis, although she conceded a bit of fresh air might do her some good. "Right then, little fella, I'd best take you for a stroll around the park," Jess was saying out loud to Elvis as she opened her bedroom door. And then she froze for a moment as she took in the scene of carnage. Bottles and cans and more bottles and cans covered just about every surface, accompanied with plates of left over curry.

Jess decided that she would tackle this clean up job after a blow of fresh air, although she did clear a section of the kitchen work top in order to get to the kettle. At that moment, she picked up the empty champagne bottle Jake had brought along to the party and was just about to throw it into the rubbish bin when she stopped. She stood frozen to the spot for a moment staring at the bottle as if it held some kind of hidden message, which of course it did. Well kind of! Though not of course a message, it was more of a reminder, and for Jess the reminder was of a fragmented memory of kissing Jake. "Holy shit, I kissed Jake!" Jess placed the broken bottle on the work top and continued to stare at it as her memory tried to recall information that was diluted with alcohol. No she hadn't kissed Jake, he had kissed her and as intoxicated as she had been and as hungover as she was now, she could remember enough to know it been the most sensual and exciting kiss of her life. It was at that moment that she realised that her dream had not in fact been about the gorgeous Gerard Butler and that it had actually been about the equally gorgeous Jake. '*What a mess I've got myself into again*', Jess was sorrowfully thinking to herself. However, her self-pity was interrupted by an eager puppy scratching at the door to go out. So she decided to give the cup of tea a rain check, opting instead for a bottle of coke from the fridge and headed out of the door.

Jess had been going over the kiss time and again whilst she walked Elvis, and the thing that she was finding really annoying was that whilst it was totally inappropriate, primarily because he was already spoken for, she knew she had enjoyed every moment of it.

She was still mulling over this inner conflict as she made her way around the top of the park that lead towards the exit. It was then that she came across the women with the Cocker Spaniel sitting on the bench, head in her hands. Jess realised two things; firstly that she still didn't know the name of the woman that she had been swapping pleasantries with for the last couple months and secondly, that she was out at a different time to her usual morning routine. Clearly something was not right and it was obvious to Jess that the woman was not aware that Jess was approaching her. As she drew closer,

Elvis stopped to make pleasantries with the Cocker Spaniel. Jess could not remember the dog's name but it gave her the opportunity to stop and assess whether to try and make conversation with the woman. Jess had a sneaking suspicion she knew what the situation could be, and so using the excuse to kneel down to fuss the dog, Jess quietly asked the woman if she was okay.

Months of pleasantries had passed between the two without a substantial conversation emerging, as this woman was always agitated and in a rush and Jess felt a little uncomfortable in forcing a conversation. However, if her suspicions were correct, then this could be the only opportunity she would have to engage her in a conversation. At first Jess wondered if the women had heard her as for a moment, she did not respond. Then slowly, she lifted her face from her hands, looking at Jess and in between quiet sobs she managed to mumble, "No." Having looked at Jess for just a moment, she lowered her head into her hands again and continued to sob. She may have only glanced at Jess momentarily but this gave Jess long enough to see the black eye and split lip, reinforcing her suspicions of the woman's situation.

Her suspicions had begun shortly after their first few encounters. The woman was friendly but always in a rush to get back home and have her husband's breakfast ready. Twice when she had spent a little longer than normal chatting to Jess, her husband had rung her and Jess could hear a raised voice insisting she come back home. However, it had been the bruises that Jess had observed on a couple of occasions, even though the woman always had the hood of her jacket pulled down low, that had aroused her suspicions further.

"I'm a good listener you know," Jess replied, testing the water to see if the friendly but enigmatic women would take the bait. Although the woman didn't reply straight away, she did stop crying. Jess sat down beside her and waited quietly for what must have been just a few moments but seemed much longer. She did not speak as she did not want to force

182

her into a conversation, merely waiting until the woman was ready to speak.

Slowly, she raised her head from her hands and made eye contact with Jess. Her injuries were more extensive than Jess had initially observed and her worst fears for the wellbeing of the women now sat dishevelled and lost on a bench in the park became a reality. Along with the two black eyes and bust lip, she also had a swelling forming above the brow of her right eye and a faint cut could be seen along her cheek. Tears started to run involuntarily from her eyes as she quietly said, "I can't go home. I can't go back there."

"No, you can't but you can come home with me. We'll get you cleaned up and then come up with a plan."

For a moment the women seemed resistant to Jess's offer and so Jess calmly continued. "I'm Jess by the way and this, as you know is Elvis."

"I'm Ruth and this is Copper," she replied in a monotone voice, gesturing at the Spaniel.

Jess got to her feet and took hold of Ruth's hands, "Come on Ruth, let's get out of this park and get you fixed up."

Ruth attempted a smile although had to abandon it as it was clearly too painful for her. Still holding onto Jess's hands, she got to her feet, wincing in pain at each movement. *My god*, Jess thought inwardly, *what on earth has that monster done to her*? As she linked arms with Ruth. She wouldn't normally have done this with someone she hardly knew, however not knowing the full extent of her injuries, she was not convinced that she would make it safely back to the shop even though it was only a short distance. Making their way slowly, Jess could see a few people stare as they passed them but fortunately, Ruth seemed not to notice. Jess had never been so pleased to enter her little shop. It had always felt homely to Jess but today it truly felt like a place of sanctuary with its pleasant floral aroma and Mrs Jacobs humming along to the radio in the back room. Jess had forgotten that Bettie had offered to come in for a couple of hours to prepare for a large order they had for the morning.

As Jess closed the door behind them she shouted through, "Bettie could you put the kettle on please?"

"Well you cheeky Madam, don't I do enough for you as it is?" Mrs Jacobs replied merrily as she came through to the shop, stopping in her tracks as she observed the scene before her. "Oh dear lord, what on earth has happened? Come here pet, let's get you sat down and warmed up with a cup of tea." Bettie put her arm around Ruth who was trembling and led her into the store room where she sat her down on the chair and immediately put the kettle on. Meanwhile, Jess pushed the shop door slightly closed, and speaking as quietly as possible, she phoned for back up. "Hi Mum, is Dad in. I need his help."

"Why, what's happened is everything ok?"

"Not really, or I wouldn't be asking for his help, but don't worry I'm okay. Mum, I can't explain now, I'm in a rush, can you just get him to come over."

Having made the call, she then went into the store room where she found Bettie helping Ruth out of her coat which was clearly causing her some discomfort. "I think we should take Ruth upstairs Bettie. It's nice and warm in the flat."

"Good idea love, you go on upstairs and I'll bring these cups of tea up to you."

"Is that ok with you Ruth? It's warmer in the flat and I can make you something to eat."

Ruth tried to produce a faint smile again, "Thank you. That would be great, although to be honest I'm not that hungry at the moment."

Leading the forlorn figure of a female broken both psychically and mentally Jess guided Ruth up the stairs to her place of sanctuary, and guided her into the living room where she put the fire on at full and plumped up the cushions. "There you go, sit yourself down. It's not exactly a palace but this sofa is incredibly comfy, by the way my flat doesn't normally look such a mess I had a party last night," she added as an explanation for the state of her home.

Ruth sat down with some degree of difficulty and Copper came and sat beside her feet, "What a mess we're in Copper. What are we going to do?"

Jess could see the tears forming again as Ruth gently stroked her clearly devoted pooches head. "It might not seem like things are great right now, but honestly Ruth they will be okay. I'm going to help you get through this, starting by making you something to eat and then why don't you have a long soak in the bath and later we can come up with a plan." In response to this suggestion Ruth did not speak and simply nodded her head.

Jess had struggled with what to prepare for Ruth to eat; having considered that eating even a sandwich would be difficult, she decided on soup. She placed the bowl on a tray and carried it through to the lounge along with the pot of tea Bettie had brought up to the flat. Jess left Ruth attempting to sip the soup while she started running the bath, adding some of the 'relaxing' bubble bath she had treated herself to the day she had rescued her Gran. She had been somewhat surprised that she had actually felt much more relaxed after bathing in it, and so she added a generous amount in the hope that it would help ease any discomfort. Jess was sure she had some camomile shampoo and conditioner and, sure enough, found it at the back of the bathroom cupboard. She considered this would be soothing for Ruth to wash her hair in as she had noticed a patch of her hair was missing. Finally, she put clean towels over the radiator to warm, along with a change of clothes.

Jess hoped that Ruth would not be offended at having to wear another person's clothes. She had noticed blood splattered down the front of her t-shirt and concluded that her recovery would be impeded by wearing a visual reminder of her husband's crimes. Jess made her way back into the living room and took the tray from her, pleased to see that she had finished all of the soup and the cup of tea. Walking into the kitchen, Jess then placed the tray on the counter and came back into the living room, carrying a glass of water and two painkillers. "Right then, you take these. They might help ease a little of your discomfort. And the bath's ready for you now, take all the time you need. While you're having a soak I'm just bobbing back down to the shop."

Ruth got slowly and painfully to her feet with Jess's help and once standing, she gave her a hug, "Thank you for all your help. You're so kind," she mumbled before making her way to the bathroom.

As soon as Ruth entered the bathroom Jess found herself on the verge of tears so she took a deep breath to compose herself before heading back downstairs to the shop just as her Dad came through the door, followed by her Mum. *Oh no! Not Mum*, Jess almost spoke the words aloud. She did love her mum dearly but she had a habit of fussing and overreacting which Jess really could not deal with now. She was glad her Dad was here though; he was very practical and calm and would know what to do.

One look at her face and Jess's dad knew something was seriously wrong. "What on earth's the matter love," he asked calmly, as he came to give his precious daughter a hug. He surmised whatever it was must be bad because Jess was not in the habit of asking for help. Before Jess could answer, Mrs Jacobs did it for her.

"It's such a mess Allen; Jess has rescued some poor lass who looks like she's been beaten within an inch of her life."

"Heavens above! Do you think it's safe keeping her in your flat? What if whoever did that to her finds out she's here," her mother exclaimed in the dramatic way Jess had anticipated.

"Shut up Joan, where do you expect the poor lass to go? Jess did right to try and help her; we just need to figure out what to do now," her dad retaliated in a manner Jess had not heard for a very long time. Jess could not remember a time

186

when her dad had challenged her mother and when Jess looked across at her, she was standing open-mouthed.

"I was only trying to point out that it's potentially dangerous to provide refuge for the poor girl. I didn't mean to send her back," replied her mother somewhat sulkily, having recovered from the shock of being challenged by her husband. Mrs Jacobs, clearly trying her best to diffuse the situation intervened by suggesting they all have a pot of tea whilst they came up with a plan.

After ten minutes they all agreed that it would be best if Jess and Ruth, plus both dogs decamped to her Gran's house as the consensus was they would both be much safer there. Mrs Jacobs telephoned her husband to say she would be slightly later home in order that Jess could stay upstairs and keep Ruth company and find out a little more detail of the crime. And Jess's Dad suggested that he and her Mum would stay around for a little while just in case the violent husband should show up.

"Do you think you'll be safe if he does show up?" Jess anxiously asked the cherished group, who were all prepared to protect not just her but someone they did not even know. She felt very blessed at that moment.

Finishing his pot of tea, Jess's dad stood up from the stool he had been perched on. "I don't think he'd start with us all even if he did turn up. Guys like that are just pathetic bullies," he said with conviction before continuing. "I would see if you can talk the lass into pressing charges though, and into going to hospital for a check-up."

Jess made her way back upstairs and quietly made her way into the living room. At first she thought Ruth was sleeping as she had her eyes closed and seemed restful. However, as Jess approached, she opened her eyes with a start and quietly told Jess that she felt much better having had a bath and changed into fresh clothes. Jess sat down on the far end of the sofa feeling a little uncomfortable at having to broach the difficult subject. She decided to start the conversation on a positive note. "You look much better now you've had a soak in the bath and some rest and Copper looks snug in front of the fire, although if he gets any closer he's going to be in it!" Jess was glad that she had managed to make Ruth smile as she looked at her beloved dog, although it only lasted for a moment.

"He does that at home," she paused for a moment before adding, "Did do that at home. Now we don't have a home."

It was no good, Jess was aware that nothing was going to cheer Ruth up today and they really did have to come up with a plan. Trying to sound calm and confident Jess broached the subject. "Ruth I hate to have to push you but we're going to have to discuss what to do next. There's no way I'm letting you go back there, but I don't think we should stay here either just in case he works out where you are." Jess could see the fear flash through Ruth's eyes. "Don't panic, I won't let him anywhere near you. If it's okay with you I think I already have an idea. I'll make us a cup of tea and then I'll run it by you and see what you think."

As they sipped their tea, Jess outlined the plan her dad had come up with the hope that Ruth would agree that it would provide them with a place of sanctuary until a more viable solution could be found. Jess hoped that Ruth would agree, although she suspected that given her unfortunate present circumstances, Ruth would agree with anything Jess put forward at this moment in time. As anticipated, she did agree and although Ruth did not say so, Jess suspected that she was relieved to be staying somewhere that was well away from the vicinity of her husband. Jess tried to touch upon the subject of her pressing charges against her husband, although she would not be persuaded; neither would she go to hospital for a check-up. However, Jess was incredibly relieved to hear that she was adamant that she had no intention of returning to her husband.

Having made a preliminary plan, Jess talked Ruth into letting her parents come up to the flat so that they could finalise the arrangements. She went back down to the shop, locking the door before warning her mother not to make a fuss or be overdramatic before they headed upstairs. "We won't be long Bettie," Jess said as she headed towards the flat, before turning round and giving the lovely old lady a hug, "Thanks for stopping. You're always there for me when I need it and I do appreciate it."

"You're welcome dear. You're always there for other people and that includes me. You've closed up shop and come to help on more than one occasion when our Jack's had one of his funny turns. One good turn deserves another, and I'd do anything to help you. Now you get yourself back up those stairs and sort that lass out and I'll make myself another pot of tea."

Jess ran back up to the flat realising that Ruth would now be enduring her mother. However, she need not have worried because her mother was on her best behaviour, showing kindness to Ruth that Jess had rarely experienced herself. After ten minutes it had been agreed that her parents would leave now and go put the heating on to warm her Gran's house as it had been standing empty for some time now. After collecting provisions for the girls, they would then take them to the temporary safe house. The collective that had now formed recognised they were being over cautious because as yet Ruth's husband did not even know that she was with Jess but even so, they felt it was best not to create anything suspicious. Tomorrow Jess's parents would work in the shop so that Ruth would not be on her own and it would give the girls extra time to think about what to do next. Having arrived at their plan, Jess accompanied her parents back down to the shop.

"Thank you both so much. I really didn't know what to do. I feel much more confident now though."

You're welcome sweetie," her dad said giving Jess a hug. "I'm not happy about you staying here on your own until we get back, though. That is clearly one nasty piece of work. If he can do that to someone he's supposed to love then I'm damn sure he won't think anything of hurting you. Maybe you should lock up the shop now."

At that moment Bettie intervened. "It's fine Allen. I'm not going anywhere and just let that bully try anything while I'm here." Jess's dad looked at the fierce look on Bettie's face and gave her a fond smile, "I don't doubt it Bettie! Okay then girls, we won't be long."

As it turned out, it did not take Ruth's brutal husband long to work out where his wife had sought sanctuary. Only half an hour after her parents had left, the door was opened with such force it slammed into the wall. Inwardly Jess's adrenaline kicked into action. However, she managed to retain a calm external image. She recognised the man walking arrogantly towards her immediately. Jess had never considered him to be an attractive man when she had seen him previously walking Copper and now with his face contorted in anger, he looked like a monster. In Jess's opinion, exactly what he was.

He came to a halt in front of the counter, and then leaning across to within inches of Jess's face he snarled, "I believe you have something that belongs to me!"

It was clear that he was intending to intimidate Jess and although inwardly it was having the desired effect, she calmly answered, "I think you'll find I don't have anything *that belongs to you*," ensuring that the comment, 'that belongs to you' was emphasised.

"Don't get clever with me, you little bitch. You're the only person that she's mentioned in months so I know full well she's here. Now go and get her. She's coming home with me."

Jess was incensed with anger. Not only had he been rude to her, but he could not even be bothered to refer to his wife by her name. "If you mean Ruth by 'her', then yes Ruth is here. Though you can threaten me as much as you like, she's not going anywhere with you. Not now, and not ever again. So I suggest you leave or I'll call the police and have you

190

arrested for the wife beater that you are. You should be ashamed of yourself."

At this point Bettie came out of the store room holding a vase like a baseball bat and stood beside Jess behind the counter. "You heard her. I suggest you leave this minute. I've come across the likes of you before and you're nothing but a bully."

Jess took one look at the man's face and it was clear that this disgusting specimen of a male did not like being challenged by females. Instinctively she moved in front of Bettie. It was a wise move, because just as she did so, he went to hit her. He failed in his attempt though because just at that moment, Elvis, who had been sitting beside Jess's feet, sprang up knocking flowers and Jess's business cards out of the way as he landed on the counter. His throaty growls led the startled villain to retreat slightly.

"The lady told you to leave and I suggest that you do just that before I make you!"

In all the commotion, Jess had not seen Jake enter the shop and she had never been so pleased to see him. He strode confidently towards the two women who he could see were attempting to be brave whilst dealing with a difficult situation. Coming to stand beside them, he reiterated what he had said. "I told you to leave and I won't tell you again. I will count to five and then I'm going to make you leave."

Clearly the wife beater did not relish the thought of having to contend with a guy who could look after himself and whilst fixing Jake and the women with a look of pure evil he began to retreat. As he reached the door he turned, "I want my wife back and I *will* be back to get her."

Jake took a step forward, "If I find out you've been anywhere near this shop again I will hunt you down and make you regret it." Ruth's husband did not hang around any longer and left the shop, slamming the door behind him.

Once he had left both Jess and Bettie visibly relaxed. "Are you two okay? What the hell is going on?" Jake demanded with concern evident in his voice.

"I think it's time for another cup of tea, although I swear I'm going to have a drop of brandy tonight. That is one nasty man. I can't begin to think what that poor woman has gone through living with him," Bettie mumbled as she went back into the store room.

Jess had never been so pleased to see anyone and for once she was not overwhelmed by his presence. "I think I've had enough for one day," she responded, "Can you lock the shop door and then I'll tell you all about what's been happening."

Jake was enraged when he heard what had unfolded. "Well I'm glad I turned up when I did. Although I think Elvis had the situation under control, didn't you little fella?" Elvis was still perched on the counter, relishing being lavished with attention from Jake.

"I know! I can't believe he did that. I haven't seen him jump that high since he jumped my parents' gate and I've never seen him be aggressive," replied Jess before planting a kiss on the top of Elvis's head.

"He's not aggressive at all. He was just protecting you. You have yourself a good, loyal dog there."

"I know," Jess answered, somewhat absent-mindedly as she had just had an idea.

"Listen Jake, I'm not sure if she'll be up for it, but seeing as you're medically trained, I wonder if Ruth might consider letting you check her over. I'm really concerned that she won't go to hospital."

"If you can talk her into it, then yeah, that's fine with me. If she took a beating as bad as that then really she should be checked out. You go and see if you can talk her into it. I'll stay here and chat to this lovely lady," he responded, gesturing to Mrs Jacobs who was returning with yet another pot of tea.

"I'm not in any rush because I'm not going anywhere until you're safely out of here for the night."

As Jess left the shop to go upstairs she paused at the door. "Thanks Jake. You always seem to be saving me or my friends and family."

"Any time babe."

Chapter Twenty Four

Jess decided to keep from Ruth that her husband had tracked her down for the time being. Instead she focused on persuading her to have a check-up. It took some doing however but after about ten minutes, Jess had talked Ruth into letting Jake give her a quick health check. Jake had assessed many injuries in his time including many women who had been beaten by their other halves. However, this woman's injuries were some of the most severe he had seen. Knowing that Ruth was resistant to being medically examined Jess took the opportunity to get organised. "Right I'm going to pack a few things in my bedroom. Give me a shout when you've finished."

It didn't take long before there was a gentle knock at her bedroom door. Without even thinking she shouted, "Come in!" Jess was placing items from her wardrobe onto her bed when Jake entered her room, and as he did so the air seemed to leave it. Now that Jess had had time to calm down, his presence was beginning to affect her again.

Jake noted the flush creep into Jess's cheeks and at any other time he would have been pleased that he was having an effect upon the object of his affection, particularly in her bedroom. However, he was not the kind of guy to take advantage of any woman, especially one who had been through so much. He knew what Jess needed now was practical support and so he casually reported to Jess that whilst Ruth's injuries were severe, and that shit of a husband of hers had clearly intended to cause some real damage, he considered that she would most likely be fine with rest. Ideally the cut above her eye could have done with some tape to secure the wound in order that it healed correctly, he also suspected that her ribs were bruised although not cracked, however he could not be certain without her having them x-rayed. All in all though, he considered that she had been very lucky to escape with her life.

Jess listened to his findings as she continued to place items into her bag, then sat down on the edge of her bed and put her head in her hands. She suddenly felt very tired and could feel tears trying to force their way into her eyes. "It's a bit of a mess isn't it? I knew I didn't like him, but whoever heard of a guy with a Cocker Spaniel being a wife beater. I tried to just think he was just uptight, although deep down I knew what he was, and what Ruth was most likely going through. I should have intervened sooner."

Jake came and sat down beside Jess, and put his strong arm around her shoulders, pulling her into him as he did so. "Hey, come on. You know no one could have done anything. She had to make the decision to leave the cretin on her own and as soon as she did, you helped her. And now I'm here to help, so you're not on your own."

Jess felt safe and comforted being held by Jake and she knew she was falling even more deeply for him. Thank God Brandon was up this weekend. She would have to speak to him about this and get his perspective. She took a deep breath and looked into Jake's brilliant blue eyes and for a moment they just held each other's gaze. Jess was the first to break the moment. "Thanks Jake, I'm very fortunate to have you in my life." Taking a deep breath she added, "Now I think it's time I got Ruth out of here and to safety."

Jake could see the tears trying to escape from her beautiful green eyes as she battled to contain her brave exterior and was overwhelmed with a desire to protect her and those she cared for. He was not sure whether she could recall anything about last night, he had been aware that she had been incredibly drunk, which is why he had not taken her to bed. And whilst he was desperate to find out her feelings towards him, he knew now was not the time. So he stood up, bringing her to her feet with him and said, "Come on my brave Jess, let's get you and Ruth out of here."

He helped Ruth out of the flat and down the stairs where they were met by Jess's parents, who like Jake were enraged to discover that Ruth's monstrous husband had threatened Jess. Unfortunately Ruth overheard this information and started to shake uncontrollably. At which point Jake put a protective arm around her and tried to reassure her that she was now safe.

"Right we've been over to your Gran's and put the heating on, so it should be nice and warm by the time you get there. And we've just called in at the shop and got some groceries so you can have some supper. But Jess, listen. I think it would be a good idea if you left your car here tonight just in case that scoundrel tries to find you again." Seeing the look of fear on Ruth's face Jess's dad quickly added, "I mean it's unlikely he would, but just to be on the safe side I would prefer it if you did. "I know what you're saying Dad, but it will be a right pain in the morning trying to get here to open the shop."

"You won't have to, me and your mum plus Bettie are going to cover the shop. We all agreed that you girls could do with the rest."

Jake was in agreement. "I think what your dad is saying is right. Plus the sooner you're out of here, the better." Jake turned to Jess's dad, "I'm happy to run the girls over, though it going to be a bit of a squeeze in the mini with the two dogs as well."

"Good idea lad. Well if it's ok with you, then you take the girls and I'll put the dogs in the boot and we'll meet you over there. Here pass us your bag Jess. I'll take that in my car.

Right, you set off then, and we'll lock up and see Bettie back home and then me and your Mum will meet you there."

Jess relaxed immediately upon entering her Gran's house. It was one of those properties that for some reason just felt homely, along with so many happy memories. It was clear that it had the same effect on Ruth as Jess could see her visibly relax a little. Jake made himself busy putting the kettle on, whilst Jess gave Ruth a quick tour of the house. Jess then insisted that Ruth made herself comfortable on the sofa while she went and joined Jake in the kitchen. He had managed to find the cups, as well as tea and coffee and with perfect timing her parents arrived with the other provisions, including milk. Jess helped Jake make drinks for everyone and then carried them into the living room.

They all sat quietly for a few moments before Ruth was the first to speak, "I just want to thank you all for all your help today. I hate that you've all been put to so much trouble because of me. And Jess I can't begin to thank you for everything you've done," she said, firstly looking at Jess, and then each of the group in turn. Collectively, they each muttered that she needn't thank them at all.

Jess took another sip of her tea before broaching the subject that she had been contemplating on the journey to her Gran's. "Ruth, I hate to push you on this when you've had the day you've had, but I've been thinking that it might be a good thing if I rang that shit of a husband of yours and told him to bag up your things. I just think that maybe it's a good idea to cut all ties with him as soon as possible and you're going to need your possessions from your house."

Ruth, as Jess had anticipated, responded nervously that she could not go back there, ever. "It's ok I'll ring him and tell him to bag them up and then I'll go and pick them up tomorrow. At least that way it's one less thing to have to deal with later."

Jake had been listening to Jess's reasoning intently and was the first to voice his concerns. "I agree with what you're saying Jess, but there is no way I would let you anywhere near that man. I'll ring him myself and go and pick up Ruth's things tomorrow."

"And I'll go with you, lad. I don't want you going there on your own." Jess's dad quickly added, "I know you can look after yourself, but that guy seems crazy. I think it would be best if you took someone along with you."

"I agree Dad. I know; I'll ring Brandon. He and his partner are here for the weekend. I was planning on meeting up with them tomorrow. I know they won't mind going along, and maybe Paul too; I'll ring them now. Jake got the number of Ruth's husband from her, before going into the kitchen to call him. From the living room the rest of them could hear Jake's slightly raised voice, but other than that could not make out what he was saying. Just a few minutes later he came back and calmly said it was organised for Ruth's possessions to be collected tomorrow at 2pm. "Do you want to call the troops then? I'd best be going to check on the dog."

The mention of Jake's dog was a stark reminder to Jess that Jake was not simply Prince Charming here to save her or Ruth, and that he most likely had to get back to his partner. Getting to her feet, Jess smiled politely and said, "I'll call them now."

Jake sensed the change in her and guessed what had fuelled it, reinforcing his urge to stop the nonsense that she believed about him sooner rather than later. As Jess entered the hallway her parents were waiting for her by the door.

"Now, not to worry sweetie. You'll be safe here until things settle down and me and your Mum will call over tomorrow after we've closed up the shop. That nice young lad will sort everything else out. I think you've got yourself a good one there Jess."

Before Jess could explain, her parents gave her a quick hug and then left. Jess shut the door behind them and turned to go back into the living room, discovering Jake standing there. She wondered whether Jake had overheard her father. Whilst she would have preferred he hadn't, after the day she had had, her father believing Jake to be her boyfriend was the least of her worries.

If he had heard he was giving nothing away and for a moment he just stood looking at her, smiling before walking towards her and taking her into his arms, hugging her tightly. Jess didn't resist. It might be an odd situation but right now she simply relished feeling safe in his arms.

"Right babe, I'd best be off too," he said quietly, though without letting go of her. When he did let go of her, Jess felt cold and vulnerable, remaining in the same spot without moving or saying anything. She wondered if he was able to read her mind because in the next instance he took her chin and tipped her face up so she had to meet his gaze. "You've been incredibly brave today. Jessica Wainwright you are one incredible female. You're just tired now, so get some rest and stay strong. I've left my number with Ruth. If you need me, just call and if not I'll be back tomorrow." With that, he kissed the top of her head and opened the front door. Just as he was about to exit he turned around, "Do you know, I wasn't supposed to be working that day but I'm really glad I did. I must remember to buy Nick a pint next time we're out for talking me into swapping shifts with him." He left, closing the door behind him and leaving Jess seriously confused.

Chapter Twenty Five

The next day Jess woke feeling slightly disorientated at not being in her own bed. She had slept surprisingly well and upon wakening had momentarily forgotten about yesterday's events. As soon as she did remember, she jumped out of bed relishing the warmth of her Gran's house as opposed to her own cold flat. She put on socks and a hoodie, a habit now entrenched in her morning ritual and tip toed across the landing, quietly opening the door to the bedroom which Ruth had slept in. It looked as though Ruth was still sound asleep so Jess headed downstairs to make breakfast. After letting the two excitable dogs out into the garden, she put the kettle on and got the bacon out of the fridge. She planned on taking Ruth breakfast up to her room as a treat, suspecting that she had been unlikely to get many treats off her husband; however, just as the bacon had almost finished cooking, Ruth appeared in the kitchen, looking much more rested than the previous day.

"Morning. Did you sleep well? I was going to bring your breakfast up to you," Jess said cheerily.

"The beautiful smell of a bacon sarnie is enough to raise the dead from their sleep," replied Ruth with a smile that Jess could see was still painful.

Ruth had never made a humorous comment in the time they had chatted in the park and Jess wondered if this morning was the beginning of her becoming the real Ruth once more.

"Well there you go. Tuck in. If you're hungry there's some more bacon in the oven warming."

Just then a scratching could be heard at the kitchen door so Jess let both dogs into the kitchen and then tried to calm them down by bribing them with food. "There you go guys. A treat for you too," she jovially said to the two eager dogs as she offered each of them a piece of bacon before joining Ruth at the table. For a moment each of the girls were silent as they tucked into her breakfast.

Ruth was the first to speak, "I've been thinking Jess. Maybe I should press charges after all. Though I'm really not sure I could cope with all the hassle."

Jess was secretly pleased at Ruth's change of heart; though she was aware it had to be her decision. And so she waited for a moment and then replied that she thought it was the right thing to do. She reinforced to Ruth that if she did decide to go ahead and press charges against him, then she would support her all the way and so would everyone else. As an afterthought Jess added that it might be best to wait until after the guys had collected her things in order not to aggravate him further though. And so, as they finished their breakfasts, it was agreed that once the all clear had been received that the guys were safely away from Ruth's former home, they would report her husband to the police.

Shortly after lunch, Brandon and Justin were the first to arrive at her Gran's house as part of the posse to retrieve Ruth's possessions. Jess had not seen Brandon in months and surprised herself by how pleased she was to see him. He came through the door first, giving her a big hug, "Hi sweetie. It's good to see you," he whispered as he continued to hug her. He finally let her go and Justin made his way in next, also hugging Jess affectionately.

It's a strange world, Jess thought to herself as Justin gave her a peck on the cheek and warmly said, "It's good to see you, kiddo."

Brandon had made his way into the kitchen and was already chatting with Ruth as Jess and Justin made their way through. "No we don't mind at all honestly, anything to help," Brandon reassured Ruth in response to her concerns that she had put them to too much trouble.

Jess had already updated Ruth that morning on her relationship with her ex and his new partner. "I know it's a bit of an unusual set up, but Brandon was my best friend and I do like Justin. We just grew apart; it was no-one's fault really. In fact, now I think it was for the best," Jess had explained over breakfast. Ruth had responded that she thought it was great they had remained friends and they had both agreed that Ruth trying to be friends with her (soon to be ex) husband would be out of the question.

Brandon knew the layout of Jess's Gran's house as he had been there many times before; as such he made himself busy making everyone drinks. "So who is it that's coming with us today? Though I really don't know why you thought we would need back up. I'm sure me and Justin could manage one guy on our own."

Jess recognised Brandon's petulance at the suggestion they would need extra support. She wondered whether he assumed Jess saw him as being less capable of dealing with a situation like this just because he was now openly gay. This was an absurd idea to Jess, as she was fully aware that Brandon could look after himself. "I simply thought it would be a good idea to have two cars as we have no idea how much of Ruth's stuff he will bag up. And anyway, it'll be nice for you to meet some of my new friends," she reasoned.

This seemed to pacify Brandon and he smiled at her, knowing that she had sussed out his grievance, "So who are your new friends then hun?"

"Well there's Paul who's Kate's new boyfriend. He's really nice, she met him at the gym we joined – "

Before she could continue, Brandon interrupted, "Crikey! Is that really you Jess? Because the Jess I knew wouldn't have been seen dead in a gym." Justin and Ruth smiled at each other as they observed the easy banter between the two.

"Funny aren't you! Now if you don't mind, I'll continue what I was saying. And the final person joining you is my new friend Jake who just so happens to be gay. In fact, I was hoping to have a chat with you later about him because I'm a little confused to be honest."

Brandon knew Jess well and recognised that she really did want to run something by him. She may no longer be the partner for him but he did still love her. "Of course you can. We'll have a chat when we get back and you can tell me what's bothering you."

Next to arrive was Kate with Paul. Being Jess's best friend, Kate knew Brandon well. Although at the time she had not been happy with the fact that he had run off with someone else, like Jess she was happy now to forgive and forget. She had always liked him, when all was said and done. And so they hugged each other before introducing their new partners to each other. As they waited for Jake to arrive they all made their way into the living room which faced out onto the front garden and drive.

As a car pulled up, Brandon looked out of the window. "Would your new friend look like Gerard Butler by any chance?" he said, smirking at Jess.

"Yep, that would be him. I forgot to mention that he's gorgeous, just unavailable to me," Jess replied in as casual a manner as possible as made her way to open the door.

As Jake stepped through the door he too gave her a hug. Jess felt truly indulged in affection today. Remembering belatedly that the house was full of people, he let her go. Something he was not fond of doing. "Afternoon gorgeous. Judging by the number of cars in the drive, I'm guessing I'm the last to arrive."

Jess was pleased to see him and smiled animatedly up into those gorgeous eyes, as always feeling less composed when she was in his presence. "You are the last to arrive, although you're not late. Follow me and I'll introduce you to my ex-husband and his boyfriend, and of course you'll know the others."

Jess had turned to make her way into the living room and so she did not see the look of realisation on Jake's face. He had been bemused as to why she had misinterpreted him as being gay. Even though his mate Tom had pointed out that on the basis of their initial meetings, the evidence had been a little suspicious. He pondered the notion that perhaps Jess's ex-husband also drove a ridiculously floral car and had a Chihuahua as a pet. When Jake entered the crowded living room, he initially greeted Kate and Paul as well as asking Ruth how she was feeling. Lastly, Jess introduced Jake to Brandon and Justin. "Jake this is Brandon my ex-husband, and this is his partner Justin. Although, they'll soon be more than partners as Brandon's just been telling us about how they're getting married later in the year." And then gesturing to the party gathered in her Gran's living room, she said "And this is Jake who I was telling you about."

"All good things, I hope?" Jake asked jovially, as he shook hands with Brandon and then did the same with Justin, "And congratulations."

Jess was feeling slightly uncomfortable and offered to make Jake a cup of tea before they went to collect Ruth's belongings. She was met at the kitchen door by Brandon who whispered, "Where did you manage to find a guy like that round here? If I wasn't so happily in love with Justin, I'd be tempted myself."

"And you might be in luck, because I mentioned earlier Jake is gay. That's what I want to talk to you about," Jess whispered back.

"Really!" replied Brandon, with a bemused look.

The guys left as soon as they had finished their drinks, and the girls waited anxiously for their return. Kate tried to alleviate the tension, "Honestly, this is ridiculous. You'd think they had gone off to war, and not just to collect some items from a bloke, albeit a nasty one."

Ruth smiled at her comment, "That's the trouble Kate He is a nasty one, and unpredictable. I feel awful having put everyone to so much trouble."

Jess immediately tried to waylay her concerns, "Don't be silly. You'd do the same to help someone if they needed it, I just know it. Now don't fret, they'll be back soon."

Jess was right. They were back within the hour with two cars full of Ruth's belongings. The heroic warriors seemed calm and in good spirits and relayed that it had been really straightforward, although they all agreed the guy was a complete arse. They had decided not to tell the women that there had been an incident whereby Jake had had to be restrained by the others in response to Ruth's husband goading that, "The little bitch deserved everything she got."

They had all agreed this would be best kept between them so as not to upset Ruth further.

After unloading the cars and putting the items in the garage, they all convened in the kitchen while Ruth rang the police. Collectively they decided to wait with Jess and Ruth until the police had been to interview her in order to provide moral support.

It was a couple of hours before the police arrived to take Ruth's statement. They advised her that her husband would be arrested and more than likely he would then be bailed. The police were pleased that Ruth had so much support and was not on her own; however, they advised her to get a Solicitor first thing in the morning.

It was early evening by the time the police left and Jess could see that the day's events had taken their toll on Ruth's energy levels. She was concerned that Ruth had not eaten anything for hours and neither had the rest of them, so she suggested that they order a Chinese before they disbanded. The food arrived a little after seven and they sat amiably around the kitchen table, chatting animatedly about many subjects other than Ruth's ordeal, in order to try and take her mind of the situation.

Jake was reluctant to leave. Even though it had not been the best of situations in order to spend time with others, he was enjoying their company. And though he knew the girls were safe, he was still uneasy about them in the house on their own. However, he considered that Jess would most likely want to spend some time catching up with Brandon and Justin and so shortly after Kate and Paul left, he made his exit, having agreed that next time they all met up it would be in the pub for a drink.

Jess saw him to the door, whereby he put his arms around her and held her close for a few moments. She no longer felt uncomfortable being hugged by Jake, although it did reinforce her confusion with regard to her feelings for him. She was pleased that she would have the opportunity to discuss the situation with Brandon. Jess sensed Jake's reluctance to leave and although under different circumstances she may have invited him to stay longer, she really wanted to speak with Brandon. Releasing herself from his hold she looked up and noted that he looked troubled.

"What's the matter? We'll be fine you know. Brandon and Justin have agreed to stay on for a few days, and if we need anything I promise I'll call."

Jake was concerned for the girls' welfare, but had also been distracted with the notion that the situation could not continue and had been silently brooding on a plan. He forced a smile, "I know you will, babe. Right, I'll be off. Call me if you need anything." With that, he kissed the top of her head and left.

"Babe!" Jess muttered to herself as she made her way back into the living room, "Why does he insist on calling me that?"

As soon as Jess entered the living room Ruth thanked everyone again for everything they had done for her and then retired to bed. Jess insisted on making her a hot water bottle to ease the pain, plus a hot chocolate and offered to bring them up to her with some painkillers.

When Jess came back downstairs she found Brandon and Justin in the kitchen tidying up, with Brandon in the process of pouring three glasses of wine.

Jess plonked herself down on a chair and let out a sigh. "God, I'm exhausted! What a stressful couple of days. I'm so glad you're here guys. I feel much better having my friends around me."

Brandon came and sat down at the table, handing over a glass of Chardonnay to Jess. "Here sweetie, get that down you. You've earned it."

Justin came to join them at the table and they simultaneously each took a drink of their wine. And then Brandon, with a silly grin on his face asked, "Talking of 'friends' Jess, now he's gone are you going to tell us how you managed to bag Mr 'Spitting Image of Gerard Butler' in Bradford."

Jess giggled, "He does look like him, doesn't he? But I told you earlier, I haven't bagged him because he's gay."

Brandon and Justin looked at each before turning back to Jess and chorusing, "He is not!"

Jess looked at them both to assess whether they were kidding her. They seemed genuine, but she had convinced herself of the facts. She had hoped that they would have been able to shed some light on her attraction to him. As it was, they were not helping and in fact, were just making matters worse. "Come on guys! I was counting on your help. Since that guy came into my life he has done nothing but confuse me. I mean I have to admit between just us that I do like him and I haven't even told Kate that. But come on, who wouldn't? He ticks all the boxes except for the bit where he's unavailable because he has a boyfriend."

Jess took another sip of her wine which was going down a treat, and when she placed her glass on the table Justin topped it up. Brandon watched Jess from across the table taking note of how cute she was, plus funny and sweet natured. It was no wonder that Jake had fallen for her. He suddenly felt a stab of guilt and hoped that she was not going to ruin the rest of her life by assuming that every potential suitor was going to run off with a guy.

"Jess, sweetie, the reason you're attracted to him is because that guy is one hundred percent definitely not gay. I have no idea why you've told yourself that he is but I can assure that he is not. And, what's more, that guy is only interested in one person and that is you. He's like a love sick puppy. Don't tell me you haven't noticed."

"That's right Jess. I'm with Brandon one hundred percent. It's obvious the guy is crazy for you. It's as plain as the nose on your face," Justin agreed.

"Cheeky! Are you saying I have a plain nose?" giggled Jess as the wine began to take effect.

"Stop changing the subject, Missy," intervened Brandon in a tone much more serious than he had intended. "Now, we are not leaving this table until you have told us everything and we have your love life in order. So open another bottle of wine will you, Justin, because I have a feeling this might take a while."

Chapter Twenty Six

Three days later, and Jess's life had resumed some degree of normality now she and Elvis were back in her flat. Ruth had left Jess's Gran's house the next morning. Her brother had driven up from 'down south' in order that she go and stay with him for a while. One of Ruth's neighbours had got word to Ruth that her husband had packed up and left the property.

"He always was a Mummy's boy. She'd never see any wrong in him," Ruth had told Jess upon hearing the news. They had been pleased to hear he was no longer in the area. The women had hugged affectionately and promised to remain friends. Jess had been sad to see Ruth go. Though she knew being out of the area for a while would be better for Ruth, once she and Copper had left even Elvis seemed despondent.

Later the same day, Brandon and Justin also departed. They too had hugged Jess warmly and she had shed a tear as they drove away. Both men had promised not to leave it so long next time to meet up and Brandon had insisted that Jess keep him posted on any developments in her love life.

"I will, although I wouldn't hold your breath," she had promised. Then as soon as everyone had left, Jess had immediately packed up her things and gone home.

Wednesday morning and Jess was back in her beloved shop. She had slept soundly, primarily because Mrs Jacobs had been into her flat to ensure it was nice and warm. As she had anticipated, everything was as it should be with regard to the shop as Mrs Jacobs had been running the business a long time and could deal with every eventuality with her eyes shut.

That afternoon, they closed the shop early as usual on a Wednesday. However, as opposed to doing her usual thing of shopping or having an indulgent lunch, Jess put on her trainers and went for a run. She didn't get very far though, as Elvis insisted on stopping every two minutes to have a wee or smell something of interest. In addition, people kept stopping her for a chat. *Or a nosey*, Jess considered as the women that stopped her were only interested in hearing Ruth's story. *Small villages,* Jess mused. *They can be great, although on the downside everyone knows everybody's business. No doubt fuelled by my mother!*

Jess had abandoned her run and was just making her way back to the flat when her mobile rang. "Hi hun. What are you up to? You sound out of breath."

It was Kate and she was clearly in high spirits. Before Jess could answer that she was in fact out trying to jog, Kate continued excitedly, "Listen, I hope you don't mind but I've changed the venue for this week's walk. Instead of the woods I've arranged that we all meet on the greenway. That way we can call off at that pub which is a couple of miles into the route."

"No, I don't mind at all. In fact, I think it's a great idea. Do you know how many are planning on coming along?" Jess asked enthusiastically, glad that life was beginning to return to normal and secretly curious as to whether Jake had decided to join them this week. She had received text messages from him enquiring whether she was safe or needed anything, but she had not actually spoken to him and was aware that she would have been pleased if he had called in to see her at the shop. Following her drunken night with Brandon and Justin she was just as confused as before, but now she had resigned herself to the fact that she would be happy if they did just remain friends because she was happy just being in his company.

In any event, Kate did not expand on who was coming along, just instructing Jess to be at the greenway for eleven-thirty. That way they could walk for a while before the pub opened for lunch. "Great, I'll see you then. Must dash now though. I have to get back to work. Oh, and Jess, we won't have to wear silly wellington boots or dog walking clothes as we won't need them on the greenway. I'll be wearing something nice for a change to walk the dog. I just thought I'd let you know in case you want to make a bit of an effort," and then she ended the call before Jess could say anything further.

How bizarre, Jess mused, questioning whether since owning Elvis she was beginning to look like she lived in wellies. She didn't get a chance to dwell on it though, as before she managed to get back home, she was stopped twice more by people wanting to know of Ruth's situation.

Chapter Twenty Seven

On Sunday morning Jess got up earlier than usual, in order to make an effort as Kate had suggested. She didn't know whether to be a little upset at Kate's comment as Jess didn't think she had turned into a bag lady. Granted, the extra time it took to accommodate looking after a dog did mean that she very rarely had much time to apply make-up. And yes, she had recently had a bit of a crisis with the situation with Ruth, but even so she had not considered she looked too bad.

Jess decided she would have words with Kate about it later. After deliberating for a while, she opted for a cream vintage dress that floated around her knees. Although it was a lovely spring day, there was still a chill in the air most days so she decided that layering would be a good idea and wore a cardigan under her denim jacket. Finishing the look, she opted for her favourite cowboy boots. Because Jess had risen earlier than normal, she had time to clip her hair up, to even put polish on her nails, and at eleven o' clock she and Elvis left the house and headed for the greenway.

As she pulled into the car park with Elvis buckled into the passenger seat, Jess could see that this morning there seemed to be a large turnout. Kate looked radiant and Jess could see her whisper something to Paul as she and Elvis got out of the car. Also present this morning were Sylvia and James, along with Suzie and Luke and Nathen the fireman. There was also Lucy from the gym and Pamela and Patricia.

One face that Jess registered was not present was Jake, and although Jess felt a stab of disappointment she did not have time to show it because she was enveloped in hugs and well wishes from the group, who each in turn said how pleased they were to see her. "Thanks guys, that's really sweet of you. Still, it's lovely to see you all. I'm really looking forward to this walk. It's a lovely day for it. Shall we make a move now? I think there's a pint with my name on it," Jess giggled.

"I hope there's a pint with my name on it too."

Jess pivoted round so fast she nearly lost her balance. She recognised the voice, and was unable to hide her pleasure that Jake had decided to join them. Jess had convinced herself that she was no longer bothered that he was unavailable; she was just contented to be in his company.

Jess had always been the kind of person who had difficulty hiding her emotions, stood transfixed. She gazed into Jake's beautiful blue eyes, savouring how gorgeous he truly was. Although for a moment she did not speak, the huge smile on her face made it clear to everyone around that she was obviously pleased to see him, in fact, so pleased to see him that she had not initially registered the very attractive woman standing beside him. Jake could see Jess slowly register this fact and he knew she would be too polite to ask who his guest might be. He also knew full well by now that Jess was incredibly quick in forming misconceptions in regard to him, something he had noted she did not do with anyone else. He was not about to let her form any more crazy notions about him and so he decided this confusion would stop now. It was, after all, why he had invited his companion along. That, and the fact he had been dying to introduce Jess to her.

"Jess, there's someone I'd like you to meet. This is Charlie." Jess's brain was in a whirl as she tried to recollect where she had heard that name before.

Jake observed how pretty Jess looked with the bemused look on her face; however he decided to put her out of her confusion. "Charlie is my sister, it's actually Charlotte, but Charlie suits her better," he stated in a matter of fact manner, although with a slight grin on his face.

Jess looked from Jake to Charlie and then back again, recognising at that instant a distinct family resemblance. They had the same eyes and dark hair, and matching dimples on their cheeks when they smiled.

Charlie was finding the situation both amusing and bemusing at the same time. It was clear that these two were mad for each other. Yet why would Jess not acknowledge it? Charlie had decided immediately that she liked Jess and could see why her brother was so taken with her. She just hoped that the situation would be resolved soon because she was getting a bit fed up of Jake moping around like a lovesick puppy. Instead of shaking hands as Jess had anticipated, Charlie stepped forward and gave Jess a warm hug. "It's lovely to meet you. I've heard a lot about you." Seemingly as an afterthought, she turned and gestured behind her. "Sorry hun. I almost forgot you were there."

"No change there then," muttered the tall, attractive man coming towards them, carrying Chico in his arms. As he came to stand beside them he put his arm around Charlie's waist in a casually affectionate manner, "It's okay, love. I won't take offence; I'm used to it now." He placed Chico on the floor and shook hands with Jess. "Pleased to meet you at last, I've heard a lot about you."

"Really?" Jess asked looking a little bemused, and then added, "I hope it was all good."

"Yep, it certainly was," Charlie and her boyfriend replied in unison. Jess then noted a look pass between brother and sister and promised herself that she would ask Jake later, what it implied.

At that moment Kate came to join them and after quick introductions, she suggested they all set off. "It's a fabulous day, guys. I'm thinking if I timed it right, we should just about get to the White Bear for one o' clock, just in time for some liquid lunch." They all agreed this sounded perfect and the group set off on their walk.

The greenway was a beautiful walk. Since being regenerated from the abandoned railway line, sculptures had been strategically placed along the route. A stream ran alongside the greenway and it was a relaxing environment to go for a walk with a friendly group of people plus their dogs. Jess decided that she would arrange this venue again as everyone seemed to be enjoying the change. For the first fifteen minutes, Jess walked alongside Jake, Charlie and her boyfriend Blake chatting amiably. Jess felt comfortable in their company, and it was clear that Jake thought a lot about his sister as they relayed silly adventures from their youth. Although Jess would have been happy just to walk with them, she was aware that she had not seen some of the other members for a couple of weeks. Now that it was turning into an official group with members willingly paying a small fee, Jess was aware that it was her duty to make sure everyone was enjoying themselves and had someone to chat to. With this in mind, she made her way to the front of the group to chat with some of the newer members.

Lucy was chatting to James and Sylvia and just behind them were the two sisters Pamela and Patricia. They seemed happy enough chatting between themselves and Jess could hear them swapping ideas on how to stop dogs from chewing. Behind them was Nathen the fireman with his Bearded Collie who was talking to a man Jess had not seen before and it seemed that he had not brought a dog with him, or at least it was off the lead and exploring somewhere.

Jess decided she would introduce herself to the potential new member. "Hi Nathen it's good to see you."

"It's good to see you too, Jess. I heard about the incident with Ruth, is everything sorted now?" Nathen enquired sincerely.

Jess was a little bemused, "It is kind of sorted, although I didn't know you knew Ruth."

215

"I only know her a little. She used to work with my sister before she got together with that shmuck. To be honest, I'm just glad she's out of that relationship at last. We all knew he was a wrong 'un. Next time you speak to her tell her I was asking how she is, will you?"

"I definitely will Nathen. I'm sure she would be glad to hear people want to know she's ok." In order to move the conversation to something different, not because she didn't care about Ruth's situation, but because she wanted just for today to relax and not worry about anything, she turned to shake hands with Nathen's companion. "Hi, I'm Jess. I don't think we've met before have we?"

"No, we've not met before or I'm sure I would have remembered. I'm Adam and I also work at the station. I was at a bit of a loose end today so Nathen suggested I tag along with you guys. Although he did promise me that there would be lots of bikini clad hotties walking their dogs."

"I did not! Take no notice of him Jess. Stop showing me up Adam, or it'll be you doing the cooking on shift all week," Nathen protested, while getting his friend in a playful headlock.

Jess laughed at the laddish banter between the two mates who had most likely seen all kinds of dreadful sights in their work, and knew the comment had not been made in a sleazy manner. Joining in the light-hearted banter, Jess responded by commenting that when the weather warmed up she would suggest it to the other members, although she wasn't hopeful. She chatted to them for a little longer, then went to talk to Suzie and Luke who were also chatting to what Jess assumed was a new member.

"Jess I'd like you to meet Rosie. You remember me mentioning Rosie, we used to work together in a night club a few years back when I was at college. Rosie's the one I told you about who was dead clever and studying to do a PhD," Suzie chirped, clearly fond of her friend.

"Hi, pleased to meet you. Suzie did tell me about you. It's nice to put a name to a face at last."

"Pleased to meet you too. I've heard a lot about you too, all good in case you were wondering. Oh, and this is Sampson my gorgeous little fella," responded Rosie. Sampson, Rosie's 'gorgeous little fella' was in fact a burly, white Bull Terrier. Jess had never seen such a stocky dog. He happily trotted alongside his owner on his chunky little legs, tail wagging. Until they got chatting, Jess would not necessarily have placed Suzie and Rosie as being friends. Suzie was always immaculately presented with hair, nails and make up finished to perfection, whereas Rosie wore no makeup whatsoever, not that she needed it as she was an attractive woman without all the trimmings. What they did have in common however, was that they were genuinely lovely people who were both interesting and intelligent. It was no wonder that Luke was besotted these days with Suzie. This got Jess wondering if Rosie was single. Maybe Jess could work her matchmaking magic once again.

Jess walked along enjoying the feel of warm spring sunshine on her face. As she had envisaged, she got a little warm and stopped to take off her denim jacket and tie it round her waist. Just as she was doing so, she heard Patricia shout, "Oh no! It's a squirrel! Quick Pam, I need to get Rufus back on his lead before he notices it." There then followed a degree of excitement as Patricia went scurrying off shouting, "Rufus! Come on, Boy, look what Mummy has for you." This, Jess could see were some treats that she had pulled out from her pocket. It was too late though, as Rufus had seen the startled little creature and gave chase. The poor little animal paused for a moment and suddenly it was too late. It became an early lunch for Rufus, who came trotting back up to his owner with a squirrel tail dangling from his mouth.

Jess could not help herself and the words had left her mouth before she had time to think, "Oh that's gross! I think I'm going to be sick!" Elvis seemed just as disturbed at the scene before him and unlike the other dogs went nowhere near

Rufus. "Thank God! Unlike the real Elvis, you're not fond of a squirrel or two. I don't think I could cope," said Jess as she bent down to stroke Elvis in order to distract herself from watching Rufus finish off the remains of his snack.

"Rufus, you are such a naughty dog! You can stay on the lead from now on," Patricia exclaimed.

"You ok babe?" came the unmistakeable voice of Jake from beside Jess.

Once again, Jess found herself looking into those gorgeous eyes. "I'm okay thanks Jake. In fact, I feel like a bit of a fool. When I get the chance, I'll have to speak to Patricia and apologise for overreacting. I mean it's not like *she* ate the squirrel and I suppose Rufus is just behaving like a dog, albeit one with a poor choice for appetisers."

"I wouldn't worry yourself Jess. If Rufus has eaten them before then I'm quite sure she's used to people's reactions. I mean seeing Squirrel Nutkin eaten for starters isn't something most people see every day and you weren't the only one struggling. I'm sure I could see our Charlie trying not to throw up. So come on, stop worrying and let's catch up with the others because I think that we're nearly at the pub and I for one could do with a pint."

Jess took note of Jake's calm composure and felt even sillier. Of course Jake would be unfazed by an episode like that. After all, he was a paramedic and would have seen all kinds of things in his time. "You're right. A liquid lunch sounds perfect right now," Jess replied, regaining her image as a self-composed business woman as opposed to a silly female with a weak stomach. "Let's go and catch up with the others."

As she and Jake followed the slight bend of the greenway, she could see the other group members leaving the track and heading along the path which led to the White Bear public house. The White Bear was a modest sized building that oozed character. It was painted white with neat black window sills and had ivy growing randomly around some of the windows. Although it was difficult to be precise, Jess guessed that the building must be a few hundred years old and a feature that made this a perfect venue for the tribe of unlikely new associates, was that it had a lovely large beer garden just adjacent to the greenway. It truly was a beautiful location to have lunch. You could even hear the trickle of water from the stream above the vibrant chatter of the group who had begun to acquire available seating.

"Over here!" shouted Charlie, waving her arm to grab their attention. "We managed to save you two a couple of seats with us."

"Thanks guys," said Jess, as she plonked herself down in the little gap at the end of the table with Jake coming to sit opposite her. "Oh, can you just hold Elvis for me for a second whilst I go see if I can get some water for the dogs?" asked Jess, rising to her feet.

"Sure no problem," Jake replied, taking hold of the lead. A few minutes later, Jess returned carrying two large bowls full of water for the dogs. As she made her way unnoticed towards the table, she could see the group huddled together deep in conversation. It was only when she was almost back, that Kate noticed her and the group regained their previous stances and began chatting in their small groups. The men in the group immediately got to their feet, "Right let's get some drinks," they all said in unison. Having collected everyone's drinks requests, they headed into the pub.

Jess did not have time to dwell on the odd scene that had just played out before her because as soon as she sat back down, she was drawn into an animated discussion with Jake's sister. Charlie wanted to know if Jess could possibly do the flowers for her forthcoming wedding to Blake. And, as is often the case when weddings are mentioned, it became the focal point of conversation for the next ten minutes, until the guys arrived back with the drinks.

For a couple of minutes everyone was quiet as they checked out the food menu before beginning to debate what they considered looked the most appetising.

"So what's it to be then, Jess?" Jake asked as he placed his menu on the table.

"I'm not sure to be honest," Jess replied. She was being honest because she was torn between having the salad which she considered was the ladylike option and the mega burger and chips which she really wanted but considered inappropriate given the situation. That, she decided, was a meal to have with just your friends, when dropping sauce down your chin did not matter. And so she opted for the salad, although as an afterthought, asked for a bowl of chips. *It had to be done*, she reasoned. After all what was a pub lunch if it did not involve chips. "What are you going to go for?" she asked Jake politely, suddenly feeling a little awkward with the arrangement of him buying her lunch, which he had insisted upon.

"Well," he said with a slight smirk forming on his mouth. "I was thinking the squirrel pie sounded quite nice. What do you think? Squirrel pie and chips sounds quite appetising, I think."

"What?" Jess exclaimed, picking up the menu and quickly scouring the contents in order to find the offending dish. "I never saw that on the menu. You can't have that. You must have seen it wrong. I'm sure that eating a squirrel isn't even legal in this country."

She looked back up from the menu to find Jake visibly trying not to laugh along with the other members sat around their table. Realising belatedly that Jake was jesting with her, Jess threw the menu at him from across the table. "Funny, aren't you?" she said, although she was beginning to giggle at her own naivety.

"Sorry babe, I couldn't resist," he replied and then got to his feet, followed by the rest of the men. "Right, we'll go order the food."

For the next hour Jess and the others chatted easily about many subjects, although as expected, the conversation frequently drifted back to their beloved dogs. Jess relayed to

Charlie and Blake how she had become the guardian of Elvis. Jake added that it was one of his more amusing shouts; what with her Gran dressed like an Eskimo and Jess being in her pyjamas, plus the ambulance door falling off, that had everyone in stitches. Jess noted two things about Jake's version of events that day. Firstly, that he was a great story teller, holding everyone captivated with his version of the story. Secondly, he had noted that she was wearing her PJs, and felt a stab of embarrassment that he had seen her looking like a pyjama wearing cave woman.

Charlie went on to tell the group how she had acquired Chico from a friend. Apparently, Charlie's friend had considered that a small dog would be a great addition to the family. However, she had small children and the bad-tempered little man kept nipping them. Charlie had taken him on, and over time he had settled down. Kate shared that she suspected that Mitzi was pregnant following her fun in the woods, and that she still had not told her Mum.

After finishing her lunch, Jess kept mingling with the other members in order to ensure everyone was enjoying themselves. It seemed that they were as they had begun chatting to each other across different tables. This in turn had Jess again pondering at just how easy it seemed to be for strangers to chat comfortably when a canine was part of the equation. She sat quietly for a moment just enjoying watching everyone having a fun day out and felt very pleased that the hair brained scheme of having a social group for dog owners, seemed to have worked out. However, she was brought out of her moment of quiet contemplation by Jake coming to stand beside her.

Jake had watched how Jess had easily mingled with each member and it was clear that she was held in high regard by every one of them. It reinforced what he knew now was his love for her. "Jess, I think we should make a move and maybe head back."

"Oh right. Yeah, good idea, it is getting quite late," Jess agreed, getting to her feet. "Shall we head back then?" Jess asked the various members who were seated randomly around the beer garden, as she made her way back to her table to retrieve her coat, bag and Elvis. Instead of everyone drinking up and getting to their feet as she had anticipated, the group seemed reluctant to move. Charlie was making a phone call and gestured she would catch them up. Nathen and his friend Adam had just bought themselves another pint and they too said that they would be with them soon. Kate, Paul, Suzie and Luke chorused that they had just ordered dessert and wouldn't be long and the rest of the group all decided they need a toilet visit before they set off and as the queue was monstrous, they too would catch Jake and Jess up.

"Oh well, that's ok. We can wait for you," suggested the ever-obliging Jess.

Jake was eager that his plan to get Jess on her own was not foiled and so somewhat more anxious than he had hoped to sound, he intervened. Taking hold of Jess's hand he began to lead her away from the beer garden. "I'm sure they can catch us up and look, Elvis thinks we're going now," he coaxed, trying to sound as casual as possible.

Jess did not protest to being led away. In truth she was relishing the feel of Jake's strong grip upon her hand. In fact, the sensation of his touch was beginning to give her that strange feeling again.

For the first ten minutes or so they walked hand in hand and made small talk about what a lovely day it had been with a great turn out and delicious pub food. However, little by little, the conversation began to waver until they were walking in silence. Although Jess was known for being a bubbly, chatty person, she was just as happy at times to be quiet and so for a few moments, she just walked along beside Jake, relaxed in his company. However, as the period of silence continued, she began to feel slightly uncomfortable and looked up at Jake. Jess was worried. The colour had gone from his face and he looked distracted. "Jake, are you feeling ok? You're not looking too great."

Jake stopped walking, which in turn made Jess stop. He looked down into her beautiful face and saw the worry in her eyes. "I'm fine Jess. But listen, there is something I wanted to talk to you about."

Jess waited for him to continue and for what seemed like an age whilst Jake continued to look down at her. She was beginning to worry that there was something seriously wrong as she could see the inner turmoil playing behind his eyes. And then, just as she was about to say something, she heard him say, "To hell with this!" and before she could react, he had her in his arms and she was under the spell of the most fabulous kiss she had ever experienced.

At that moment, she had little awareness of what was happening and she really did not care. What felt like electricity surged throughout her entire body as she wrapped her arms around his neck for support and totally immersed herself in his kiss.

Jake finally removed his lips from hers and gently kissed her neck whilst intimately mumbling her name. With his lips no longer on hers, Jess had a chance to breathe and take stock of what was happening. "But Jake, you're -."

"In love with you," he murmured in her ear, "And I have been since the day I met you."

Jess had a sudden surge of mixed emotions, although underpinning them was guilt at finding so much pleasure in kissing someone who was out of bounds to her. Trying to find strength that she no longer felt she had in her body, she tried to pull away. "This is wrong Jake, you're already spoken for."

Jake was not about to let her go now that he finally had hold of her, and the kiss reinforced to him that she felt the same way about him as he did her. Taking hold of her chin in order that she had to look directly at him, he stated clearly, "Jess, I'm not gay, and I don't have a partner. In fact I've not been interested in anyone since the day I met you. At first, it seemed like a bit of fun to let you believe your misconceptions of me, but I've been trying for ages to get you on your own and set the record straight."

Jess continued to hold Jake's gaze as her brain processed what he had said and then a smile formed at her lips. "I can be such a fool can't I?" she whispered and then just as their lips were about to meet again she added, "But I am a fool in love with you Jake."

Chapter Twenty Eight

Jess did not exactly know the definition of utopia. However, wrapped in Jake's secure embrace as he kissed the sensitive area of her neck and mumbled how much in love with her he was, she considered that this was definitely *her* utopia. She would have loved to have spent the rest of the day in their hotel room. However, she was conscious that they had already been far longer than they should. Prising herself from Jake's embrace, she swung her legs over the edge of the bed. For a moment, she was tempted to get back into bed as Jake was deliberately trying to persuade her to do by running his fingers up and down her spine, sending electric shocks of desire pulsing through her body. Leaning over, she gave Jake a quick kiss. "Jake, stop trying to distract me! Everyone is going to wonder where we are." Then, before he could distract her into succumbing to temptation, she quickly got off the bed and made her way into the bathroom.

Jess showered quickly and then made her way back into their room to dress. Having done so, she made her way back into the bathroom to re-apply her makeup and pin her hair up.

Jake came into the bathroom and stopped to admire her for a moment. "You look gorgeous," he said, before kissing the top of her head. "Right I'm going to get a quick shower while you finish getting ready."

"Ok love," Jess replied, taking note of his fabulous physique. She looked at her reflection in the mirror, and for a moment, she was lost in her own perfect world as she reflected on that day six months earlier when Jake had kissed her so passionately, putting an end to her misguided assumptions of him. What a perfect day it had been, well except for when the rest of the group had come around the corner and started clapping and cheering at them. To think that Jake had organised it with them to stay behind so he could do, well what he had done, which was to kiss her and begin the start of a perfect relationship. Jess smiled at her reflection. To think she had been so wrong about him. She, who considered herself to be so astute in assessing people. How true it must be that love is blind. "It's a good job I do better with the love lives of others!"

"Sorry babe, did you say something?" asked Jake above the sound of the shower.

Jess hadn't realised that she had spoken out loud. "I was just saying how good it is that everyone could make it today. It's made the day extra special and won't all the dogs look fabulous dressed up! I thought Kate was mad when she first suggested it, but it's actually quite a nice touch," Jess said loudly in order that Jake could hear her in the shower.

"I guess so. Though the guys at work think I've gone a bit soft in the head since I met you," replied Jake through the sound of running water.

"Well, they may think I've turned you a bit soft, but I'll bet Adam isn't complaining seeing as I fixed him up with Izzy, or Helena, coming to think of it. I briefly spotted her earlier and she and Rebecca looked just as loved up as they have since the day I introduced them on that walk we arranged in the Dales. They too have gone to the trouble of dressing Tilly and Pickles up," Jess giggled. "Who would have thought that a dog would like pickled onions?"

"Well, Elvis likes to share your Chinese," replied Jake as he stepped out of the shower and reached for a towel. Which Jess noted, took him a little longer than it should have.

With a smirk on her face she commented, "I know what you're trying to do, Mister. And it isn't going to work. Now, get dressed or we're going to be late."

Jake laughed, and made his way past her and into the bedroom. "I've been rumbled. Do you know, for a girl who got it so wrong when it came to me, you really are quite astute when you put your mind to it. I mean, you're right, you may have turned me a bit soft in the head, but you're worth every moment of the ribbing I took in the beginning when I joined that dog walking group. They don't take the mick any more though since you've worked your matchmaking magic on my colleagues. Even my boss was asking about the group the other day, and whether you might be able to fix him up. He was asking me how you do it and I told him that I honestly didn't have a clue."

Jess giggled at the thought of Jake and his boss discussing the concept of how walking your dog with a group of strangers could be so much fun. "Well, it's classified, I could tell you, but then I'd have to kill you," she joked, then paused for a moment before popping her head round the bathroom door and adding, "with kindness!"

"Thank God," laughed Jake, "I was beginning to wonder whether to do a runner."

"I think it's a bit late for that," replied Jess, enjoying their playful banter before turning back to the bathroom mirror to continue pinning up her hair. "Well considering I love and trust you, I shall share my secrets. Although to be honest, it's not rocket science. Though it is science to some extent I guess. However, as Jack Sparrow would say, *it's more of a guideline.*"

"You're crazy," laughed Jake from the other room.

"But you love me for it!"

"I sure do. Go on then. Are you going to tell me, or shall I get it out of you later?"

Although Jess couldn't see the look on Jake's face she knew he was smirking. "As tempting as that sounds, I shall tell you now but I'll make it quick because everyone really will be wondering where we've got to. Ok then, let me think. Who can I begin with?" Jess paused for a moment. "Well I may as well start from the beginning," she continued, as she placed the last of the clips in her hair. Making her way back into the bedroom, she perched on the end of the rumpled bed, admiring the view of Jake, who she considered looked incredibly sexy in his formal attire. Distracted from her chain of thoughts, it required Jake prompting her to continue.

"Oh right. Yes, where was I? Well it's quite straight forward really. I just construct a character profile of people which is underpinned by the breed of dog they own and then introduce them to someone with a similar profile."

Jake looked a little bemused at Jess's explanation, "Well you make it sound straight forward but I'm still a bit confused. What is it you're saying exactly? Is it that you fix people up by the type of dog they own?"

Jess laughed, and got up from the bed to straighten Jake's tie, "When you put it like that it does sound a bit silly, but yes that's exactly it. If you think about it logically, a dog can tell you a lot about a person."

"In what way?" asked Jake as he slipped his arms around Jess's waist and looked down at her with both amusement and intrigue.

"Well, a dog is an extension of the life you lead. Most of the people in the group have chosen their dogs because they fit in with their lifestyle. By that I mean things like how much spare time they have, plus taking into account how they choose to spend their recreational time so the jobs they have and how many hours they work factors into it. In addition you can even work out what kind of home they have and how it's furnished. Even the kind of car a person drives can tell you a lot about the individual."

"So you work all that out just by what type of dog they own? What are you, some kind of mind reader?" asked Jake in a somewhat teasing manner.

"Are you mocking me?"

"Absolutely not babe. It's just a lot of information to contrive just by knowing what kind of dog someone owns."

Jess paused for a moment whilst she tried to think of an example. "Well Kate and Paul don't count as they got together at the gym which was inadvertently because of the group, but obviously Paul didn't have a dog at the time so their situation is slightly different and I can't believe they'll soon be parents and, they've kept one of the puppies that Mitzi had following that embarrassing day in the woods. They're definitely going to have their hands full! Though I'm sure they'll cope. They're both so laid back I don't think anything would get them stressed."

"I'll tell you who's a good example, Nathen with his Collie and Ruth. He's very active and proactive. Even though he works shifts, having a big outdoor loving dog works for him as his mum looks after it whilst he's at work. Then, when he's not, he takes it on long walks in the country or running with him. I knew from the start he was fond of Ruth and I also know that since she came back to the village, they have spent quite a bit of time together. Ruth is taking things slowly obviously, after what she went through with that shit of a husband but they are perfect for each other. Nathen's so nice natured, as is she. They both like to be out and about with their dogs at every opportunity and they're both not bothered that their dogs like to swim in the river and bring a bit of muck back into the house. They've both got laminate flooring and leather sofas to make it easier to clean up after their pooches. Yep. In time I think they'll make a perfect partnership."

Jess was enjoying highlighting her powers of perception and seeing the look of admiration on Jake's face encouraged her to continue. "And if you decided to give a dog a home from a kennels, the same concept would apply. You still choose a pet which will enhance your life and lifestyle. It has to work for both the owner and the dog. In fact, the kennels do their own kind of profiling by matching appropriate dogs to owners. Added to that, if you give a dog a home from the kennels then it's likely that you're a compassionate person who recognises diversity, enjoys a challenge and has lots of patience."

Jake was impressed, and in such close proximity to Jess was no longer able to resist kissing her. He began nuzzling the tender area of her neck which he knew she would be unable to resist responding to. "So along with being incredibly pretty, you're also very perceptive, aren't you? I'm one lucky guy," he mumbled as Jess began to succumb to his plan. And then he stopped his manipulation of her senses and looked into her eyes, "Hang on a minute. If you're so perceptive, how come you got it so wrong with me?"

Jess giggled in response to the question, "Well it's underpinned in science but it's not an exact science. In fact as I said, it's more of a guideline and anyway with regard to you, I think I was too love struck to see straight. In fact, I don't think at the time I would have seen the wood for the trees so to speak, even when accompanied by an army of dogs. Anyway, now I've shared my secret theories with you, I suggest you go back to making me behave like a dishonest woman."

Jake laughed and gave Jess a quick kiss on her forehead. "You rumbled my plan, perceptive again. However, I made a honest woman of you about an hour ago, and as much as I would love to stay in this room all day and night with you babe, our guests will be wondering where we've got to. So Mrs Mullaney, I think we'd best make a move before they send out a search party. And it wouldn't be hard for them to locate us with twenty-five dogs plus Elvis on the case.

"Talking of Elvis, I wonder if he can do us a rendition of 'Hound Dog' as a wedding present," Jess teased, as she remembered a dream many months previously. She then took Jake's hand as they headed out of the room to join their guests.

"You're crazy," Jake laughed.

"Just crazy in love with you, babe," Jess shot back, without hesitation reiterating her own words from the day they had officially become an item.

As they made their way out of the hotel towards the marquee where all their guests plus canines were waiting for them, Jess considered herself to be the luckiest girl in the world. Not only was this kind, caring and gorgeous man her husband, but to add to it all, her favourite people were here to share this perfect day. *This really is utopia*, she thought to herself as they entered the marquee and Elvis bounded excitedly towards her wearing a bow tie.

Jess looked over at her Gran who was chatting animatedly to a new member of the group, a retired vet who had heard about the group through his daughter who now ran the clinic. Jess had high hopes that something might flourish for them. As she observed them for a moment, a feeling of deep gratitude swept over her, "I must thank Gran later for encouraging me to provide Elvis with a home," she contemplated to herself.

"You ok, babe?" asked Jake who had observed Jess in a world of her own.

"I'm fine, sweetheart," Jess replied, giving Jake a heart-warming smile. "I was just thinking about that morning eight months ago when you and I went to rescue my Gran. I was thinking that, never, ever in my wildest dreams, did I consider it would lead to love!"